THE INITIAL FOLD

NICK ADAMS

Elliptical
Publishing

For Rachel.
Thank you for your unbridled patience,
love and knowledge.

PROLOGUE

GERMAN BORDER – KROISBACH, AUSTRIA

MAY 2ND 1945, 10:38 A.M.

The lone American soldier wobbled the heavy military bicycle down the narrow lane. He'd only learned to ride the contraption a few hours ago and his balance was far from perfect. He was uncomfortable as the saddle was hard and his uniform trousers were made from a coarse material which chafed his legs as he pedalled.

Even though it was late spring now, it was still quite chilly on this overcast morning and an occasional spot of drizzle made him rue the decision of accepting this particular assignment.

He knew the apprehension he felt was justified, as, even though the majority of the remaining German forces were allegedly several kilometres away, in full retreat towards Berlin, he'd heard reports of lone German snipers hiding in order to harass the oncoming Allied troops.

He kept his eyes on the ditches and hedgerows, checking for anything unusual, looking for a particular man he hoped to find, rather than a sniper's bullet.

Sure enough, as he rounded the next bend, and approaching a wooded area on the outskirts of Kroisbach, a very nervous-looking, smartly-dressed civilian man stepped out from the trees and signalled the soldier to stop. Anxiously looking up and down the lane, he approached the American soldier.

'Myself and brother and colleagues like to surrender to American forces – are important prisoner,' he said in broken English.

'What's your name?' the American asked, even though he knew exactly who he was.

'Magnus von—'

An American military truck suddenly rounded the bend behind them and braked to a stop in the middle of the road. The German stopped mid-sentence and appeared to be visibly shaking.

'It's okay,' he said, pointing at the truck. 'It's American.'

He put his bike on the ground and walked over to the truck to speak to the driver. 'There are some important civilian prisoners here who wish to surrender to us,' he said loudly, in an American accent, so the German could overhear. 'Can we utilise your truck to get them back to safety?'

'Sure thing,' the driver said, nodding and smiling, first at the soldier, and then at the German.

The soldier turned and walked back over to Magnus.

'Are your friends nearby?' he asked.

Magnus raised his hat in the air three times and twelve other men slowly materialised out of the woods, all looking nervous and constantly checking up and down the road.

'Jump in, fellas,' said the soldier, giving the truck driver a wink.

As they trooped towards the truck, the soldier dipped his hand into his front pocket. Singling out one of the approaching Germans, who had his left arm in a cast and sling, he removed his hand from his pocket and shook the man's right hand.

'It's good to meet you sir,' the soldier said. 'We were hoping you were safe.'

The German looked surprised and nodded, and, with help from his friends, clambered aboard the back of the truck.

Finally, once they were all loaded, the soldier passed the bicycle up and hopped aboard. The driver turned the truck around and drove the short distance back to the main road and headed west.

The first time the driver crunched the gears, it got a few raised eyebrows. By the third time, the soldier noticed some of the German passengers glancing in his direction with questioning looks.

'Antonio Ascari,' he said, grinning and pointing at the cab.

The Germans all burst out laughing and gave him a thumbs-up. It seemed the tension surrounding the group suddenly lessened and the trepidation of their last few weeks began to dissipate.

It wasn't long before they came across a military police jeep parked at a café in a small village. A quick explanation of the situation, the importance of the prisoners, and they handed their cargo over to two very pleased MPs, who seemed quite excited to take charge of the now-smiling Germans.

Before too many questions were asked, they roared off back the way they came, driving a couple of kilometres before taking a right turn up a dirt track, and ditching the borrowed truck and bicycle in a small copse of trees.

They walked on through the still, silent, dripping firs to a small empty clearing and stopped to ensure they were unseen.

Once they were completely satisfied they were alone, one of the soldiers spoke softly.

'Airlock open,' he said.

Out of thin air, some floating steps and a doorway

appeared. They climbed up and entered, the doorway closed, and the soldiers were gone.

After a deep rumbling, and an unusual sudden squall of wind, the small clearing in the middle of the copse was again still, silent and empty.

The cloaked Theo starship sat in a low stationary orbit above Germany, waiting. Even from this height, smoke could still be seen emanating from Helgoland, Berlin, Lubeck and Berchtesgaden, gusting away with the prevailing wind, up into the jet stream.

The last heavy Allied bombing raids over Germany had ceased only a week before, and during the raids, the Theos had needed to be very careful where they landed their cloaked shuttle.

Even when it was fully shielded, a couple of errant five hundred pounders nearby could still damage the small ship. That, and the consequences of being discovered in this system, let alone influencing the development of such a juvenile human race, would not be overly beneficial to their plans – or appreciated by the galaxy's ruling council.

Especially if it became apparent exactly how much manipulation had been in play.

The small shuttle rose up out of the atmosphere, almost underneath the much larger, cloaked starship, the two Theos allowing the sentient computer to pilot the small ship.

The computer uncloaked the shuttle and commanded one of the starship's hangar bay doors to retract. The shuttle entered the hangar, emitting a feint buzz as it pushed through an invisible atmosphere shield. It slowly turned and settled on retractable skids next to another identical ship.

The two Theos, both wearing 1945 American military fatigues of the 44th Infantry Division, exited the shuttle and hurried up through the starship to the bridge.

Two other Theos were reclining on control couches, which overlooked a giant holographic system map. One removed his strange-looking helmet and stood up to meet them.

'Did everything go to plan?'

'Yes,' said one of the arrivals. 'Although he had us worried for a while.'

'In what way?'

'He sent his brother, Magnus, to surrender.'

'But you got to meet Wernher, didn't you?'

'Yes, I did. I was able to shake his hand; the nano material was safely transferred.'

'How was his arm?' their commander asked, glaring at the other arrival, who looked down at the floor in embarrassment.

'It had to be re-broken and set properly a couple of weeks ago.' He smiled and scratched his nose. 'Well, properly as far as this planet's primitive medicine goes anyway. But to be fair to my partner, he had no idea the nanos programming would have that reaction and cause his driver to fall asleep at the wheel.'

'No, I suppose not.'

'The good news is,' said the first arrival, 'Wernher von Braun is alive and he's with the Americans. He's fit and ready to carry on with his rocket research influenced towards space exploration, rather than weapons, and the Saturn Five nanos will activate in about fifteen years' time. So, the mission was a success.'

'Yeah, you're right,' he said, sitting, then reclining back on the control couch. 'Next, we need to start looking at the American politicians.'

'How long do you think it will be?' asked the first arrival.

'For what?'

'The Americans to venture into space.'

'About ten or so of their years; that's why we need

to start influencing the most likely White House candidates.'

'Have we written off the Russians?'

'Absolutely not. Although with today's little push in the right direction, I'm betting on the Americans. Especially if we can get similar contact with a future president.'

'And what about instigating jump capabilities?'

'That'll need to be at least a hundred years away. Anything less will appear suspicious. As has been our brief for centuries, we need to make all this look like natural scientific progression.'

'Okay – so what's our next project?'

'Have you heard of an American family called the Kennedys?'

1

DEPARTMENT OF ASTROPHYSICS, CANTERBURY UNIVERSITY, ENGLAND

NOVEMBER 27TH 2049, 3:39 P.M.

'Ah bugger,' said Edward Virr, glancing up from his monitor at Andrew Faux, who was reclining on the small two-seater sofa in the corner of his study. He noticed he was reading the latest edition of *Classic Sports Bike Monthly*, most likely dreaming about which 1400cc petrol-powered missile he'd rebuild – and try to kill himself on next.

'What have you screwed up now?' Andy said, without looking up.

'It's a vmail from NASA.'

Andy looked up, puzzled. 'Yeah, so? You've been waiting to hear from NASA for a month now. What's the big deal?'

'It's from James.'

'James who?'

'James Dewey, you idiot. It's not going to be James

Dean, is it? He's been dead for over ninety years,' said Ed, rolling his eyes and shaking his head.

Andy looked up suddenly. 'What, the astronaut? The guy who first walked on Mars?'

'Yes, he is the Administrator of NASA now.'

'I know that. He's actually sent *you* a personal vmail?' Andy asked, suddenly very interested.

'Yeah,' replied Ed, now sounding a little nervous.

'Are you sure it's not James the chef, as one of his practical jokes?'

'Of course I am. It's from Kennedy Space Centre, for heaven's sake,' said Ed. 'In Florida, where the Mars project space planes are,' he added sarcastically.

'That's really cool,' said Andy, tossing the magazine back on the table. 'Does he mention me?'

'I don't know, I haven't looked at it yet.'

'Well, in your own time then – it'd be nice to know if I'm gainfully employed in the near future,' he said, crossing his arms and raising his eyebrows.

Ed looked up from his desk, over Andy's head and out of the double-glazed corner window above the sofa.

It was late autumn in the south-east of England and the tree branches looked empty and stark against the grey sky, the stubborn last leaves having only recently fallen. The gardeners had been busy raking the majority of them into piles, but a stiff breeze had picked up and begun distributing them all back out again.

The air temperature struggled to reach four degrees and a light drizzle had been falling for what seemed like weeks.

Ed glanced back at the flashing icon in his inbox. It was a month now since his meeting with Kurt Haynes, the NASA Director of Engineering at the Armstrong Flight Research Centre in the Mojave Desert. The weather had been a lot warmer there and Ed had enjoyed getting away from the cold and damp, if only for a couple of days.

NASA, being NASA, had given nothing away at Ed's presentation. He was excited, and convinced the math and physics all checked out. The lab tests had proven positive and he knew this could be a monumental leap forward for the human race. It could change the world forever.

It had been his project right from the start and he didn't want to be left in the wings as others took that first flight.

Edward was originally from Cambridge and for the past ten years he'd run the Department of Physics and Astronomy at Canterbury University.

He'd been a leading physicist for sixteen years, with a PhD in Physics and a Masters in Aerospace Engineering. He'd spent the best part of the last ten years working on FTL – Faster than Light – theories.

The Alcubierre Drive Theory, with all its supposed insurmountable difficulties, was the starting block.

He always believed a fully operational FTL system could be achieved in his working lifetime as new technologies began to bloom in the early to mid-twenty-first century.

For the last few years, his work had been highly confidential. Neither the Dean of the university or Ed's parents had any idea of the breakthrough. Only his colleague, Andy Faux, and a handful of senior NASA management knew that history was possibly in the making.

The healthy funding that NASA injected into the university's budget ensured that Ed was left alone. Both Ed and Andy fully appreciated that if any knowledge of this project's potential success got out into the media, their safety would be severely compromised. It was commonly known that all the major superpowers and several smaller countries were also experimenting to achieve the first FTL technology.

Ed's worry was that he didn't want to be left out of the team that made the first jump, or 'fold', as was his preferred terminology.

Now, eighty years after Neil Armstrong landed the Eagle on the Moon and twenty years after James Dewey landed the Falcon on Mars, he believed he had finally made the breakthrough. He prayed that the newly-self-named Virr Drive would be given the full funding and go-ahead from NASA. All that really had to be done now was to build a ship around a full-size Virr Drive and find someone brave enough to press the 'go' button.

Part of Ed's proposal to NASA was to include Andy on the team. Andy had been a part of the project for seven years and was quite simply the best mechanical and electrical aerospace engineer Ed had ever worked with. He was as much his friend as he was colleague. He kept Ed sane with his madcap sense of humour and colourful language, especially in the early years when it seemed to be a case of hitting brick wall after brick wall, and the threat of losing funding was a distinct possibility.

Andy was a local to Kent. Growing up in a small village near Maidstone, he had an encyclopaedic knowledge of all the best country pubs and what real ale they served.

'What if they turn us down, Andy? What if they find a flaw in the maths?' said Ed, frowning and glaring across the room at his friend.

'No, they bloody won't,' said Andy. 'You know everything's top drawer. NASA is fully aware the Russians, Chinese, Japanese and Indians are way off with this tech, so you're firmly in the driving seat, my old friend.'

With that, Ed turned back to his desk screen, crossed

his fingers and voice-instructed the machine to open his vmail with playback via his personal BlueScape. He sat staring at the screen for several minutes and could see Andy fidgeting in his peripheral vision.

'For crap's sake, Edward, any time soon would be just fine. Do they love our work or not?' he asked, putting his feet up on the coffee table and his hands behind his head.

Ed looked up at Andy, pushed his chair back and walked over to open the window, allowing some fresh air to blow in. After taking a few deep breaths and trying to slow his heart rate down so he wasn't shaking so much, he turned and looked at Andy.

'Is your passport current?' he asked, seemingly taking Andy by surprise.

'Err – yeah.'

'How would you like a free holiday to Florida?'

Andy looked at his friend dubiously. 'Tell me this isn't another wind-up, Edward, or you're a dead man.'

'No joke, Andy – NASA want to fly you and me to Kennedy Space Centre tomorrow morning.'

'You beauty – I'll pack my sunglasses.'

2

BIGGIN HILL AIRPORT – BROMLEY, ENGLAND

NOVEMBER 28TH 2049, 11:04 A.M.

Ed and Andy stepped out of an auto taxi that had parked itself on the hangar pad adjacent to a NASA personal executive twelve-seater ScramLake G5.

It was still drizzling in the late morning light and neither of them wasted any time grabbing their backpacks and hustling to the aircrafts steps.

'Cool – a ScramLake,' said Andy. 'Have you been in one of these before, Ed?'

'Are you bloody kidding me?' said Ed, laughing. 'I have a three hundred million dollar G5 at my beck and call, twenty-four hours a day.'

'I'll take that as a "no" then. Dewey must be really excited over our project to send this baby to pick us up,' he called back, jumping up the stairway with the boyish enthusiasm of a ten-year-old on his first rollercoaster ride. He paused at the doorway for the compulsory iris scan, grinned at the flight manager and bundled himself inside.

'Wow, full harnesses, Ed, and the seats are shape-adapting. Awesome.'

Ed shook his head at the flight manager standing at the top of the stairs who appeared completely nonplussed by Andy's adolescent behaviour.

'I'm terribly sorry about Mr Faux. He hasn't taken one of his adult pills today,' said Ed, smiling.

'That's quite all right, Mr Virr. I'll make sure his harness is so tight it'll hurt just breathing,' said the flight manager.

'Have you got a strap that goes around his mouth?' asked Ed.

'No,' the manager replied. 'But we do carry Amobarbital for the more… troublesome passengers.'

With the slightest hint of a smirk on his face, the manager began to prepare the cabin. Ed and Andy dropped into two front seats after stowing their rucksacks in the sealable side bins.

There were no overhead compartments that could drop open unexpectedly on this aircraft. The seats automatically moulded around them, ensuring a perfect fit, which they both agreed was a bit sci-fi. The manager gave them a small bag each for any loose personal items such as keys, small change and personal tablets. The bags were made of a magnetic material that sealed and then stuck to a small metal strip on the side of each personal luggage bin. Anything left loose in the cabin during the flight would very quickly become a lethal airborne missile and guaranteed to make them highly unpopular with any other passengers.

The small carbon stairway retracted into the fuselage and the door powered closed, then sealed. The flight manager checked both of their harnesses were fastened and tight, pulling Andy's harness adjuster so hard it made him grunt, and then took his own seat at the back of the small cabin.

Donning a matt black headset that completely covered his head and face, he instructed the aircraft to return to Florida. Although a ScramLake was fully automated, international flight regulations dictated that all automated passenger aircraft had to employ a qualified flight manager to ensure the safety of the aircraft and passengers.

Part of the bulkhead in front of Ed and Andy lit up into a panoramic screen view of both fore and aft. It had been proved in early tests that passengers were a lot less nervous if they could have some idea of where they were going, even if for most of the journey all it showed was varying shades of blue.

The fully automated ScramLake was the fastest passenger vehicle on Earth, capable of around Mach 20, although the NASA and military Scram Jets w achieving escape velocity of more than Mach 25. This one advance had made space so much more affordable. Reusable entry/re-entry vehicles meant no large disposable rocket boosters were needed. Scramjet space planes could now deliver several tonnes of cargo into space and return in a few hours laden with rare minerals mined on Mars.

The three passengers in the ScramLake were pushed back deep into their seats as the plane rose into the cloudy morning sky, turning and gaining altitude much faster than a commercial airliner. When it achieved fifty thousand feet the scrams kicked in, producing massive amounts of thrust.

'Bloody hell,' said Andy, through clenched teeth.

Ed was unable to turn his head and his reply came out more like a gurgle.

This continued for about three minutes until maximum altitude and speed were achieved, and then as abruptly as it had started, it ceased.

Ed and Andy slumped forward in their seats and looked across at each other.

'Fuck me, this thing's certainly got more go than my bike,' said Andy.

'Pretty amazing, isn't it?' said Ed, pointing at the screen that indicated the speed as Mach 17.98.

It was also a lot quieter without the scrams bellowing behind them. Just a pronounced hissing from the thin atmosphere passing by at over thirteen and a half thousand miles per hour. Four minutes later they felt the nose dip and the view on the screens went from deep blue to light blue as the plane began its descent.

'Ah crap, we're descending,' said Andy. 'What happened to the inflight movie? And we haven't been served breakfast yet and – hey look, my arms are floating.'

The aircraft was descending so quickly, right from the edge of space, that they were now weightless, and spent the next few minutes waving their arms and legs about, giggling like children.

As the plane got lower, it began to glide in big sweeping turns to lose speed, and both Ed and Andy realised why their harnesses had to be so tight. They were pulled forward hard and noticed the seats were gimbaling around under them to hold them centralised.

'That's cool,' said Ed. 'If we get the go-ahead, could we incorporate something like these into our ship?'

'Don't see why not,' said Andy. 'There's going to be a lot of G-forces involved when we're playing around with the Goertz Jets and Ion drives.'

'If they give 'em to us. We might just get an old decommissioned Apollo – if we get anything at all,' said Ed, laughing.

Ten minutes later, the ScramLake glided in and landed at Kennedy Space Centre.

The Florida facility had undergone a massive expansion over the last twenty years to facilitate the servicing of both the Mars supply space stations – one orbiting Earth (Armstrong Station), and the other orbiting Mars (Shepard Station), which in turn supplied the Mars colony known as Station Anseris Mons, or SAM. Astronauts affectionately referred to a Mars colony deployment as a holiday with Uncle Sam.

Ed and Andy thanked the flight manager for a smooth, safe journey. Although his flight input had been virtually zero, it still seemed the polite thing to do.

As the door opened, the heat and humidity invaded the cabin, taking them both by surprise.

'Now this is more like an autumn I can live with,' said Andy. 'No cloudy, drizzly, depressing shit here.'

'You're just wet all the time from the humidity instead,' said Ed, as the stairs powered down.

Almost immediately, a NASA-decaled auto van drew up. Andy quickly jumped inside to the air-conditioned coolness within, closely followed by Ed.

'Hypocrite,' said Ed.

'Who is?' said Andy.

'The man who was first into the air con, that's who.'

Although the vehicle was fully automated and the roads were completely clear, it still took the same amount of time as their flight to get across the enormous facility to the main administration complex. Even though they'd undergone iris scans as they boarded both the ScramLake and the auto van, security staff subjected them to further DNA and iris checks before allowing them entry to the building.

They were issued with security bracelets, and escorted up to the fourth floor and through to a smart restaurant area that contained eight tables. A waiter sat them by the window and instructed them that the Administrator would arrive at nine o'clock; in the meantime a full breakfast menu was at their disposal.

'I'll have the full English,' said Andy.

'Do you mean the full American?' replied the waiter, giving Andy a wry smile.

'Err – yeah, probably.'

'When in Rome, Andy, when in Rome,' said Ed. 'Two full Americans would be perfect, thank you – it seems Mach 20 has made us both very hungry.'

'Of course, gentlemen. Help yourselves to tea and coffee,' the waiter added, pointing to the relevant machines on a table at the side of the room.

An hour later, after gorging themselves on enough fried food to sink a battleship, they sat sipping coffee and staring out the window.

There seemed to be plenty going on, with an almost continuous flood of traffic coming and going between the construction warehouses over to the west and the launch runways running parallel to the east boundary.

Supplying two space stations and a mining exploration colony on a planet that was anything between fifty-five million and three hundred and sixty-two million kilometres away from Earth, was a complicated undertaking.

The perfecting of Ion drives in the mid-2020s made everything possible within a much-shortened timescale. The technology brought the Earth-to-Mars flight times down to around forty days, which would occur every seven hundred and eighty days when the planets were closely aligned, and with almost zero fuel usage. This led to the first manned Mars missions in 2027, with the first manned landing in 2029. It had long been known that Mars was an almost limitless rare minerals depository, just waiting to be exploited. NASA on its own didn't have the huge funds required to undertake an outer space mining operation on such a scale, so a conglomeration of multinational companies, along with NASA, signed the biggest exploration and mining contract in history. The International Solar System Mining Corporation – known as the ISSMC – was formed. Everyone accepted there would be little to no remuneration from the project for at least twenty years; it was a long-term investment, and not for the faint-hearted.

The timescale had proved to be fairly accurate as the

first minerals mined from the permafrost on Mars arrived back to Earth in 2048.

Ed and Andy both stood up a little too quickly, knocking the table as a smartly-dressed woman approached them, smiling.

A pepper pot fell off and Andy knocked his coffee over.

'Good morning, gentlemen. My name is Theresa Dean. I'm Administrator Dewey's Personal Assistant,' she said, with a slight smile. 'If you would like to follow me, the Administrator is looking forward to meeting you.'

'Thanks, Theresa,' they both said in unison.

'Sorry, we're both a bit nervous and excited,' said Ed.

'That's quite understandable,' said Theresa. 'I'd be nervous too if I was about to take my first space flight.'

She strode off across the restaurant, leaving Ed and Andy looking at each other with surprised expressions on their faces.

'Did she just say...?'

'I think she did,' said Ed.

They both grinned and hurried to catch up with her.

She led them through to the elevator, up to the top floor, and sat them in a small lounge area.

'If you could wait here a moment, I'll check he's ready to receive you,' she said and disappeared through a set of double doors.

'Whatever he says, don't laugh,' said Ed.

'What are you on about?'

'He has a habit of saying things twice.'

'How do you know that?' said Andy.

'Kurt Haynes told me. They all try to ignore it, but it can be a bit funny at times, so no laughing. I know what you're like when you get started.'

'Don't know what you're on about. When do I ever laugh at someone else's afflictions?'

'When that guy dropped a whole tray of drinks in the pub last year, you fell about laughing. I thought he was going to punch you through the window,' said Ed.

'Yeah, but I—'

'Gentlemen – the Administrator will see you now. He's excited to know you're here,' said Theresa, as she peered around the door.

She led them through an outer office, which contained her desk, and into the Administrator's office. On the right-hand side was another door, which she opened, and they strode through into a small boardroom containing six people.

Theresa remained near the door. 'Ladies and

gentlemen, let me introduce trainee astronauts Edward Virr and Andrew Faux.'

Ed stood rooted to the spot and saw a look of absolute shock on Andy's face – one he was sure he also wore.

All six seated at the table – four men and two women – stood as one and gave them a round of applause. Ed recognised Kurt Haynes from his previous meeting, and James Dewey was the most famous man in the world, so they both knew who he was. The other four were unknown to them.

Dewey came around the table with a big smile on his face. 'Gentlemen, gentlemen, come in please. Come in please,' he said.

Haynes winked at Ed and gave him a nod.

'Meet the team, meet the team,' said Dewey.

Andy just burst out laughing.

'Sorry about my colleague, everyone. He laughs when he gets nervous,' said Ed.

'Quite understandable,' said Dewey. 'Well, as you may have realised, we have some good news for you two – good news indeed.'

3

XAVIER LAKE'S OFFICE – LAKE AEROSPACE, DUBAI

NOVEMBER 29TH 2049, 9:10 A.M.

'With all due respect, Mr Lake – this is taking a big risk,' said Dale Copeland.

The two other men in the room looked up from their notes and stared at Dale. He had been the Financial Director for Lake AeroSpace since day one. He had also been a leading contributor to the taking of the company from a two-plane, low-orbit tourist trip provider, to a world leader in reusable space planes.

He still felt like an outsider, though, no matter how hard he worked or how successful the company became. Xavier Lake never gave him any praise – not once patted him on the back and said, 'Good job, Dale.'

'You seem to be putting a lot of trust in our Research and Development Department,' he said. 'We're pumping tens of millions into a dream that may not happen. I mean, the whole planet has tried to overcome the FTL barrier for several decades with no success, and we're building a one-off FTL ship with no bloody engine. Why are you so convinced that one of the biggest advances in human history is just around the corner? Not just that, it's just around our corner?' said Dale, regretting the forcefulness of his tone immediately.

'Dale, have I ever failed you before?' said Lake, glaring.

'No, you know you haven't. I – I just don't want this to be a first, as it could drop the share price like a stone,' said Dale, nervously.

'You're just going to have to trust me on this one, Dale,' said Lake. 'I do what I want to do with my company. I do have a few tricks up my sleeve, but it's too early to go public yet. As far as anyone's concerned, it's not an FTL ship; those words do not get spoken. Are we clear on that point, Mr Copeland?' Lake growled.

Dale nodded, a little overenthusiastically, and clenched his fists to try to cover up the shakes he could feel coming on.

'As far as the media is concerned it will continue to be a personal space plane for a super-rich client,' Lake continued.

'Yes – yes. I'm – I'm cool with that,' said Dale,

desperately trying to think of some other topic. 'Ah, I nearly forgot. Do you remember that pretty young lady journalist that came to see us last week, asking about the special space ship and, later, security caught her taking photographs inside the construction facility?'

'I understood that the police arrested her, escorted her to the airport and put her on a flight back to London, with the message, "don't come back",' said Lake.

'Yes, that's correct,' said Dale. 'Only, on the news this morning, they said she'd been murdered last night in a bungled robbery at her apartment in North London. Nothing stolen apart from her laptop and cameras,' he continued.

'That's awful – how utterly dreadful. London can be such a rough town at times. Can you ask my PA to organise some flowers on your way out? I need to have a private chat with Mr Herez,' said Lake.

Dale nodded and gathered his notes together, and left the boardroom as swiftly as he could, exhaling after closing the door. He told Lake's PA about the flowers for London and headed directly for the lift.

Lake's office was on the fifty-sixth floor. All the outer walls were floor-to-ceiling glass. Dale hated heights and every time he looked out the window his legs went weak.

Returning to the Finance Department on the third floor was his immediate concern.

'ARE WE SECURE, MR HEREZ?' asked Lake.

'Yes, boss. Your rooms were scanned this morning.'

Lake nodded, walked to the window and looked out at the view of the Dubai coastline which stretched away for miles. He turned back to face Herez.

'Is Copeland still cool?' said Lake.

'Yes, boss,' said Herez, in his heavy South American accent.

Floyd Herez had been Head of Security and Mr Lake's personal bodyguard for eleven years. He was ex-Colombian Military Special Forces and had the uncanny ability to magically make problems disappear with absolutely no trace. Nobody got near Xavier Lake without his approval.

'The surveillance we use on all our senior staff is total. Anywhere they go, anything they say, the algorithms will alert me to any transgression and also provide us with a lot of information to ensure they, err, how you say—'

'Remain loyal to the cause?' said Lake.

'Yes, Mr Lake,' said Herez, a predatory smile creasing his features.

'I understand the London problem was brought to a successful conclusion.'

'Correct, sir. I have an old friend at the London

embassy who is always susceptible to a little cash work.'

'Is he discreet?'

'He is after he saw a little video I acquired in Soho that clearly shows he's a man of – how you say – questionable sexual habits. It was pointed out to him that his wife's continued ignorance of this should be high in his priorities, especially as she is the daughter of one of the most senior generals in the Columbian military.'

'Love your work, Mr Herez. Love your work,' Lake replied, turning back to the view. 'Any new information from Canterbury?'

'Virr and Faux are in Florida. We can't activate the software on his tablet when he's at a NASA installation as the security systems would probably detect the intrusion. We will, however, check them after they leave.'

'Where are we with the jump drive?'

'About a week from testing.'

'And the construction technicians?'

'Construction is spread over six facilities in three countries. Not one of them has a clue as to what their particular unit does. It's to be flown here for installation very shortly.'

'The Chinese, are they peeping?'

'Only at NASA, as far as we can see. They know

something's in the wind, but I don't believe they have any strong intelligence yet.'

'That's good, Mr Herez,' said Lake. 'Just make sure they remain ignorant of our little toy's true purpose. We're going to need their space station facilities before too long.'

4

JOHNSON SPACE CENTRE – HOUSTON, TEXAS

Two weeks after the meeting in Florida, Ed and Andy had been flown to the Johnson Space Centre, Astronaut Training Facility near Houston in Texas.

The centre had trained astronauts from all over the world for almost ninety years. There was no other place on Earth that could better prepare people for the rigours, both mentally and physically, of a prolonged space flight.

At the Florida meeting, Ed and Andy had learned that NASA had known right from the start that this day would come, hence they had already undergone preliminary preparation, and a basic design for their ship was already under construction. As with any project of such complexity, budget constraints dictated that a ground-up design was not viable; a conversion from an existing vehicle was the best way forward.

NASA had a Mark VIII ScramJet entry/re-entry space plane at Armstrong Station. It was one of three emergency evacuation vehicles permanently attached to the station. It was due for replacement as they were up to the latest model Mark XIs now.

James Dewey had pointed out that it saved them the expense of buying a new vehicle, because the replacement for the Mark VIII was already budgeted into the Mars mining contract. It had already been tried and tested in space, with a full service record, and had been sitting idle, attached to Armstrong Station, the biggest space engineering facility known to man.

The Virr Drive components were in construction at several locations across the globe under the guise of advanced mining equipment for the Mars contract. The ship was being stripped of its three chemical Scramjet boosters and retro-fitted with two large Ion drives. The attitude thrusters were replaced with the new self-replenishing Goertz Jets and a large dome had been fabricated on top of the main body of the vehicle that would house the Virr Drive.

The engineers had been told it was for testing a new design of scanning array, which also explained why all the latest interplanetary scanning arrays were being fitted to compare the two. The cargo bay was converted into basic accommodation for the crew and the undercarriage was removed and replaced with retractable skids.

ED AND ANDY were in their fourth week of compressed astronaut training.

Normally, an astronaut recruit would undertake at least a year's basic instruction and then a further few months of field specialisation courses. The length of these depended on the complexities of their particular field.

They had to be flight-ready in six weeks, which was when the ship would be ready. Their flight up to Armstrong Station was scheduled for the first of February. It was now mid-January and they were both suffering from lack of sleep and brain overload. The sixteen-hour days were as tough as they come; the romance and excitement of becoming proper astronauts had now very much lost its sheen.

Sitting in the canteen, they were trying to face some dinner, after having spent the day undergoing inertia training – and filling sick bags.

'What's with the wet weekend face?' Andy asked.

'Ah, there's no fooling you, Sherlock. Well, apart from my breakfast and lunch popping by for a second visit and blacking out four times in the centrifuge, Steph called it a day over not being invited here. She's convinced herself that we're on a university-funded holiday and I chose to bring you instead of her,' said Ed. 'So, I'm eligible again.'

'Girls, eh! Can't live with 'em, can't kill 'em. What's a man to do?' joked Andy. 'In a few weeks' time when you're suddenly the most eligible, famous – and let's face it – rich physicist on the planet, you're going to have to beat them off with a light sabre,' he said, grinning, and slapped his friend on the back.

'That's what you're hoping for, isn't it, Mr "Play the Field" Faux. How does that saying go? "Is that an oxygen hose in your space suit, or are you just pleased to see me"?' laughed Ed, feeling a little happier for the first time that day.

'That's more like the Ed I know.'

'What's making you so bloody cheerful then?'

'You remember those amazing seats in the ScramLake?'

'Yeah.'

'We've got 'em – and that's not all. They agreed to fit the latest holographic star charting system, full flex screens for the cockpit and the new Perkins Baker zero gravity toilet,' said Andy, giving him two thumbs up.

'Only you could enthuse about a toilet.'

'Well, you know, little things and all that.'

'You said it.'

'Have you thought of a name yet?'

'A name?'

'For the ship. It has to have a call sign,' said Andy. 'You know? "The Eagle" or "The Falcon", and such like.'

'Yes, I get it, Andy, and no, I hadn't given it much thought. But now you come to mention it, how about "The Cartella"? It's Italian for folder and Tuscany is my favourite place.'

'How the hell do you do that?' said Andy. 'I spent half the night lying awake, trying to think of a cool name for the ship and the best I could come up with was "Initial Fold". I guess that's why you're the physicist and I'm the spanner monkey.'

'An Olympic standard spanner monkey, though,' answered Ed, looking at his plate and trying to find some enthusiasm for the now almost-cold lasagne.

'Absolutely, old friend. Where would you be with a broken clutch cable in Alfa Centauri?' he asked, stuffing his face with a fork full of French fries.

'Unable to change gear,' said Ed, prodding his dinner with a knife.

'Shut up, smart arse, and eat something, for heaven's sake, instead of just intimidating it with cutlery.'

He quickly leaned to one side to avoid the pea that Ed hurled past his ear.

'I think I'll go get some sleep. We've got docking

drills tomorrow and we don't want to be screwing that up,' said Ed, standing up and heading off across the canteen.

'Night, night, sweet pea. Give me a shout if you need tucking in.'

'Bollocks,' called Ed, as he exited the room with one finger raised.

5

THE OVAL OFFICE, THE WHITE HOUSE – WASHINGTON DC

JANUARY 20TH 2050, 11:20 A.M.

The President stared across the coffee table at the three people sitting opposite him.

Administrator of NASA, James Dewey, NASA Director of Engineering, Kurt Haynes and CIA Director, Donna McGuire had finished updating the President about the potential ground-breaking discovery made by Edward Virr regarding his FTL research.

Right from the start of his term, President Alastair James had been a huge advocate for space exploration and a big influence in cajoling Congress to agree to fund the research into new space technologies.

'Are you sure, James? We're only a year out from an election. This would be a huge embarrassment to the administration if it were a failure.'

'Yes, Mr President. We have undergone extensive testing in controlled laboratory conditions and everything points to the breakthrough we've all been longing for. The next logical step is to do a full-size ship test – a full-size test, indeed,' said Dewey.

President James raised his eyebrows and looked at Kurt.

'I concur with James, Mr President. There is only so much you can achieve in a small lab. The first space tests will be completely classified and only a handful of engineers – whom I will pick personally – will know the true nature of the trials,' said Haynes.

The President moved his gaze to Donna and again raised his eyebrows – a cue that she should contribute to the discussion.

'Err, what I think James and Kurt are telling you, Mr President, is that no one would know if it was a failure,' she said. 'And until a working system has proved to be completely safe, we wouldn't announce it anyway, even if initial tests proved positive.'

Kurt sat forward. 'We have no real idea of the jump range yet or how big we could make a ship and still jump. Does the size of the ship change the range, et cetera? All these factors have to be fully addressed before we can safely present this as a working system and possibly put it to the market.'

'Okay, you've convinced me,' said the President. 'But the other thing that concerns me is – would putting two civilians into a ten-billion-dollar spacecraft be the most sensible option? I can understand their point of view completely. It's their baby, putting money where their mouths are. It's – how can I put this? Wernher von Braun didn't fly the Apollo. He left it to professional astronauts and I feel it could get out of hand very quickly if these boys have even a small problem in the vicinity of Armstrong Station,' he added, looking at the three of them in turn.

'You're quite correct, Mr President,' said Haynes. 'I had this conversation with James last week and we've drawn up a shortlist of pilot candidates to do the actual – err – flying around, for want of a better term,' he said.

'So, you're saying there will be three in the test vehicle, Kurt?' said James.

'Correct, Mr President. A professional pilot and the two scientists.'

'That's very good news, guys,' said the President, looking at his watch. He stood and pointing at McGuire. 'Donna, can you make sure that the chosen pilot and any engineers who are in the fold – pun intended – fully understand their responsibilities as to the security of the project please?'

'Don't worry, Mr President. I'll provide that little chat personally. Having the Director of the CIA knocking on someone's door always gets their full attention.'

'It would certainly get my attention – attention

indeed,' said Dewey, also standing and shaking the President's hand.

The other two stood and were in the process of shaking hands with the President when a knock at the door disturbed them. The President's Personal Secretary slid into the room and pointed at his watch to remind him he had another engagement in five minutes.

As they were making their way down to the waiting vehicles, Donna took James's arm and steered him towards her limousine.

'Can I have a few moments with you alone, James?' she asked.

'No problem,' he said, signalling to Kurt that he'd be along in a couple of minutes. He dropped down into the armoured limousine. As the heavy doors clunked shut, the deadening of sound was total and the sweet musky aroma of Donna's perfume filled the interior.

'Sorry to drag you away, but I need to ask a favour,' she said.

'Fire away. What do you need?'

'Xavier Lake,' said Donna, through clenched teeth.

Dewey winced at the name. 'What's that little shit done now?'

'Well, I was hoping you might be able to tell me or at least fill in a few gaps regarding our intelligence on what he's up to in Dubai,' she said. 'We recently obtained information that he has a special one-off space plane being constructed for a private client,' she added.

'So what?' said Dewey. 'He does that all the time with his Scramjets. Even we've got one of his.'

'Yes, but this is a space plane that bears a close resemblance to our Mark VIII,' she said, a trace of concern in her voice. 'Also, he's having strange parts constructed all over the globe that could very easily be fabricated in one place. I don't like it when dodgy trillionaires start playing smoke and mirrors.'

She opened her case and retrieved a file. 'Have a look at these and tell me what you see.'

James read through the six copies of executed contracts in the file and looked up at Donna, a sick feeling in his stomach.

'Where the hell did these come from?'

'Let's just say a little bird in Dubai flew them into our possession. Can you tell me what these orders are for?'

'Yes, I can,' said James. 'These four are to raise the height of a space-plane body by about 400mm and fabricate a dome on top of that, and the last two are for major parts of two Ion drives. Do you realise that this is almost exactly what we're constructing up on Armstrong?'

'I've never been a believer in coincidences, but I do believe we have a leak and it's a fucking great big one.'

'For goodness sake, if Lake gets there before us, we're screwed. He'll just sell it to all and sundry,' said James. 'We'll have ships jumping off in all directions.'

'Do a full shut-down of everybody who has anything to do with the design of the Virr Drive – all computers, talk tabs, anything that could have the design schematics recorded on. They must be destroyed immediately, leaving only the original on the NASA Genframe,' said Donna. 'I take it the Genframe is one hundred per cent secure?'

'Will do. There's only six other people, other than you, me and the President and, yes, the Genframe self-analyses one hundred times a second for any intrusion, but I will order a full manual check on the system's security history,'

'I'll send some specialist psychology agents to interview the other six. They'll spot anyone playing secret squirrel with us.'

'Okay, I'm on it.'

'Daily updates please, James,' she called, as he jumped out of the limousine and hurried over to Kurt Haynes.

6

MEDICAL SUITE, JOHNSON SPACE CENTRE

JANUARY 20TH 2050, 12:10 P.M.

'Well, it's a lot cheaper *this* way,' said Andy. 'I've only just finished paying for my first BlueScape derma implant, I wouldn't have bothered if I knew we'd be getting these new super-fast models for free,' he added.

'Yeah,' said Ed. 'I've been reading up on the specs; these are military-grade nano implants, much more secure, huge range, the size of a grain of rice and, in conjunction with an app on your talk tab, you can eavesdrop on the less secure civilian models.'

'That's cool. I can check out what the girls are really saying about me,' said Andy, smiling broadly.

'Not without a court order, you can't, Mr Faux,' said Ed, waggling his finger.

'Who would know?'

'We would, Mr Faux,' said a booming voice from behind them.

They both jumped and spun round to find two security agents grinning at them.

'Bloody hell,' said Andy. 'Is that some sort of heart attack test or something?'

'No, Mr Faux,' said the agent. 'We're here to collect your talk tabs.'

'Actually, Agent Grey,' said Ed, reading his name badge, 'these are the property of Canterbury University and we're rather attached to them.'

'They will be cleansed and returned to the university,' said Grey.

'What about our work?' asked Andy.

'Save everything you need to the Genframe,' said the other agent.

'And then what do we do, Agent – is that Black, Agent Black?' said Andy. 'Agent Grey and Agent Black... Are we in a bloody spy movie or what?'

'Laugh away, Mr Faux. We've heard all the jokes a thousand times,' said Agent Grey appearing slightly irritated.

'Sorry, guys,' said Ed, looking at Andy with a glare. 'My friend sometimes visits the land of idiot. However, if you're taking our personal talk tabs, what are we to use from now on?'

'These,' said Black, giving them a box each.

'Awesome,' said Andy. 'Gentabs – the latest model too. Do you know what these cost, Ed?'

'They're also updated with military-encrypted software and carbon and titanium bodies, so they're impregnable and unbreakable,' said Grey.

'But they're not unlosable,' said Black. 'Just like a personal weapon in the military, you keep it with you wherever you go.'

'Both of you must change your passwords too,' said Grey.

'In hindsight, you both should have been issued with these from the start,' said Black.

'What do you mean "in hindsight"?' said Andy. 'Has something happened?'

'No – err – no, nothing has happened, Mr Faux,' said Grey, giving his colleague a sideways glance. 'It's just, with the sensitivities and importance of your work, it would have been prudent to have the latest and most secure equipment from the outset.'

'Talking of security,' said Black, 'when you've had your new implants fitted, report to building 51. I believe it's a CIA chat about security in space, or something like that. They don't tell us, so don't ask.'

'Above our pay grade,' said Grey, smiling again, and they both turned and left the waiting room.

———————

Two hours later, Ed and Andy were both the proud

owners of BlueScape Opus XII MD implants – MD standing for "Military Designation" and therefore not available to the general public.

They walked quickly across the campus, heading for building 51. It had been a chilly four degrees overnight and, although it was warmer that afternoon, they were both wrapped up against a cool breeze from the east.

'Why couldn't we do the training in Florida?' asked Andy. 'There are girls on rollerblades in bikinis there.'

'It's toughening us up for space, Andrew. It's quite cold up there too,' said Ed, smiling as he recalled his first attempt at rollerblading, many years ago, that ended with a trip to casualty.

'I'm not planning on going for any walks up there. I'm told it's easy to get lost.'

They walked past a sign indicating the direction to buildings 50 to 59.

'It's building 51 we want, isn't it? Or is it Area 51?' said Andy. He started whistling the theme to *The X Files*, an old TV series he used to watch repeats of in his youth. 'Perhaps they're going to introduce us to some aliens.'

'You idiot.'

'Unbeliever.'

'It's not a case of me not believing in extra-terrestrial life – the odds for it are stacked – it's just, I don't think the US government has been hiding dead ones in a Nevada shed for about ninety years.'

'Well, with that enormous supercomputer brain of yours, I'm sure you're right,' said Andy, continuing to whistle *The X Files* and looking in all directions around the sky again.

'Do you have to keep doing that? It wasn't funny the first time.'

'I'm looking out for the flying saucer. It can't be far away, unless... they're already here.' He continued to whistle, this time the famous five notes from *Close Encounters of the Third Kind*.

'Did you actually study for an Engineering Master's Degree or just buy it from a dodgy South American university?' said Ed, pushing Andy into a hedge.

———

BUILDING 51 was a nondescript office block amongst a dozen other nondescript office blocks in the centre of the campus. As they entered the building, a security guard scanned their bracelets.

'Agent Scarlet, is it?' said Andy, smiling at the guard, who gave him a quizzical look.

'I'll scarlet your nose if you don't shut up,' said Ed.

They were shown to a small waiting area and two

black-suited men, both with sour expressions entered the room.

'Mr Virr, come with me please,' said the first man, pointing to a side room.

'And, Mr Faux, could you come this way please?' said the other, indicating to a different room.

'Don't admit a thing,' called Andy, as they were escorted through separate doors. 'They'll never find the body.'

Ed walked into a small, windowless room and, just before the door closed, he heard Andy laughing in the next room.

'Likes a joke, your colleague, does he?' said the agent.

'I'm sorry,' said Ed. 'I didn't catch your name?'

'I didn't offer it,' said the agent. 'Sit down please, I have some questions for you.'

'Okay,' said Ed. 'If that's the way it is, I'm not going to sit down. A few things are going to happen next. One; you're going to provide me with some identification, so at least I know you have the clearance necessary for me to talk to you. Two; I'm not talking to anybody who refuses even the basics of everyday manners. Three; you're going to give up on this pathetic, heavy-handed, seen-it-all-before, dark suit, separate interrogation rooms, intimidation bullshit, because I'm not intimidated at all. Finally, number four; you're going to start talking and, not just your name, but your rank and number. You're going to tell me what's going on with our talk tabs and why they've suddenly got everyone all pissing their pants?

The agent gave Ed a malevolent glare.

'You can speak now,' Ed added, nodding and folding his arms across his chest.

The agent continued the glare for a second and then looked up at the camera set into the top corner of the room. As he opened his mouth to speak, the door burst open and a smartly-dressed lady strode into the room.

'Thank you, Agent McGrath. I'll take it from here.'

The agent quickly stood, almost to attention, mumbled a 'yes, ma'am', and shot out of the room as if fired from a gun.

'Good morning, Edward,' she said, smiling. 'I apologise for my somewhat abrupt colleague. I believe he is used to – for want of a better term – interrogating the slightly less intelligent members of the herd. My name is—'

'Donna McGuire,' said Ed. 'You've been the Director of the CIA for the last nine years; you've been married to your partner for I believe five years now and your father is retired Senator McGuire of Connecticut.'

'Wow, Edward. That's most impressive. If you ever get bored with physics there is most certainly a job for you this side of the Atlantic,' said Donna with a big smile.

'Thank you, Director. And I apologise for being a little grumpy with your agent. I have a very low threshold for rudeness.'

'So do I, Edward, so do I,' said Donna. 'And talking of manners, please have a seat. I have got to sit down; we had to run to get the Scramjet over here as soon as we heard and my legs are tired.'

'Heard what, Director?'

'Call me Donna, please. And can I call you Ed? We're old friends now, after all,' she said, grabbing one of the chairs and sitting.

'Fine by me,' said Ed, taking the chair opposite.

'Okay, Ed, the situation is, we received information that details of your recent project success may have leaked.'

'Ah shit,' said Ed. 'The Chinese or the Indians?'

'Not as far as we know. We believe it to be Xavier Lake.'

'Xavier Lake? Bloody hell, how on earth?' said Ed, his eyes wide with shock.

'After we exchanged your talk tabs this morning, we scanned the software. It was very cleverly hidden – simply the best spyware we've seen yet. It can detect the approach of scanning software and become inert in a millisecond.'

'Was it on Andy's too?'

'No, his was clear.'

'I feel really bad, like I've let people down.'

'No, don't,' she said. 'You don't live in my world. You wouldn't be expecting it. But we would like to find out how they got it on there in the first place.'

'I really don't know... I've never let my talk tab out of my sight. I have two layers of security, unless it was already on there when I was issued it.'

Donna reached for her bag and extracted a manila folder from it.

'Have a look at these photographs and tell me if there's anyone here you recognise,' she said, placing them in front of Ed, one at a time.

Ed stared at all six pictures even though he recognised one at first glance. It made his heart sink. He looked up at Donna.

'The second one?' she asked.

'Yes.'

'Where did you meet him?'

Ed looked at the camera then back to Donna. He felt sick to his stomach.

'I know how you feel, Ed. Even at my level we get scammed all the time and it makes you feel like shit. You just have to pick yourself up, sharpen your mind and get back at it.'

'He came to the university – told me he was

thinking about sending his son from Brazil to study physics. I remember because, as I was showing him around, the fire alarm went off. I had to organise getting the students out and, as you can imagine, it's like herding cats. He went back to my office to grab his bag.' Ed looked at the floor. 'That bastard. That's when he did it, wasn't it?'

'Most likely,' she said.

'I saw him stroll out only a couple of minutes later. He gave me a wave and a smile, the cocky little shit. I watched him walk across the car park and get in a chauffeur-driven limousine. I remember thinking, "He can afford the fees. No auto taxi for him…"'

'I'm going to put out a warrant for him,' she said. 'Might slow him down a bit.'

'What's his name?'

'Floyd Herez,' she said. 'And he's from Columbia, not Brazil. He's Xavier Lake's Head of Security.'

'Oh, bollocks.'

'For this reason, we've decided to alter the schedule slightly.'

'In what way?'

'You and Andrew will fly to Armstrong Station tomorrow morning.'

'Double bollocks.'

7

KENNEDY SPACE CENTRE – FLORIDA

JANUARY 21ST 2050, 10:04 A.M.

Ed had risen early the following morning and had to drag Andy out of his bunk so they could board a military plane over to Kennedy Space Centre.

The problem had been that the pair of them had spent the previous evening at a large pub on NASA Parkway, a decades-old favourite with the astronaut crowd and particularly renowned for its international draught beer collection. There was an old tradition for patrons, on the completion of their astronaut training, to work their way down all the hand pumps.

Which is why, after the quick flight over to Florida, the pair of them were finding it a struggle to don their flight suits.

'Don't give me that look, Mr Faux,' said Ed, attempting to put his left glove on his right hand.

'"There's only five more to go, Andy",' said Andy, impersonating him in a whiny voice and glaring at him. '"Let's show them how Brits drink, Andy".'

'I don't remember having to force it down your neck,' said Ed. 'And whose idea was it to attempt their whole selection of tequila as well?'

'Don't remember. It couldn't have been me. I don't drink spirits.'

'No, you don't, do you. I think it was the sixteenth shot that put you on the floor and the staff requested the auto taxi.'

'Ten minutes, guys,' said the attendant, sticking his head around the door.

This sobered the pair up very quickly. They realised that, in a few minutes, they were going into space for the first time. They spent those ten minutes checking each other's suits.

The modern suits were a lot less clunky than even ten years ago. The advances in both nano-fabric technology and electronics had ensured that full EVA suits were now a tenth of the weight of the old space shuttle days and they enabled astronauts to be more dextrous. They could walk, run and maintain around ninety percent of normal agility, even in a standard 1 gee environment.

The attendant returned and escorted them both out to

an auto van. Ed was glad for the air con as the suits were naturally designed for the absolute zero of space and not a twenty degree, January, Florida morning.

Neither of them spoke as they boarded the auto van. Both were lost in their own thoughts and spent the short five-minute journey staring into space. Ed realised the irony – as that's what they would be doing a lot of before very long.

The auto van stopped at another administration building and picked up three more similarly-suited astronauts: two men and one woman.

They all nodded at each other and exchanged pleasantries, then all five sat in silence as the auto van continued over to the hangar pads.

'Oh, for fuck's sake,' said Ed. 'Has someone died? It's like a morgue in here.'

'Say, are you the two Brits going up for the first time?' said the woman.

'Guilty as charged,' said Ed.

'Which one of you is the Tequila King?' she said, grinning.

'Ah, shit,' said Andy, looking out the window and putting his hands over his face.

'You're famous already, Andrew, and you haven't even got off the ground,' said Ed, giving the new girl a thumbs-up.

'I'm Linda,' she said. 'Linda Wisnewski, but most people call me Slopes.'

'Hi, Linda,' said Ed, shaking her hand. 'Good to meet you.'

'Hello, err, Slopes,' said a sheepish Andy, shaking hands and pulling his baseball cap over his face.

'That's something very rare,' said Ed.

'What is?'

'Mr Faux, in the company of a lady for five minutes, and he hasn't attempted to acquire your talk tab number. I've never known him this sick,' said Ed, laughing and punching Andy on the shoulder.

'Bit of a player are you, Mr Andrew? Like a little flirt with the girlies, do we?' she said, laughing and winking at Ed. 'If this is your first time up, then you won't have tried weightless sex then? A space virgin, no less.'

Andy nearly fell off his seat and stammered, 'No – err, no, I've not had the pleasure. Why, is that an offer?'

'Heaven's no, Andrew. I'm far too expensive, but don't fret about that,' she said. 'There are plenty of lovely girls on Armstrong just looking for some fresh stock,' she added, laughing out loud and receiving high-fives from the two men, who looked at Andy, grinning and nodding enthusiastically.

'Somehow, I think I'm being played, Edward.'

Ed realised the handful of tablets he'd taken earlier that morning had started to kick in and he was beginning to function a little more efficiently.

'Top deducting, Sherlock,' said Ed. 'There's no fooling you,' he added, rolling his eyes as the auto van arrived at hangar 10.

'All change please,' said a straight-faced loadmaster on opening the auto van door. 'Mind the gap and please walk directly to your spacecraft. Can you also leave any plants, seeds, live animals and bottles of tequila in the bin provided?'

Everyone smiled and looked at Andy, who looked away, pretending not to hear.

Seats were allocated to ensure the correct weight distribution for the flight. Most of the orbital planes were a five-seat configuration in the small front cabin, with cargo at the rear.

'You're the pilot?' said Andy, as Linda took the front seat and started prepping the plane for departure.

'Well done, Cactus,' she said.

'Cactus?' said Andy, looking perplexed and fastening his belts.

'Every astronaut has a handle or call sign,' she said. 'They're never allocated; they just become apparent sooner or later – you've normally got them long before you get near space. But because the two of you have kind of bucked the trend and undergone the speed-readers' astronaut course, you didn't have one. Everyone's been watching closely, though, and last night, with your heroic tequila rampage, you were at last awarded your call sign.'

'What about me?' said Ed.

'Nothing yet, Mr Virr. I'm sure you'll do something before long. Believe me, it's just a matter of time.'

With the checklist completed, Linda signalled the loadmaster who made one final check around the cabin, ensured all the belts were tight, helped them on with their helmets and stepped over to the door.

'Don't throw up in your helmet, Cactus,' he said. 'It'll float around in there with you until you're in a gravitational zone, which is about two hours from now. Have a great flight.'

With that, he swung out the door and was gone.

Linda closed both the outer and inner airlock doors and informed flight control she was all set to taxi.

The take-off was almost identical to the ScramLake that took them to Florida the previous year, except this time they wore spacesuits, the pilot was sitting in front of them and they had a windscreen to see through.

Again, the flight was fully automated, so although Linda was capable of a manual flight, she was busy observing and checking the systems to ensure nothing went awry.

At fifty thousand feet, the three huge scramjets lit up.

Ed soon realised that the ScramLake from last autumn was a poor cousin to this fiery monster. Just when he thought the G-forces pushing him deep into his seat couldn't get any stronger, they appeared to throttle up and go even harder, so hard in fact it made his eyes hurt.

The full throttle burn took just over eight minutes and accelerated the space plane to an orbital speed of over seventeen and a half thousand miles per hour.

All five astronauts watched as the sky turned from a light sunny blue to a dark royal blue and finally black.

Ed grinned as a thousand stars appeared outside the windshield.

The scramjets finally shut down, causing them all to jerk forward in their seats, and then it was suddenly quiet, except for the occasional rattle of the attitude thrusters. The space plane was programmed to turn on its axis and face back towards Earth for no particular reason other than it was one hell of a view, and they had an hour to wait for Armstrong Station to come close enough for docking.

'Wadda ya reckon, boys?' said Linda. 'Have I parked in a pretty spot, or what?'

'Is there a nice pub nearby with a beer garden? I could look at that view forever,' said Ed.

'Relax,' said Linda. 'There's a nice station due along in a minute; it doesn't have beer, but the coffee's pretty good.'

In his vision, Armstrong Station started as just another star, indistinguishable from all the others, but gradually the point of light grew and Ed realised that the ship had moved slightly to show the Station as it approached. From his vantage point, with Earth still in the background, he had a good perspective of where they were, where they came from, and where they were going.

The Station had been constructed in stages over an eleven-year period, with its current configuration commissioned a little over six years ago. It sat at an altitude of approximately one thousand kilometres in a low earth geocentric orbit and travelled at around 7.4 kilometres per second. It took up an area of almost one cubic kilometre and comprised a revolving habitation ring, with a circumference of twelve hundred metres, ten docking rings, three huge space workshops that could swallow Mars Ore Freighters for regular servicing, and twenty-seven vast ore storage bins.

Forty minutes later, the sudden machine gun rattle of the attitude thrusters woke Ed from his romantic dream world and started manoeuvring the ship in towards the looming station.

The usual friendly banter between Ed and Andy

had been noticeably absent for the last half an hour. They had been staring in awe at the gargantuan display of technology hanging almost motionless above the planet. The only movement was from the habitation ring, slowly rotating like a lazy bicycle wheel.

The thrusters rattled again and the station swung out of view as the computers brought the ship about to align its docking ring, in the ceiling of the cockpit, with its counterpart on the station. A few seconds later, they heard – and felt – a couple of clunks, a loud bang and finally an electric whirring, then silence – apart from Linda speaking to flight control, confirming to both Earth and the station that the ship had successfully docked.

'Okay, campers,' she said, finally, 'the seatbelt sign is off. Newbies beware, no vigorous movement until you've gained some weightless skills. It's not as easy as these other guys will make it look and please keep your helmets on until you're safely in the gravitational habitation areas.'

The two newbies in question tentatively undid their harnesses and Ed gave what he thought was a gentle shove against the seat, but what was in fact in weightless conditions, quite a hard shove. His intended gentle waft up to the ceiling of the cabin became an uncontrolled spin and – subsequently – a spectacular crash, head-first, into the ceiling, right next to where Linda was preparing the airlock for disembarkation.

'Are you picking a fight with my baby, Mr Virr?' said Linda. 'Because you know what they say about a mother protecting her offspring.'

'Oops,' said Ed, feeling a bit foolish. 'I got a little carried away with the thrust.'

'Quite common with physicists, along with your hard equations,' she said and carried on with the hatch opening procedure with a deadpan expression.

Ed gave her a sideways glance to see if the pun was intended, but she gave nothing away.

Andy floated up beside him and grabbed the adjacent hand hold. The other two guys had zipped across the cabin and were waiting patiently for the airlock to equalise and open.

'Let these guys go first,' said Linda, 'and you two follow. They'll show you to the Station Commander's office where I've just been told he wants to check you in personally.'

'I'm terribly sorry, Your Majesties. We had no idea of your royal status,' said one of the astronauts, bowing as Linda opened the airlock and they floated through.

'After you, Your Highness,' said Andy, attempting a flamboyant bow, which only succeeded in making him spin off across the cabin. 'Ah shiiiit.'

Linda reached over, grabbed his ankle to stop his

wayward motion, and launched him back through the airlock feet first.

ONE WHOLE DAY of their astronaut course had been an orientation of the layout of Armstrong Station. So, they knew where they were and roughly where to go.

The airlock took them to a fifty-metre long corridor with a plethora of handholds along the way that made it easier to traverse without losing control, then a second airlock that opened into the central hub of the habitation ring.

One of the other astronauts showed them the control for the elevators. The habitation ring had eight spokes with an elevator in each. The Station Commander's office was nearest to elevator 6, so they pressed the corresponding button and floated up above the hub gear housing, which was humming quite loudly, and waited inside the elevator recess. When 6 came around they all floated up inside and spun upside down to place their feet on the ceiling. The door-floor-ceiling slid shut and the elevator began its journey up the spoke. An audio message instructed them to ensure their feet were firmly planted in the illuminated end of the car as the centrifugal gravity gradually came into play as they travelled down or up the spoke.

The habitation ring used a lot of power to initiate the spin for such a huge structure. Although it could spin up to produce 1.2 gees, it was routinely kept at about 0.85 to conserve precious power, and the consensus of opinion was agreed on the fact that it made you feel light-footed and fit. The downside, though, was going back to Earth, where they would feel heavy and sluggish for days.

Ed felt the gravity beginning to push him into the floor and turned to smile at Andy.

'I'll be very glad to get this fishbowl off my head,' said Andy.

'Same here, mate,' said Ed. 'All I'm looking at is a big imprint of my nose on the inside of the visor from when I made friends with the space-plane ceiling.'

The elevator door, this time in the side of the car, slid open, and with slightly wobbly legs they all bundled out into a five-metre wide corridor. It stretched off left and right with a slight uphill curve in both directions.

Ed and Andy both removed their gloves and helped each other with the removal of their helmets.

'Normally, you would be checking in with the Purser over there in the security office,' said one of the astronauts from their shuttle, pointing across the hall. 'But Your Majesties have to go to the Commander's office which is down that way, about fifty metres on the right. His name's on the door.' And with that, he sauntered off across the corridor to the security office, his colleague following.

Ed and Andy stumbled off down the corridor.

It had been less than two hours since launch, but even with such a short period of time weightless and, although the slightly lower gravity did help, Ed's legs were still feeling a little bit disconnected.

8

CONSTRUCTION FACILITY, LAKE AEROSPACE – DUBAI

JANUARY 22ND 2050, 9:51 A.M.

'What do you mean, they've gone up?' shouted Lake. 'Gone up, where?'

'To Armstrong,' said Herez.

'Virr and Faux are on the station?'

'Yes.'

'When the hell did this happen?'

'Last night.'

'They've got two weeks of training to go yet. What the fuck are they playing at? Their test ship can't be ready,' Lake bellowed.

'They could be finishing the training on the station,' answered Herez quietly.

Lake noticed several construction engineers had stopped what they were doing and were listening. Herez opened a door and beckoned him into a small deserted drawing office at the side of the construction hangar and shut the door.

'Just in case they've brought forward their schedule, I've had a conversation with the Chinese,' said Herez. 'They've agreed to let us dock our test ship up on Tiangong in a couple of days and we can finish the final construction there.'

'You're sure they have no idea what it is?' said Lake, calming slightly.

'Yes, as far as they're concerned, it's still a prototype executive spaceplane.'

'Good,' said Lake, looking a little happier. 'I want you to go up with it.'

'ME – in space?' choked Herez, looking horrified.

'Yes, Mr Herez. The space plane. Tiangong. Tomorrow.'

'What about my work here?'

'You seem to have forgotten about the international arrest warrant the British Government have posted for you. Although I'm sure it was the Americans' idea. This will get you safely out of the way and keep nosy people away from that jump drive. Don't forget, I'm paying them a shitload of cash for the use of their workshop on the station. So, you put it in a corner somewhere out the way and stay in it day and night. Only our engineers get to touch it, is that clear, Mr Herez?'

'Yes, sir.'

'You could sound a bit more enthusiastic,' said Lake, glowering.

'I've never been into space.'

'You're not going alone. Two engineers are going up with you and they've been up before. Do what they do. Let them use the accommodation at the station and you bunk down on the ship. The sleeping module is state of the art and distinctly better than the Chinese cabins anyway. Remember to run the life support and seal the ship when you have to sleep. They won't be expecting you to be there and they usually depressurise the service bay to move ships in and out during the sleep cycle.'

'Okay, boss. When will you be coming up?'

'When the ship is ready for the first test, which the engineers promise me will be in about three days. Then we can go for a little joy ride and make history.'

'We?' Herez stared wide-eyed at Lake. 'What do you mean, "we"? If you need to take anyone on a test flight, surely one of the engineers would be the better call.'

'Your lack of backbone is beginning to irritate me, Mr Herez. Should I have a problem with your lack of enthusiasm?'

'No, sir. Not at all. Everything will be ready for your arrival.'

'Make sure it is.'

Lake left the office, leaving an unusually nervous Herez behind.

9

ARMSTRONG STATION – ORBITING EARTH

JANUARY 21ST 2050, 4:45 P.M.

'I'm sure I can smell bacon,' said Ed as they walked down the corridor towards the Station Commander's office.

'Fried mushrooms and grilled tomatoes,' replied Andy.

'It's not just me then; this place does smell like a transport café.'

'I could murder a fried breakfast right about now.'

They approached a closed door with a sign that read 'Colonel Jim Rucker, Station Commander', and pressed the intercom button. They heard a faint *ding dong*, like an old English doorbell from the last century. They looked at each other with raised eyebrows.

The door clicked open and they walked into a medium-sized office, decorated in the style of a twentieth century gentlemen's club: dark green walls, a large oak desk with a high-backed green leather chair and a three-seater green leather Chesterfield to one side. Although all the furniture was bolted to the floor, it did take them a little by surprise and made them wonder how such large pieces of furniture came through such a small door.

'I bet you're wondering how I got them in 'ere,' said a smiling man who entered through a side door. He extended his hand. 'Colonel Rucker,' he said, shaking their hands as they introduced themselves in turn. 'But please, call me Jim. I had them put the furniture in when the unit was in construction. I don't know what'll happen if it ever wears out,' he said. 'And don't expect to have similar fixtures and fittings in your quarters either; you'll find yours are a bit more basic,' he added, offering them a seat on the Chesterfield.

After issuing them with their personal ID bracelets and explaining how everything worked, he then walked them over to the mess hall, where they could at last get their bacon fix.

If anything on the station was better than they had imagined then it was the food: no sucking on weightless pouches of mush, but proper chefs preparing good, wholesome grub.

Ed agreed with Andy that it was a very good development.

'Okay,' said Jim. 'Regarding your ship. The

engineers have been running double shifts to get it completed. This new scanning radar whatnot you're testing must be very high priority because Dewey handing out overtime is something that almost never happens.'

'It is,' said Ed, trying to look nonchalant. 'Did Dewey mention anything to you about providing us with a pilot?'

'Yes, he did. And, as a matter of fact, here she comes now.'

Ed looked over his shoulder to see Linda walking into the mess.

'It's you,' said Andy.

'What's me?' she said, looking around at the group and nodding at the colonel.

'You're our pilot,' said Ed, smiling.

'So it seems,' she said. 'Any problems with that, gentlemen?'

'None whatsoever,' said Ed.

'You could have told us earlier, though,' said Andy.

'I've only just had the order. It came through on my Gentab when I got back to my room. I'm sorry, did you think I was holding out on you, Cactus?' she said.

'Well, I'm glad you guys are getting along,' Jim said.

'Actually, talking of holding out,' said Ed, 'Linda, could you sit with us please?' He looked around to check they weren't going to be overheard. 'We've been given permission by James Dewey to give only the two of you the following information.'

Linda sat down next to Jim and they both looked at each other with raised eyebrows.

'Ooh, intrigue,' said Linda. 'Can't beat a bit of that.'

Ed spent the next ten minutes explaining the reason for their test flights was to test a jump drive and nothing to do with scanning radar, only having to stop once when a crew member came in to grab a coffee.

'Knowing what you know now, Linda. I have to offer you the chance to say no,' said Ed. 'I'm confident we won't be in any real danger, but I can't guarantee it's without risks.'

'Are you bloody kidding me,' said Linda, almost falling out of her chair. 'It's the chance to be on the next Eagle or Falcon – of course I'm in. In with a capital "I".'

Jim leaned forward and stared at Ed and Andy in turn.

'Although I'm a bit annoyed about not being informed from the start,' he said, 'I can understand the secrecy necessary with a project as huge as this and that does explain why the engineers working on your ship have been – how do I say – less than chatty about their work. What concerns me most, though, is what we tell everyone here in flight control if your ship disappears.'

'There's no "if", about it, Jim,' said Ed. 'The Cartella will disappear. It's the reappearing in the right place that's the hard bit – and that's the bit we need to test. What you tell your crew, I'll leave up to you. But new stealth technology would be a good one.' Ed paused for a second. 'Can we take a look at the ship? I want to check the current state of play, make sure everything is where it should be and perhaps run some initial diagnostics.'

'It's getting a bit late in the day up here, but it shouldn't be a problem,' said Jim. 'If you go around to your rooms and change out of your EVA suits, I'll contact service bay 3 and let them know we're on our way.'

'What do we wear when we get out of these?' said Andy, indicating to his EVA suit.

'In your room will be NASA station suits, shoes and everything else you should need for your stay with us. Watch out for the underwear though; they can be a bit scratchy,' he added, with a smile. 'We'll all meet back here in twenty minutes and go play with spaceships.'

As they all filed out of the mess, Ed and Andy looked left and then right, wondering which way they lived. Before they could say anything, Linda pushed past.

'This way, fellas. The station is only at one-third

capacity, so at least half the rooms haven't been fitted out yet. We're all bunked in the same area.'

ED STORMED out of his allocated cabin and banged his fist loudly on Andy's door.

'Look at this, just look at this,' he said, thrusting a station suit into Andy's face as Andy answered the door in his underwear.

'Yes, Ed. It's a station suit and they're all grey. It suits you. It goes perfectly with your mood.'

'No, no. What's written on it.'

Andy grabbed the suit and read the NASA name label on the chest patch: 'Edward "Head Butt" Virr', and he burst out laughing.

'I don't feel so bad about mine now,' he said between bouts of laughter.

'Head Butt – I mean – how did they make these so fast? I've got to live with this for the rest of my life,' said Ed. 'I'm traumatised. What's my mum going to think and then later in life: "What was your NASA call sign, Grandad?" It's a nightmare.'

'Head Butt and Cactus save the galaxy,' said Andy, in his best Hollywood-movie-advert voice. 'It's a guaranteed box-office smash, Ed.'

'I'll smash you if I find out you had anything to do with this, Andrew Faux.'

'Hello, Head Butt. Having an underwear party?' said Linda, leaning around the door. 'Can I play?'

'Don't you bloody start,' said Ed, snatching his suit back from Andy.

'Something I said?' she said innocently.

'Mr Grumpy Pants doesn't like his call sign,' said Andy, grinning.

'You don't know how lucky you are,' said Linda. 'There's an engineer on the station with the call sign "Wet Dream" and it's sewn onto the front of all his clothes.'

ED, Andy, Jim and Linda took a spoke lift down to the central hub.

This time, they floated off in the opposite direction of the docking area, down another fifty-metre corridor and through another airlock. They emerged into an even wider corridor, which was so long they could barely see either end. Stiff handles, which resembled the ones on buses and trains dangled down from the ceiling and moved in both directions. A sign signalled that service bay 3 was off to the right, so they all in turn grabbed a handle as it passed and were dragged off in that direction.

Service bay 3 was at the far end, so five hundred metres later they all let go and grabbed the handles around the entrance airlock. They entered a large office where the Service Bay Supervisor floated in front of a control panel and was gazing out a window that took up a whole wall overlooking the service bay. She nodded at them as they entered.

'Evening, boss.'

'Evening, Kelsie,' said Jim. 'How's the ship coming along?'

'Well, we're almost there, boss,' she said. 'Although it's a hell of a squeeze getting all this new gear to fit in and I must admit that's the weirdest scanning array I've ever seen.'

'Yeah, it's a completely new concept,' said Ed, quickly. 'May we go in and have a tour?'

'Eno and Terry are about to call it a day. I'll let them know you're coming in while you gas up,' she said.

Ed and Andy both looked at each other and in unison said, 'Gas up?'

'That's a big hangar in there,' said Jim. 'You don't want to be free-floating in an area that big. We wear these little gas jet packs.' He unhooked one of several which were attached to the side wall where they were recharging. 'They don't take up much space or long to get used to. Have a practice when you first get inside – before you go too near the ship – and if it starts beeping at you, you're running low on gas. Come straight back here for an exchange or a recharge.'

They all strapped on a gas pack and floated over to the airlock, which Kelsie opened for them. Jim and Linda both zipped off through, making it look easy. Ed and Andy tentatively toggled the control arms and slowly emerged into the bay. There was a sudden *whoops* and Andy flew past Ed backward and upside down.

'Release the control arm, Cactus,' shouted Linda.

He did so and stopped, righted himself and grinned at Linda.

'Piece of cake,' he said, pirouetting and taking a bow.

'Idiot,' she replied.

'Takes one to know one,' he called as he flew by upside down again.

'What is this, kindergarten?' she said, shaking her head.

Ed laughed as Jim high-fived Andy as he floated by.

'If I had my way there'd be no men on the station at all,' said Linda.

'Amen to that,' boomed a voice over the tannoy and everyone looked up at a smiling Kelsie in the control room.

'Nosy cow,' Linda whispered to Ed.

'I heard that,' Kelsie replied, not smiling anymore.

'It's not a good idea to piss off the person with the outer airlock control, Linda,' said Jim.

'Sorry, boss. Sorry, Kelsie,' said Linda, waving at the control room.

'Apology accepted. You may continue breathing,' she said, smiling again.

THE CARTELLA WASN'T EXACTLY what you'd call a pretty ship, with bits and pieces bolted on here and there. It was obviously a conversion and not a new build, but both Ed and Andy thought she was beautiful.

They floated around her, savouring the reality of their design. It looked so much better and bigger in the flesh than on the ship design schematics they'd been shown a few weeks earlier.

'What stops it floating around the bay?' said Ed.

'The floor can be lightly magnetised,' said Jim, 'enough to stop the ships from moving about. It gets turned off when you want to fly, plus, if you commit the heinous crime of losing a tool in here, it will eventually turn up stuck to the floor.'

'That's good,' said Ed. 'I misplace Andy now and again.'

THE TWO ENGINEERS that had been working inside the ship both appeared. They gave everyone a thumbs-up and jetted over to the control room airlock to go on a sleep break.

Ed did not need an invitation and immediately jetted in through the cabin airlock to have a look round. What he found inside made all the hairs on the back of his neck stand up.

'Wow, that's freaking awesome,' said Andy from behind him.

'I can't believe this,' said Ed, looking at the layout of the control cabin.

Three of the very latest, form-fitting, gimbaling seats sat in semi-circle around the nose of the ship, with flat screen control panels in front of each one. The middle one was for the pilot, the right one for the ship's engineer and the left, nearest the airlock, for the Virr Drive operator. Behind the control cabin was a sealable door that led to a small galley that specialised in preparing weightless rations. It had storage containers in every conceivable spot, so no amount of space was wasted.

'There'll be enough food on board to last about six months, just in case you get waylaid somewhere for a while,' said Jim. 'It's the standard default larder on our

Mars freighters, as that's where we thought you might be going.'

'If we break down where we're going, I don't think six *years*' food would make any difference,' said Ed.

Beyond the galley was a small dressing room, containing three large lockers for stowing their EVA suits and after that, three tiny crew cabins. The back of the retired station lifeboat was full of Goertz control equipment, Ion and Virr drive systems, upgraded life-support equipment, air scrubbers and scanning array paraphernalia.

'Now I'm really excited,' said Ed as he floated back through to the control cabin, getting used to where the hand holds were around the ship. He pulled himself down into the left-hand seat, which immediately formed itself around him, before reaching up and powering on his control display. It lit up with a faint audible chime and he proceeded to run a self-diagnostic program.

'You seem very familiar with the panel already,' said Linda.

'We designed these Touchlite panels right from the start,' said Andy as he descended into the right-hand seat. 'Or the basic layout anyway. This is the first time we've seen them in the real world, though.' He lit up his panel, only to get a battery of red warning symbols. 'Looks like they've still got a bit of work to go yet. The Goertz kit isn't operational and the Ion propellant management system has yet to be configured.'

'I like a man with big words,' said Linda, dropping into the centre seat.

Ed gave her a sly glance, but again she had the perfect deadpan expression.

'They've just transposed the original button dash into one of your Touchlite screens. Everything seems to be in the same place,' said Linda. She powered up her screen and watched as it went through a full ship-flight diagnostic. 'This is way cool,' she said and touched a blue lit button.

Immediately, the flexi screen powered down over the windscreen and lit up with a view of the hangar from all angles, which included a good view of Kelsie in the bay control room. She seemed to be swaying around, almost as if she were drunk, with her mouth open.

'What the hell is she doing?' asked Linda.

'Hang on,' said Andy and brought one of the scanning arrays to life, adjusting it to receive audio. Suddenly out of the cabin speakers came the sound of Bon Jovi's 'Livin' on a Prayer.'

'Ah, she's a girl who likes the classics,' said Jim.

'Same 'ere,' said Andy. 'Though I'm more of a Genesis guy.'

'Pink Floyd,' said Ed, putting his hand up like a schoolboy.

'Pretenders,' said Linda, lifting both arms up.

They all looked around at Jim – at the same moment – with expectant expressions.

'Ah, err, Rolling Stones, I suppose – if I had to pick one,' he said.

Andy was busy at his console for a second.

'What are you doing now?' asked Linda.

'Watch this,' said Andy, pointing at Kelsie on the screen. 'I've got a feed into the sound system in the hangar. Everyone be quiet for a second.' He'd configured his BlueScape into *The Cartella*'s systems and, in a very official voice, said, 'Living on a Prayer? You'll be living on unemployment benefit if you don't get back to work!'

Kelsie's face went ashen and she stared around the room. The music stopped and, in a little voice, she said, 'Who's there?'

They all fell about laughing in the cockpit as they watched the confusion on her face.

Twenty minutes later, they all left the ship and floated back to – and through – the bay control room, replacing the gas packs to recharge on their hooks as they went.

'Thanks ever so much, Kelsie. We'll see you in a couple of days. Could you ask the engineers to let me know as soon as they're done?'

'Err, okay, boss,' said Kelsie, still looking a little rattled.

They all floated out into the corridor and prepared to grab the moving handles.

'One other thing,' said Andy, as Jim pressed the airlock close button. 'Unemployment benefit is quite generous these days, so don't worry.'

'You fucking bast—' was all they heard before the airlock sealed.

10

TIANGONG SPACE STATION –
ORBITING EARTH

JANUARY 23RD 2050, 1:36 P.M. + 8HRS

The engineers thought the flight up had been without drama, although Floyd Herez wouldn't agree with that.

The pilot hadn't docked at Tiangong Space Station but had manoeuvred the ScramLake straight into the vast engineering bay. The ship had to be tethered for the time being as the rubber tyres had yet to be replaced with metal skids, so the ship would adhere to the magnetic floor.

The engineers got to work almost immediately – after checking in to their accommodation and changing out of their EVA suits. Most of the fit-out had been done at the hangar in Dubai, but now the ship was in orbit the main engines had to be swapped out for the Ion drives and a few other upgrades were needed.

Herez didn't like weightlessness at all. The constant falling sensation made him permanently nauseous.

Unlike Armstrong, Tiangong didn't have a rotating artificial gravity wheel, so the staffing cycles had to be shorter.

The Chinese hadn't signed up for the Mars mining program. Instead they had set their sights on plundering the asteroid belt between Mars and Jupiter. Originally, they'd made plans for Ceres, the largest dwarf planet in the solar system. But the three unmanned craft – all landed in different areas – discovered that before they could get down to anything even remotely worth mining there was between one and three kilometres of ice crust.

They changed their plans and focused on Vesta, which had been attributed as a minor planet and second only in size to Ceres, although, at five hundred and twenty-five kilometres in diameter, it was certainly no small rock.

The three test craft they landed there produced hugely promising results. Almost immediately, they set about the process of establishing a permanent mining settlement on the surface. With the disappointment of Ceres – which had put them back a decade –and the vast distances involved, it would be at least another eight to ten years before they'd be likely to show any return.

The two Lake Aerospace engineers annoyed Herez greatly. They showed him no respect and seemed to consider him an underling. This he was most certainly not used to, but up on the station there wasn't a lot he could do about it. So, he spent most of his time either sleeping, eating the dreadful food or reading the scanning array manuals, trying to ignore the bumps, bangs and general racket of the ship being rebuilt around him.

Later that day his Gentab chimed, which was unusual and made him jump; up to now it had remained completely silent. He'd begun to think it didn't have reception up here on the station, but obviously it did.

The unread vmail flashing on the screen was from Lake.

'Trust him to be able to get through when no one else can,' said Herez and pressed play.

'Good morning, Floyd. I hope you're having a pleasant holiday,' said Lake, smiling and making a big show of taking a sip of a glass of wine.

'Patronising bastard,' said Herez.

'Now, now – that wasn't a very sporting thing to say about your employer, was it?' said Lake, chuckling.

Herez glanced down at the settings to reassure himself this was a recording and shook his head in bewilderment when he confirmed it was.

'I don't know how secure this is,' continued Lake, putting on a more serious face. 'So I'll keep it brief. I'm informed by your two engineer colleagues that the scheduled work will be complete during the day cycle tomorrow. I'll plan to pop up tomorrow afternoon for a full systems check. Make sure you're ready, Mr H.'

Herez stared at the screen long after the recording had finished and wondered if it wasn't too late to find alternative employment.

11

TIANGONG SPACE STATION – ORBITING EARTH

JANUARY 24TH 2050, 4:15 P.M. + 8HRS

The Chinese-made Scramjet orbital plane docked at ring seven on Tiangong Space Station.

Xavier Lake was first off the ship and floated his way through the various airlocks and corridors on his way to the central control module. There weren't any elevators or drag handles on this station; visitors had to pull themselves around while trying not to collide with anyone coming from the opposite direction.

It took Lake a good ten minutes to find his way. He had been up here twice before but had had a guide on both of those occasions and hadn't memorised the route.

Colonel Xiong Yu, the senior officer on the station, welcomed Lake into the control room with a bow and floated over with his hand outstretched. Lake, returning the bow, grabbed his hand.

The control room was, as with every room on this

station, quite small, but designed for function rather than comfort. There were four other junior officers on duty, all strapped into seats in front of their relative control panels and screens.

'Colonel, so good to see you again,' said Lake.

'Likewise, Mr Lake,' said Xiong. 'I trust your flight up was comfortable.'

'It was. Thank you, Colonel. An exceptionally smooth transition as always,' he said, smiling.

'If you would like to follow me, Mr Lake, we can talk in my office – through here in the next module.'

Lake followed the colonel through an airlock into another module that seemed to contain nothing but computer hardware. The colonel turned left and keyed a password into a pad on the wall. A small hatch opened and they both floated through into a sphere five-metres in diameter. Lake looked around and was amazed to see the majority of the outer wall was made of thick Plexiglas. The view was spectacular.

He floated up to the glass and marvelled. It was like spacewalking without a suit and helmet.

Outside and to his left were rows of station modules and docking rings. He could see his recently-docked space plane sitting with two others and, below them, a huge construction area where he could see the flashes of welding torches and make out several space-suited figures busy with the building of the ore storage hoppers. The freighters from Vesta would one day fill these with valuable minerals. But best of all, straight out in front, was the Earth, slowly turning, big and blue and beautiful.

'Can I say, Colonel, the view from your office window is outstanding.'

'I call it my revenge window,' said Xiong, floating over to Lake with his arms crossed and a sly smile on his face.

'Revenge window?'

'When I go back down to Jiuquan or Beijing, there are certain members of the party faithful who seem to enjoy finding fault with anything and everything I do. Not because anything is wrong, but just to remind me where I stand. So, I come in here now and again and wait for the People's Republic to come around, I stick out my foot and pretend to stand on them, like bugs,' said Xiong, looking back out at the view.

'That's my kind of thinking, Colonel. Excellent. Do you mind if I wait for the USA to come around? I've got a bit of bug stomping of my own to do,' he said, laughing.

Xiong Yu joined in and they both chuckled away, staring out at the amazing view.

'I nearly forgot. I have something for you,' said Lake, slipping off his backpack and, after rummaging inside for a moment, presented Xiong with a two-litre bottle of a well-known brand of Chinese water.

'Water?' said Xiong, looking thoroughly underwhelmed.

'The water bottle is just for show; I refilled it with something you might appreciate a little more. Your favourite, I seem to remember.'

Xiong unscrewed the top very carefully, took a sniff, a little sip and immediately capped it again. 'How did you get this up here?' he said with a big grin on his face. 'Xi Feng Liquor – thank you, my friend. We shall share some of this a little later when there are less – how you English say – nosy parkers around.'

'I like that plan. Talking of plans, how's my ship coming along?'

'Why don't we go over and have a look?'

'Excellent, show me the way and I can get out of this EVA suit too.'

Fifteen minutes later, Xiong and Lake emerged out of the airlock and into service hangar 2. They'd picked up a couple of jet packs on the way so they could navigate around the large space. Both men had used them many times. They zipped across the hangar and cruised around the space plane, inspecting the new additions to the ship. Lake paid particular attention to the new Ion drives, attitude thrusters and the large extension to the roof of the vehicle.

'That's something I haven't seen before,' said Xiong, pointing at the bulbous roof.

'It's a new, experimental scanning array,' Lake lied. 'Something I'm hoping will prove interesting to all the spacefaring nations.'

He quickly jetted down to the ship's doorway and disappeared inside. As Xiong approached the door, Lake stuck his head back out.

'I'm going to change out of this suit and have a meeting with my staff. I'll come up to the control room later to find you. If you can get away, I'll help you with your bottle of water,' Lake said, and with a small wave, he disappeared again.

Inside the ship, Lake glanced over at a monitor, which showed the view of one of the many external cameras. He watched as Xiong, outside, stared at the ship's door for a second and then up at the strange roof line of the ship, shrugged his shoulders and jetted back up to the airlock.

BACK IN THE CONTROL ROOM, Xiong floated over to his Executive Officer and Security Chief, Lang Xia.

'Anything new on that ship?' asked Xiong.

'No, sir,' said Lang. 'We weren't able to get near it because of that nosy South American, although the results of the photographs and scans we took of the equipment going into that strange bump came back from Beijing. They confirmed that it's not a scanning array.'

'Were they able to identify what it is?'

'No.'

'Lake's up to something and I need to know what,' said Xiong. 'I don't care how much he's paying for the privilege. When he starts lying to me on my station, his business becomes very much my business. Tomorrow morning, when that ship goes out, scan it with everything. Don't take your eyes off it for a second.'

'No, sir.'

LAKE CHANGED out of his EVA suit in his cabin and into something a little less restricting and returned to the flight deck.

He sent the two engineers back to their cabins with instructions to stay on the station until the flight-testing had been concluded, then floated over to the flight controls and turned to study Herez.

'Have the locals been paying much attention?' he said.

'At first they did. It was the Executive Officer, Lang. He was the nosiest, but he soon got bored when we told him nothing. They've got cameras all round this hangar, so I'm sure everything was photographed as it was installed and sent back to Earth for analysis.'

'They won't have a clue, but I'm sure they'll be scanning us with everything they've got in the morning. I'd love to see their faces when the ship disappears.'

Lake pulled himself down into the pilot's seat, brought the control systems online and asked for a full systems diagnostic. Very few people knew that Xavier Lake was, in fact, a very competent pilot. He test-flew all his own aircraft and, a few years ago, had paid to put himself through the rigorous orbital space-plane pilot training course with the Chinese.

The engineers had done well; he received a glowing screen full of green lights. The ship was ready to fly.

'Are you up to speed with your responsibilities, Mr Herez?'

Herez sank down into the second seat and flicked on the scanning array screen.

'I don't know about up to speed but I'm pretty sure I know what I'm doing now,' replied Herez. 'I've spent two days reading the manuals and operating the systems in training mode. I think I know my way round most of it.'

'We'll give you a trial in the morning, then, and you

can show me what you've learned,' said Lake, powering down the ship. He floated out of his seat and headed for the main door.

'Don't wait up. Just be ready to make history at eight in the morning, station time,' he said, as he slipped his gas pack back on and jetted out the door, all set for an evening drinking expensive rice wine with the Station Commander.

12

ARMSTRONG STATION – ORBITING EARTH

JANUARY 25TH 2050, 7:39 A.M.

Ed hoped that today would be remembered forever in the annals of human space history, alongside July 20th 1969, and May 9th 2029, to name only two. Unlike those dates, both having been anticipated for months – if not years – by the majority of the human race, today's imminent history-making was known to but a few.

Ed and two others of those few had just had breakfast and were hanging on to the moving toggles, taking them down towards service hangar 3.

'Have you thought up a good tag line, Ed?' called Andy.

'A tag line?'

'You know, "One small step for a man..." Or, "Alien planets are now within reach..." Something along those lines.'

'All aboard the colonisation express. Tickets please,' said Ed.

'Do you think it will be like that?' said Linda, 'I mean, if we were to find Earth-like habitable planets, I'm not sure I'd want to leave home for good and set up on an alien world.'

'You'd be surprised,' said Andy. 'Remember the Americas, Australia, the Wild West... And when they advertised for engineers to go to Mars, people flocked. If they thought for a minute that the grass was remotely greener then they packed up and went.'

'Not much grass on Mars,' said Linda.

'I don't think a lot of the original settlers in Australia had much of a choice either, Andrew,' said Ed, looking over his shoulder. 'But I do agree with what you're trying to say.'

As they arrived at the bay door, Linda operated the airlock and they all floated into the control room. Kelsie was on duty again and turned towards them, away from the control desk, and glared at Andy.

'Did you miss me?' he said.

'I miss pushing you out an airlock, you arsehole,' growled Kelsie, still glaring and with her hands balled into fists.

'Isn't love a wonderful thing?' said Linda with a dreamy expression on her face.

'Enough of the Mills and Boon,' ordered Ed. 'Everyone gas up and get over to the ship.'

Ed noticed Linda exchange a questioning look with Andy.

'He gets all authoritative when he's nervous,' said Andy, moving across the office to the jet packs. 'Whereas I laugh a lot,' he added.

'I can hear you, you know,' said Ed, becoming more pissed off by the second.

'I don't know which of you is more annoying,' said Linda.

'I do,' said Kelsie and punched the airlock control with a loud bang that made everyone jump. She stared menacingly at Andy as he managed to jet through the door as far away from Kelsie as possible without actually hitting his shoulder on the door frame.

Once inside the ship, they all went to their relevant cabins to suit up. They then returned to the cockpit and strapped themselves into their designated seats. The engineers had completed all the upgrades and installations, so the system diagnostics showed green lights on all three of the control panels.

Linda called up Flight Control.

'Cartella, this is Armstrong Flight Control, you're coming through loud and clear – over.' She gave them a basic flight plan and testing area and proceeded to seal the ship.

'Are you guys good to go?'

'All good,' said Ed.

'Same 'ere,' said Andy.

They all sat in silence as Kelsie prepared for depressurisation of the hangar. Sirens sounded and red lights flashed their warnings, before the service bay slowly lost its atmosphere and the huge outer airlock doors began to gradually retract. The magnetised floor under the Cartella was deactivated, and Linda expertly raised and turned the ship, then jetted through the door and into open space.

'Cartella, you are clear to proceed to preselected testing co-ordinates,' said a voice from Armstrong Flight Control.

Linda acknowledged this and, once they were far enough from the station, she turned the ship away from Earth and ignited the Ion drives. The huge Mars Ore Freighters had three of these same design ion engines. The Cartella was a tiny fraction of the mass and had two of them, so the result was quite spectacular.

'Holy cow,' shouted Linda. 'A racing spaceship. This is epic.'

She gradually opened the throttles and they were pushed back harder and harder into their seats. The Cartella shot away from the station, accelerating towards the agreed test zone.

'When you told me it would take about two hours to

reach the test area, one hundred thousand kilometres away from Earth, I thought you were bloody joking,' said Linda.

'It's faster than an Imperial Cruiser,' said Andy with a suitably straight face.

'That's very true,' agreed Ed, nodding with a similarly knowledgeable expression.

'What the hell are you two on about?' she said, trying to turn in her seat to look at them but failing because of her harness and helmet.

'Ah, it's kind of physicist stuff,' said Andy.

'Involves a lot of math,' said Ed, trying not to laugh.

'Involves a lot of nerdy ancient movie bullshit, more like,' said Linda. 'I'm getting to know you two better than you think.'

'Strong, with this young padowan, the force is,' said Andy.

'God help me,' whispered Linda, making the sign of the cross.

'Cartella, this is Mission Control Kennedy. Do you copy? Over.'

'Shit, did they hear that?' said Linda, quickly lifting her arm up and hitting the transmit icon.

'Kennedy, this is the Cartella. Receiving you loud and clear – over.'

'Cartella, I have The President at the White House wishing to say a few words – over.'

'Copy that, Kennedy. Go ahead, Mr President.'

'Yes, good morning, Cartella. This is President James calling from the Oval Office. I just wanted to say good luck with your tests today. Although the public is unaware, there are a few good people back here who know of your endeavours and are really supportive of you guys. If your experiments are successful, this will open up the human race to the galaxy. The opportunities from this are endless. Again, good luck today and I look forward to meeting the three of you here at the White House on your safe return – over.'

'Thank you, Mr President,' said Linda. 'I think I can speak for the three of us in saying that we are very aware of the significance of these tests to mankind today and we're all very honoured to play a leading role in such a historical moment. Thank you for taking the time out of your day to speak to us – over.'

'You're welcome, Cartella. Have a momentous day – President James out.'

'Wow,' said Ed. 'Little Miss Diplomatic, a career in politics beckons.'

'All hail, President Slopes,' said Andy, smiling.

'Shut it, you two,' said Linda. 'I was only being polite.'

'Cartella, this is James Dewey at Kennedy Mission Control. Do you copy? Over.'

'Yes, we copy, Mr Dewey. Go ahead – over.'

'Cartella, I would just like to reiterate what the President said and, from all the team here, we wish you all a safe flight today. A safe flight indeed – over.'

They all smirked.

'Thank you very much, Mr Dewey. Would you like us to bring you back a present? Over.'

'That would be much appreciated, Cartella. A nice bottle of Rigil Kentaurus Burgundy would be very nice – over.'

'No problem. Although, I will have to put it on the NASA account as I don't seem to have any cash on me – over.'

'No problem, Cartella. Just mention my name for a discount – Dewey out.'

'What the hell is Rigil Kentaurus?' asked Linda.

'It's the astronomical name for Alfa Centauri A,' said Ed.

'I'm the career pilot astronaut,' said Linda. 'Why don't I know that?'

'Classified information,' said Andy.

'You do realise that I have the override to your oxygen supply, Mr Faux?' growled Linda.

Andy looked across at Ed, grimacing, and, for once in his life, he stayed very quiet.

Sixty-eight minutes later, the Cartella entered the designated jump zone. They'd all been lost in their own thoughts for most of that time, but at least it gave Andy time to test and programme his new scanning array ready for the first jump. Ed had also been busy checking, and double-checking his co-ordinates. He was paranoid about ensuring he didn't emerge the Cartella into a solid body or a strong gravitational well, one that they wouldn't have time – or enough power – to pull out of.

'Cartella, this is Kennedy – over.'

'Kennedy, receiving you loud and clear – over.'

'Cartella, you can proceed with the initial fold, when ready. And good luck – over.'

'Copy that, Kennedy. Initial fold in sixty seconds and thank you – Cartella out.'

'Good to go, Andy?' said Linda.

'I have the scanning arrays on maximum forward detection, so all good at my end.'

'If there's anything in our path when we emerge, I want to know immediately,' she added, reinforcing what were now the new folding standard procedures.

'Don't worry,' said Andy. 'If there's a grain of sand in our way, you'll know about it.'

'Okay, Mr Virr,' said Linda. 'Time to prove your mettle.'

'Roger that,' said Ed and glanced across at Andy,

who gave him a thumbs-up. 'Right then. Good luck, everyone. Folding in five, four, three, two, one.'

Ed held his breath and lightly touched the big flashing purple icon on his console.

A light green haze enveloped the ship and the Cartella vanished.

13

TIANGONG SPACE STATION

JANUARY 25TH 2050, 8:03 A.M. + 8HRS

Xavier Lake hadn't named his ship. He didn't believe in any of that sentimental crap, so Test Plane 71 sat in Tiangong Space Station's service bay 2, magnetically anchored to the floor on the recently-installed retractable steel struts that replaced the standard undercarriage.

Floyd Herez had woken early; he found that sleeping comfortably in weightless conditions was a skill he lacked. When you woke several times every hour with a falling sensation, it made you permanently tired and extremely irritable. He knew, however, to keep those emotions in check around Lake; if he annoyed him, even mildly, taking a walk out of an airlock was a very real outcome.

Herez underwent another system diagnostic on his scanning arrays, the third time this morning. It kept him busy, made him more proficient with the equipment and stopped him brooding over what was to come later that morning.

His concentration was disturbed by a call from the service bay office, asking him to unseal the main cabin door. Lake jetted in before the door was even half open, removing his jet pack mid-flight, and threw himself down into the pilot's seat, which retracted around him.

'Morning, Mr Herez,' said Lake. 'Do something with this for me.' He projected his jet pack across the cabin towards him.

'Morning, boss,' he replied, trying to hide the contempt in his voice. 'Did the evening go well?'

'Surprisingly well, thank you,' said Lake. 'I now believe rice wine to be an excellent intelligence gathering tool, it's—'

A loud *ping* erupted from Herez's console, indicating that the conversation wasn't private.

'Just a second,' said Herez, sealing the airlock doors and activating the jamming suite. 'Okay, all secure.'

'Thank you, Mr Herez. I'm pleased to see you're getting quite intimate with the ship's systems. Now – as I was saying – it's the opinion of Beijing that we're working on a new stealth system. I didn't deny or confirm anything, so when the ship disappears it'll make them think they're correct. So, I'm going to change our jump co-ordinates and go a little further out where it'll be impossible for them to see us emerge.'

Herez looked horrified.

'When you say, further out – how far exactly?'

'Neptune.'

'Neptune?' shouted Herez. 'I thought we agreed on the Moon so if anything goes wrong, we can be back here in a few hours with the conventional Ion engines.'

'Fortune favours the bold, Mr Herez.'

'It's no fun being rich posthumously, though,' Herez replied.

'Just have all the cameras online,' said Lake as he started to activate the ship's propulsion systems.

'Are we not suiting up?'

'You can if it makes you feel better,' said Lake as he continued prepping the ship for launch.

Ten minutes later, Lake requested permission to exit the service bay. Thirty seconds after that, the bay depressurised, the huge doors slid slowly open and the magnetic floor was deactivated.

He lifted, turned and jetted the ship through the bay doors, retracting the landing struts as he went.

'Belt up tight,' said Lake. 'I'm going to light up the Ions in a few minutes.'

Herez did as he was told. As with Lake, he hadn't bothered with the EVA suit. His reasoning was it would be better to die quickly than float around in a suit thinking about it, knowing the inevitable was only a couple of hours away.

The Ion drives lit a few minutes later and they both grunted as they were pushed deep into their seats.

'Full scan forward, if you please, Mr Herez,' said Lake. 'Don't want to run into anything, do we?'

Herez slowly forced his arms up and activated the array, knowing Lake had done that deliberately to make it difficult. But he was a long way from home and way out of his comfort zone, so there would be no complaints today.

Five minutes later, the acceleration ceased as suddenly as it had begun. They could both breathe easier and operate their consoles without any effort again.

Herez programmed his array to give an audible alert in case of any debris in the path of the ship. Now they were out of Earth's orbital gravity influence, it would be unlikely. But even the smallest particle hitting the ship at this speed would be potentially catastrophic; it would be better to know in plenty of time and undertake a minor course adjustment.

'That's strange,' said Herez.

'What is?' said Lake, glancing over at the array screen.

'Every so often, there's just a trace – almost like a murmur – of a return directly behind us.'

'How far behind?'

'Five hundred kilometres.'

'Could be a system glitch; it's new and untested,' said Lake. 'I'll get the engineers to check it out.'

'Always a possibility,' replied Herez. 'There it is again and this time only four hundred and eighty-seven kilometres back.'

'On the same course?'

'Seems to be.'

'I'll change course by a few degrees.'

'There it is,' said Herez, a few minutes later. 'Still directly behind and still closing. It's changed course with us.'

They both looked at each other and frowned.

'It's not just a shadow of our own ship, is it?' said Herez.

'Not now, it's not,' said Lake. 'It's closing and it altered course with us. If it was a shadow glitch it wouldn't have changed course until the point in space that we did.'

'Has anyone perfected space stealth technology that you know of?' asked Herez.

'Everyone's been working on it, including us,' said Lake. 'I don't know of—'

A shrill pinging sound cut him off mid-sentence.

'I have a hard return now, accelerating towards us –

much smaller,' said Herez. 'It's an incoming missile. I think we're being fired on,' he shouted.

'Shit, the fucking Chinese have double-crossed us,' said Lake, gritting his teeth.

'The Chinese could have done it anytime; they don't need a stealth ship all the way out here.'

'How long to impact?' Lake asked as he put in a severe change of course that had their gimbaling seats lurching to the left.

'Twenty-five seconds,' said Herez, grimacing against the sudden G-forces. 'Can we jump?'

'I haven't programmed any emergence co-ordinates.'

'I read the manual on the system; doesn't it have an emergency jump facility that gets you away from trouble and into random clear space? Fifteen seconds to impact.'

'Shit. Yes, it does.' Lake hit the jump standby icon and watched as the system powered up, his shaking hand hovering over the initiate icon.

'Five seconds,' said Herez.

'Come on, come on,' bellowed Lake, staring at the icon, which remained stubbornly unlit.

'Three, two...' Herez shut his eyes.

The icon lit up a bright purple.

'One,' shouted Lake and punched the lit icon.

A green haze enveloped the small ship and it disappeared.

On the pursuing stealth ship, the pilot glared at his tactical weapons screen. Both the target and the missile had vanished off the display at the moment of impact. He waited a few moments for any returns from the debris field. Seeing none, he shrugged, sent the 'target destroyed' code and turned his tiny ship for home.

14

THE CARTELLA SPACEPLANE – LOCATION AS YET UNCONFIRMED

JANUARY 25TH 2050, 10:12 A.M.

The green haze faded from around the Cartella, no alarms sounded and, so far, they hadn't run into anything.

'Anything on the forward array, Andrew?' called Linda.

'Nothing – all clear,' said Andy and he looked across at Ed, who was activating the new Holonav system.

'Position please, Edward,' called Linda again, this time holding her breath.

'Just a second,' said Ed, waiting for the system to flash up their position. 'Oh, wow,' he said. 'Can you turn the ship on its axis, ninety degrees to port, and clear the front screens please? I want us to be able to see out the front window.'

Linda powered up the flexi screens and began spinning the ship on its axis to the port side.

As the Cartella spun, a huge ringed planet swept into view.

'Lady and gentleman,' said Ed, beaming from ear to ear. 'Welcome to Saturn.'

'Holy moly,' said Linda. 'It's absolutely beautiful. I'm – I'm getting quite, I can't believe it – is that really Saturn?' she said, trying to wipe her eyes, but realising she couldn't with her helmet on.

Andy had been very quiet and sat very still, his face obscured by the reflection on his visor. He finally released himself from his seat and floated over towards Ed.

'I need a hug, Ed,' said Andy. 'And you, Linda. Come on, a group hug is the order of the day.'

The other two released their belts, they all removed their helmets and spent five minutes cheering and hugging in the middle of the control cabin, celebrating the fact that they had just travelled 1.2 billion kilometres in a fraction of a second.

'Just a moment, I have something for just this occasion,' said Linda. She floated back to the galley area, rummaged in one of the refrigeration units and produced a bottle of Champagne. 'We'll have to open it carefully, but I believe the situation warrants it.'

'How did you get that on board?' asked Ed.

'I smuggled it up to the station a few weeks ago,' said Linda. 'It was for my birthday next month, but this would be a lot more momentous. It would've been a bit sad if we didn't have anything to celebrate with.'

'Did you bring any cigars?' said Andy, smiling, taking the bottle and removing the cork very, very gently.

They all turned towards the front window and toasted themselves, Saturn, the human race, the Virr Drive and anything else that came to mind, with careful swigs from the bottle.

'I suppose we should send a signal back to Earth,' said Ed.

'How long will it take from here?' said Linda.

'Almost eighty minutes,' said Andy.

'Wouldn't it be quicker to jump back and tell them in real time?' she said.

'Well, it would,' said Ed. 'But James asked us to do some scans of Saturn with the new arrays while we're here. NASA's had nothing coming out this way since the Cassini Probe over thirty years ago.'

'And the technological advances in scanning arrays means we can record a thousand times more information in a few minutes than Cassini did in years,' added Andy.

'You'll get no argument from me,' said Linda, laughing. 'You guys do what you have to do and I'll just sit back and enjoy this spectacular view.'

AS THE CARTELLA silently floated across the sunlit side of Saturn, Andy pushed the scanning arrays through their full repertoire, recording masses of data for James and his colleagues back at NASA.

Ed and Linda retreated to the galley and organised lunch.

'Mm, beef stroganoff,' said Andy. 'Have we got a nice Burgundy to go with it?'

'No, cranberry juice,' said Linda, '2050 vintage.'

'A very good year,' said Ed. 'No expense spared for us, eh?'

'And there's a 2049 raspberry cordial.'

'I'm welling up,' said Andy. 'How frillerous are they?'

'It's frivolous,' said Ed.

'Yeah, whatever. I'm an engineer, not a librarian.'

'Liability, more like,' said Linda, giggling.

'Just listen to her,' said Ed. 'Getting way too familiar with the English sense of humour.'

'Talking of familiar,' said Andy. 'I think we've been hanging around this planet for far too long. I've finished with the scans and the information has all been sent back to NASA. So, how about we undertake another little voyage into the unknown after lunch?'

'Shall we give it a real test?' said Ed, sinking down into his seat and letting it envelop him.

'When you say "real test",' said Linda. 'How far can this thing go? I mean, it must have a limit to its fold distance?'

'Yes, it does,' said Ed. 'Although, it's only a theory at the moment.'

'Only a theory,' said Linda, looking none too happy. 'What happens if you dial in a jump that the system hasn't enough power for?'

'Nothing,' said Ed. 'I built in a fail-safe that if the system doesn't contain enough energy to get us there, it doesn't initiate the fold.'

'Well, that's a relief,' said Linda, looking happier. 'I had visions of emerging with only half a ship.'

'This morning's fold used less than one hundredth of a percent of the full system's capability.'

'Wow, is that all? How much throttle are you going to give it next time?'

'We were thinking of Rigil Kentaurus,' mumbled Andy, through a mouthful of stroganoff.

'So, that's what Dewey was on about,' said Linda. 'The posh name for Alpha Centauri A.'

'Yeah,' said Ed. 'Jumping around your own solar system isn't of real interest; the latest Ion drives can get you around that in a matter of a few weeks anyway. It's jumping to other solar systems within our galaxy –

and maybe to other galaxies one day – that's the real deal.'

'Okay, then,' said Linda. 'In for a penny. How far is it to Rigil whatsisname?'

'Just over 4.3 light years, or – err – hang on.' Ed sat thinking for a moment. 'Around forty-one, I think,' he said eventually.

'Forty-one?' asked Linda. 'I thought it was forty-two,' she added with a sly grin.

'Forty-two?' quizzed Ed, now looking confused. 'It can't be as much as forty-two trillion kilometres, as one light year is only 9.5 trill—'

Andy burst out laughing.

'Brilliant Linda, absolutely brilliant,' he giggled. 'You got him. You're learning fast.'

Ed sat, looking between the two of them and shaking his head in bewilderment.

'What are you two on about?' he asked.

'Forty-two, Ed. It's the answer to the universal question,' said Andy.

Ed still looked blank.

'*Hitchhikers Guide to the*–'

'Ah shit,' said Ed. 'Yeah you got me. Well done, Linda.'

'Awesome,' said Linda, and high-fived Andy.

'Okay, road trip,' he said, winking at her whilst prepping the array for a fold.

Once lunch was over, Linda joined them at the front, strapped in and slowly spun the Cartella back so it was facing the direction of travel.

It had gone quiet as they all took a last look at Saturn as it swung slowly out of view.

'I'd like to make an executive decision and say no helmets during folding,' said Ed. 'The ship doesn't actually accelerate or decelerate and is no more likely to fail than at any other time.'

'I'm cool with that,' said Andy.

'All good with me,' said Linda. 'Although we best keep them attached to the seat.'

'Okay, full scans forward,' said Andy. 'I'm ready to rock.'

'The ship's all yours, Ed. Jump when ready,' said Linda.

'Hang on,' said Andy.

Ed paused, his finger poised over the purple flashing icon.

'What's up?' said Ed, looking over at Andy.

'We've run out of Champagne,' said Andy, with a horrified expression.

'You tosser,' said Ed and pressed the initiate fold icon hard.

The green haze enveloped the Cartella and, this time, there were no witnesses as it vanished.

15

THE OVAL OFFICE – WASHINGTON DC

JANUARY 25TH 2050, 1:49 P.M.

The President read the documents in front of him, but his mind was elsewhere.

After his conversation with the crew of the Cartella very early that morning, he couldn't concentrate on anything but the huge consequences of mankind having a workable star drive. If Edward Virr succeeded today, what would it really bring for the human race?

He sat back in his big leather chair and stared across the Oval Office at a large picture he'd insisted on hanging in the room.

It was a photograph of Armstrong Station above a beautiful blue Earth below, with the USA clearly visible below the station. As he gazed at the picture, he wondered how many similar Earths there were, waiting to be discovered. He knew, by being a bit of a space exploration junkie, that there were over four hundred billion stars in just our galaxy alone and the Milky Way was surrounded by billions of other galaxies.

Over the last few decades, long-range telescopes had found dozens of Earth-like planets, which orbited stars in the closest few solar systems. So, the odds for human habitable planets were quite staggering and the potential for millions of new Earths being easily reachable almost overnight was a sobering thought.

He believed mankind could evolve in two ways: one was with colonies keeping ties with Earth and forming a kind of commonwealth of planets; and the other was with colonisation ships disappearing off in all directions, never to be heard of again.

'Mr President. Mr President...'

President James started suddenly and realised his secretary had been calling him.

'Are you all right, sir?'

'Yes – yes, I'm fine – sorry. I was elsewhere there for a minute.'

'I have James Dewey and Donna McGuire on video link, sir.'

The President looked at his Gentab and then glanced at the picture on the wall again, before accepting the secure link.

'Good afternoon, Donna. Good afternoon, James. What's the news?'

'Good afternoon, Mr President,' said Dewey. 'We've

just received a signal from the Cartella, sir. A signal, yes.'

'Where are they?'

'Saturn, Mr President, Saturn. Taking pictures of Saturn and drinking Champagne,' said Dewey, laughing, completely unable to hide his excitement.

The President sat back in his chair and again glanced at his picture before looking back at the two smiling faces on his tablet.

'What are your thoughts, Donna?'

'Well, Mr President. This has to be one of the biggest moments in human history,' she said. 'It usurps everything up to now. But we have to be very careful and keep control of this technology as it could also be the end of human history.'

'I agree totally, Donna. The potential problems of losing control of this could have at least half the population of Earth disappearing off in all directions and then coming back with who knows what alien animal species, plants – diseases even – that could wipe out life on Earth in a week.'

'This technology must remain classified for the time being,' she said.

'Do you agree, James?'

'Unfortunately, I do, Mr President. Sad as it is, I too realise the consequences of this tech going unchecked. We will need a whole new government department—'

'Probably several,' said Donna, cutting in. 'With a raft of legislation governing every possible scenario – and I imagine several that we know nothing about yet. There's going to be stuff out there that'll make our toes curl.'

'So, we're in agreement then,' said the President. 'Classified at the highest level until we have some rules in place. That's good. I feel it will prove to be the right thing to do. James, I need you to select a small group of experts – people you can really trust – who can make a start at drawing up a basic rule book for the use of this tech. When you have your shortlist of candidates, bring them here to the White House so Donna and I can put the fear of god into them regarding nondisclosure. Does that make sense?'

'Absolutely, Mr President, absolutely,' said Dewey.

'Thank you, James. I'll speak to you in a few days.' The President clicked off the connection to Florida and looked at Donna with a frown.

'What's the Xavier Lake situation?'

'The stealth ship engaged his space plane around a hundred thousand kilometres out from Earth.'

'Was it destroyed?'

'We're not completely sure.'

'That doesn't sound very definitive, Donna.'

'He jumped less than a second before the missile struck.'

'Hmm, so his ship wasn't destroyed. Did we self-destruct the missile?'

'Well, that's the thing,' said Donna. 'When he jumped, the missile was so close to his ship, it jumped with him. It was included in the fold envelope.'

'Well, I'll be damned. Will it destroy the ship the second it emerges?'

'It's obviously never happened before, but we believe so, yes,'

He stared at her for a second; if she had any doubts, then she hid them well.

'Okay, then. Let's hope that's the case. He was a thief and a murderer and deserved it. Also, did the stealth ship return undetected?'

'It's back in its hangar in Nevada, Mr President, and there's been no chatter coming from any source regarding any detection of an unidentified ship.'

'Very good, Donna, thank you – and keep an eye on Dewey's selections, will you? Give them a run through your computers, just to be on the safe side.'

'Will do, Mr President.' And, with a nod, she disappeared from his screen.

16

TEST PLANE 71 – POSITION UNCONFIRMED

JANUARY 25TH 2050, 10:03 A.M. + 8HRS

Lake opened his eyes as the green haze dissipated from around the ship.

He'd braced for the missile impact that was less than one second away and nothing had happened. The jump must have been successful. If not, they'd have been a vapour trail by now.

'We jumped away from the weapon,' said Lake, starting to breathe again.

'Shit,' said Herez. 'No, we didn't. The missile – it came with us.'

'Where is it?'

'In front of us, moving away.'

'How can that be?' said Lake.

'It was travelling a lot faster than us,' said Herez. 'About fifteen thousand kilometres per hour faster.'

'If it came with us in the jump envelope then it must

have been only a fraction of a second from impact. And at its speed, that would be—' Lake thought for a moment. 'That would be two hundred and fifty kilometres a minute faster than us, which is just over four kilometres a second.'

'It passed us in the jump,' said Herez, looking distinctly alarmed.

'Or, through us. The jump computer must have regarded it as a separate entity and formed a second envelope. That's amazing.'

'Err – hang on – shit. Not again,' said Herez. 'It's turning – it's turning. It's going to re-engage us.'

'Sit back in your seat,' shouted Lake. He activated the Ion drives on full power, which squashed them both back into their seats. 'Anything on the array in front of us?'

'No, sir. There's a large object above us – five hundred kilometres out. Must be a meteor or a comet or something as it's going a lot faster than us and in a straight line.'

'Where's that missile?' said Lake, the whites of his knuckles clearly visible as he gripped the sides of the control panel.

'Still turning, still—' A whining note suddenly sounded in the cabin. 'Ah shit, that's missile lock. It's reacquired us – it's – now that's odd.'

'What is?' shouted Lake, now sounding very scared.

'It's going up over us,' said Herez, staring at his display. 'It's acquired a lock on – on the meteor.'

Lake cut the acceleration and sat up in his seat to stare at the scanning display.

'It must have a shitload of metal in it or something to enable a missile lock,' said Herez, looking a little happier now.

'I don't care, it just saved our lives.'

'Where are we, by the way?'

'Good question, Mr Herez. In all the excitement, I hadn't had a chance to see where the jump took us.' Lake checked the nav system, looked at it with a wide-eyed expression for a second and whistled through his teeth.

'Incredible,' he said.

'Well, how far did we jump?'

'One hundred and twenty-six light years,' said Lake, grinning for the first time in a while.

'You have got to be shitting me.'

'No bull,' said Lake. 'It's quite clear on the nav—'

'Not the distance,' shouted Herez. 'The bloody Meteor – it's – it's – no that can't be right. That's impossible.'

Lake looked across at the scanning display again to see Herez frantically hitting icons and frowning, his face white as a sheet.

'What's up with the meteor?'

'It's bloody slowing down.'

'Bollocks,' said Lake. 'That's impossible.'

'It is, and there — it just changed direction.' Herez looked over at Lake with real fear on his face. 'It's now matched our speed and course exactly.'

'Is it a ship?'

'It can't be. It's fourteen fucking kilometres long.'

'How far away is it?'

'Four hundred kilometres.'

'Get some cameras on it. Maximum magnification.'

The camera pod on the top of the ship panned upwards and zoomed in on an enormous dark object, following their trajectory. The only reason they knew it was there, was because of the stars it blocked out. As they stared at the monitor, a second much smaller and brighter object slowly slipped into view, heading towards the bigger one.

'Shit, that's the missile,' said Herez. 'Do we have any way to warn—'

As he spoke, a flash of light emanated from the big object, like a dead-straight bolt of lightning, and the missile exploded harmlessly, fifty kilometres short of its target.

'Well, whoever they are, they're armed,' said Lake, now unsure whether he should be enthralled or scared or both.

'Can we jump away?' asked Herez, visibly trembling.

Lake looked at Herez and back at the monitor, showing what was now quite obviously an enormous space ship. Lake wondered if someone on Earth could possibly construct something so huge in secret, but discarded the thought almost immediately. The logistics of constructing a ship of this size in plain sight would be next to impossible. But clandestinely? Not a chance.

'Do we want to jump, though?' said Lake.

'Well, I fucking do,' shouted Herez. 'They're going to think we fired that missile at them and smear us into the next galaxy.'

'That ship is hugely advanced,' said Lake. 'Their technology is light years ahead of us. I'm sure they realise that we were trying to avoid that missile and, anyway, this is first contact, something the human race has wondered about for thousands of years. Aren't you even the remotest bit intrigued as to who they—'

They were both flung around in their seats as their ship started to swing up towards the alien vessel. As they looked at the monitor, the camera panned around and kept the huge ship in view, which began to grow in size.

'They're coming closer,' shouted Herez, trying to hang on to his seat.

'I believe we're going to them.'

'Can't you jump or light the Ion drive, and get us away from them?'

'I think it would be as pointless as trying to tow an office block with a bicycle, Mr Herez,' said Lake, watching as they were dragged closer.

Herez looked at Lake with a surprised expression. 'You're giving up,' said Herez, in a shocked tone.

'It's more like knowing when you're outclassed and trying not to look too aggressive, Mr Herez,' said Lake, putting his hands behind his head and leaning back in his seat.

'Well, I can at least give their ship a full scan and see what we're up against,' said Herez, starting to punch icons on his display. 'Shit,' he said as his control display went dark, closely followed by the helm display, and then everything else on the ship, except for the cabin lights and the life-support system.

'That's a good sign,' said Lake.

'Are you bloody joking? They just turned our ship off.'

'But they left the lights and life support on,' said Lake. 'So, they don't want us dead.'

He leaned forward to see if anything was visible out of the front screen. It wasn't, but with the size of that ship, he knew they would see it very soon.

17

THE CARTELLA SPACEPLANE –

ALPHA CENTAURI A (RIGIL KENTAURUS), CONSTELLATION OF CENTAURUS

January 25th 2050, 12:01 P.M.

The green haze faded. Three faces looked over at the Holonav as Ed pressed the icon for navigation compute. It flashed up with indicators, instructing them of the three-star system they'd emerged into.

They were sixty-seven million kilometres from Alpha Centauri A which, at 1.1 times the mass of the Sun, was the largest and brightest of the three.

'Congratulations, everyone,' said Ed. 'Welcome to the triple-star Centauri system.'

'Wow, this gets better and better,' said Linda. 'Are we clear ahead, Cactus?' She glanced across at Andy who was busy studying his display.

'Yep, nothing near us within one hundred million kilometres apart from the star. I'll scan for planets around Centauri A and B as there's been controversy over those two for decades.'

'What about C?' asked Linda, gazing at the Holonav, which clearly showed the red dwarf close by.

'That's a different story,' said Ed. 'We've known about an exoplanet in the habitable zone around that little star for some time. We can have a mini jump over there in a while to check it out, but in the meantime, I need to do a full diagnostic on the fold drive.'

Linda suddenly looked concerned.

'It's working okay, though?' she said, nervously.

'Yes, it's fine,' said Ed. 'I just need to record the parameters of each jump to build up a database for the engineers back at NASA.'

'Six,' said Andy, suddenly, and a little overloud, making the other two jump. 'Sorry, guys, I get a bit carried away with all this record-breaking and history-making.'

'I take it you've found six planets,' said Ed.

'I have,' he said, looking smug. 'Although, none are Goldilocks.'

'What?' asked Linda, her arms folded across her chest.

The other two looked at each other and then down at their relative displays and data.

'That's interesting,' said Ed, looking up and smiling. 'We used 1.8 percent capability on that fold.'

'Really,' said Andy, looking pleased. 'That's awesome.'

'Hang on a minute,' said Linda. 'You two go back a bit. You can't just slot Goldilocks into a sentence, and then move on. What the hell is Goldilocks?'

Ed looked at Andy, 'You can tell her.'

'Well,' said Andy. 'It's when you discover a new planet in a solar system that's not too hot and not too cold, but just right.'

'What, you mean habitable?'

'Yeah,' said Andy.

'Why can't you just say habitable? Why do you have to make up a silly name?'

'It's a recognised NASA term and has been for decades,' said Ed.

She shook her head. 'What is it with men and stupid code names?'

'I don't know, Slopes,' said Andy.

'If I wasn't strapped into this seat, Andrew…'

'I think we are about to work out the jump capacity for this ship,' said Ed, changing the subject quickly. 'If we travelled 4.37 light years, using only 1.8 percent power, then we have a potential range of—'

Linda unclipped her Gentab from the helm display and tapped away for a moment. 'Of around 242 light years,' she said, looking up at the other two with a hopeful expression.

'Spot on,' said Andy, giving her a thumbs-up and a big grin.

Linda stuck her tongue out.

'You have to allow a little bit for gravitational effects here and there, but 242 light years would seem to be around this system's capacity,' said Ed, also giving Linda a thumbs-up.

'Can you record that into the history books?' said Linda, smiling at last.

'I think the fact that you piloted the first jump ship will make you your fame and fortune, Miss Slopes,' said Ed. 'Have you started writing your acceptance speeches yet?'

'Shit, I hadn't thought of that,' said Linda. 'I'm crap at public speaking too.'

'You're not alone there,' said Ed, with a worried look. 'And I have to give lectures—'

'I don't think these planets are going to give anyone at NASA an erection,' interrupted Andy. 'They're all either balls of lava or blocks of ice. I'm ready to jump over and have a look at one of Proxima Centauri's planets.'

'I'll charge the drive,' said Ed. 'How close do you need to be to get the most out of the array?'

'Around three hundred thousand kilometres would

be top marks, Mr Virr,' said Andy. 'I'm looking forward to scanning a potentially habitable planet – the tidal effects from the red dwarf might make the weather a little unpredictable – but it is well within the zone.'

'Okay, Linda. Be ready to spin the ship to port again – I'm hoping to emerge in a similar configuration to Saturn,' said Ed, waiting for the drive computer to accept the co-ordinates.

'I'm ready,' said Linda, looking across at Andy, who was prepping the array for the jump.

'Ready boss,' said Andy after a couple of seconds and sat back in his seat.

'Folding in three, two, one.' He hit the purple flashing icon once again.

They watched the now-familiar green haze form around the ship, heard a faint whining in the background and a clunk, and then total darkness.

'What the hell, was that the landing struts extending?' shouted Linda, from the complete blackness of the cockpit. 'Have we just blown a fuse?'

'Shit,' said Andy.

'Bollocks,' said Ed.

'That doesn't help much, guys,' said Linda. 'There's torches in a holder on the right-hand side of the cockpit wall.'

'I'll go,' said Andy. 'I know where they are.' He

released his belts and fumbled around the wall of the cabin. Finding the release handle for the emergency kit, he pulled it open and rummaged inside.

'On the left, I think. Just inside the hatch,' said Linda. 'Have you found them?'

'Yes, got one,' said Andy, and he flicked it on, swinging it around the cabin. 'Hang on, I'll get the other two.'

'Andy?' said Linda, staring at him with a puzzled expression.

'What?' he said, standing up and staring back.

'You're – standing up,' she said, pointing at his feet. Andy looked down and took a couple of paces across the cabin.

'Oh, fuck me – we've got gravity,' said Andy.

'That can't be,' said Linda, looking over at Ed.

'Not unless we're accelerating at around 1 gee straight upwards,' said Ed, looking up at the ceiling, which made the other two follow his gaze.

Linda jumped out of her seat, grabbed another torch and shone it at the front window, gazing up to see … absolutely nothing.

'There's no stars. It's completely black out there.'

'There's no planet on the port side either,' said Ed, who had also released himself from his seat and was peering out the left side of the front screen. 'Andy, see if you can get the power back on in engineering. Do you remember where the trips are?'

'Yes, boss,' he said as he walked slowly on wobbly legs back through the ship to the engineering bay.

Ed pulled open a small hatch underneath his control display and proceeded to check the local trip switches were all on. He did the same for the helm and for the engineering panel as well. All were as they should be.

Andy walked back into the cockpit with a puzzled look and bent down to pull open the same small hatch underneath his engineering panel.

'They're all good, Andy,' said Ed. 'I've checked all three panels. I take it the main trips are all on too?'

'Yep,' said Andy. 'But have you noticed everything is non-functioning, except the life-support system?'

'Shit, you're right,' said Ed. 'And Linda said the whining before the lights went out were the landing struts extending. Have we auto-landed on a moon or something?'

'The ship doesn't have anything like that built in,' said Andy. 'We were travelling at forty-six thousand kilometres per hour, so the deceleration would have been a high gee, reverse-ion burn for several minutes – so, no, we haven't landed anywhere. That's completely impossible. I'll put money on the fact—'

Suddenly, the lights came back on, which made

them all jump and, two seconds later, all three control panels began their boot-up routines.

'Did someone do something?' asked Linda.

'No,' said the other two in unison.

Then all three looked at each other in horror as they heard the distinct sound of the outer airlock door cycling open.

18

EMPOROS CLASS FREIGHTER – ENTERING THE KRIX'IR SYSTEM

DAY 413, YEAR 11269, 17:12FC, PCC

The freighter turned at the correct waypoint, in towards the planet Krix'ir. For the past three weeks, the ship had kept to its predetermined schedule and nothing had changed.

Cargo was picked up and delivered at the various ports of call, exactly as normal. No one had any idea the freighter had been boarded just before leaving Krix'ir three weeks earlier.

Captain Haarrs and his seven-man crew were rendered unconscious in a matter of seconds and secured in an unused stores hold. The eight Antistasi resistance fighters had then put into play the elaborate deception that had been years in the planning.

Major Luzin sat on one of the bridge command couches. He was alert now and a little nervous. The completion of his highly secret mission was close and the success or failure of the three-week masquerade relied entirely on the next couple of hours.

'What time do you want the crew knocked unconscious, sir?' asked his sergeant.

'Ten minutes before we dock. That will give us several hours, firstly to unload as if nothing's awry, and then time to change and disappear,' he said. 'I'm relying on the crew not being discovered and released until loading tomorrow morning.'

The sergeant nodded, turned and disappeared off the bridge.

Luzin took out a small communication scrambler that had been in his pocket for the entire mission. This was the first and only time he would transmit from the ship anything other than standard ship protocol transmissions. He set the device on the console, ensured it was functioning correctly and opened a narrow channel directly at the nearest Krix'ir communications satellite.

'Meizon reporting,' he said and waited.

Thirty seconds later he got his reply.

'Go ahead, Meizon.'

'Package delivered successfully on 395 as planned.'

'Any unforeseen difficulties?'

'Negative.'

'Thank you, Meizon. Have a safe extraction – control out.'

Luzin stood up and walked over to his navigation officer. 'Keep her on this course. Nice and steady for the next thirty minutes please, Lieutenant – standard Krix'ir orbital protocol.'

'Yes, sir.'

He strolled off the bridge, straight to his cabin and unscrewed a panel in the bathroom, then picked out a small remote control and put it in his pocket, also grabbing a pre-packed bag from under the bed. Returning to the main corridor, he strolled down as far as possible away from the bridge and quickly opened an escape shuttle hatch, threw in the bag and jumped inside, sealing the hatch behind him.

Knowing an alarm was now sounding on the bridge, he quickly slipped into the pilot's seat, removed the safety cover and immediately hit the manual launch toggle. The tiny shuttle slammed away from the freighter and, ignoring the insistent questioning coming from the freighters bridge, he steered the little ship around the freighter and accelerated so the larger ship was directly behind him. With the planet Krix'ir directly in front and, checking he was at a safe distance from the freighter, he retrieved the remote from his pocket. Next, he ensured he was tightly strapped in and there were no loose items in the shuttle. Once satisfied, he removed the cover from the remote and depressed the red button.

Behind him, the Krix'ir Emporos Class Freighter

exploded. The eleven charges he'd hidden overnight at crucial points within the ship had pulled it apart from the seams.

He rammed the throttles to the maximum for a few seconds and then turned everything off, so the only sound was the rattle of debris on the outer hull. The escape shuttle began tumbling towards the planet, surrounded by debris from the freighter.

Half an hour later, as the shuttle reached the upper atmosphere, he activated the manoeuvring jets to position the ship at the correct attitude for a safe insertion. As he dropped deeper into the blinding blue of the planet, he could make out other pieces of the freighter above and around him, plummeting with their own fiery trails belching out behind, and hoped they covered his own insertion trail.

He risked a quick scan below to find out where exactly he was.

As Krix'ir's land masses were mostly desert and he had deliberately timed the approach so the majorly-populated zone was on the far side, he knew there would be very little below to detect him.

At twenty thousand metres, he activated the anti-gravity drive and arrested his plummet to a more controlled dive, only levelling out at one thousand metres. The small mining town or settlement he had to find was around two hundred kilometres away, so he slowly made his way in that direction. Scanning for movement ahead was his main priority, as he didn't want to bump into anyone who could report his arrival.

When he began to get life readings around five kilometres ahead, so he searched below and landed the small craft in a narrow rocky valley. With one last glance at the scanner to ensure he was alone, he set the final explosive charge inside the escape shuttle, changed into local dress and began to walk in the direction of the town.

A few minutes later as he activated the charge, the low boom went unnoticed – it was an everyday background noise in a mining community.

On reaching the small town, he was pleased to find he could get a seat on a miners personnel transport the following morning to Goss'inray, the main settlement seven thousand kilometres away. He was slightly less enthused on hearing that all off-planet transportation had been postponed due to an unexplained orbital accident. The fact he might be on Krix'ir for a little longer than anticipated had been foreseen. Forever the consummate planner, Luzin had grown a beard, which was all the rage in the local mining community. He'd bought locally made clothing and ensured he had plenty of Krix'ir mining chits, and not the GDA interplanetary Prosfora currency.

Sitting back in his seat in the rear of a small café, he

allowed himself a little smile – the first for weeks. The hard work was done. Getting home and back underground where he belonged should now prove the easy part.

Other than the dust and flies that permanently invaded every orifice, he didn't anticipate encountering any problems from now on.

19

ALONGSIDE ALIEN STARSHIP – 126 LIGHT YEARS FROM EARTH

JANUARY 25TH 2050, 10:17 A.M. + 8HRS

'It appears, Mr Herez, that the answer to the age old question, "are we alone?" is an emphatic no,' said Lake, as their tiny space plane was drawn up closer to the immense matt black starship.

They both craned their necks, trying to look up out of the front screen again; only this time there were no stars above them. It was all ship.

'They must have some sort of energy beam that can disable our systems and drag us in,' said Herez. 'They haven't attached a cable or anything.'

'You haven't watched much sci-fi, have you?' said Lake. 'It's called a tractor beam – at least it is on all the movies I've watched.'

Herez just turned and stared at him as if he was insane and Lake realised, partly by the fact that Herez was visibly shaking and partly by the smell of urine in the cabin, just how terrified Herez really was.

Their ship turned and continued up the side of the alien vessel. No light emanated from any part of the vessel either: it was gargantuan, matt black and eerily menacing. They could see along its almost-featureless length, the occasional ripple or blister in its never-ending expanse.

Suddenly, a section of the hull opened – or disappeared, was a better term. One minute, it was a solid section of hull; the next, a gaping floodlit hangar was directly in front of their ship, with several strange-looking craft parked along the far wall.

An invisible barrier shimmered as they were drawn inside and the outer hull immediately reverted to its original dull characterless footing.

Once they passed through the invisible barrier, gravity pushed them down into their seats and anything loose in the cockpit dropped to the floor.

The sudden whirring of the landing skids made them both jump and the space plane clunked down in a corner of the hangar facing a wall. There was silence for a few seconds, followed by a few bangs and scrapes, then they heard the outer airlock cycling. They both remained very quiet and still, wondering what the hell was on the other side of that airlock door.

It wasn't long before the door control chimed and

went green. The inner door slid up into its housing, with a slight hiss of equalising pressure, and immediately a disc-shaped object, about a half-metre in diameter, zipped into the cabin and hung motionless in the centre of the cabin. It slowly turned, emitting flashes of light in an array of colours, which lasted about thirty seconds. Then a commanding voice boomed out from the disc in an alien language that sounded like a string of commands.

'We don't understand your language,' said Lake, in as loud a voice as he could muster without actually shouting.

There was silence for a moment and then the voice returned, speaking in English.

'Why you are conversing in Gaia dialektos?' said the voice.

'I don't understand the question, what is Gaia dialektos?' asked Lake.

'Gaia is a class PV planet and is on katapato list red,' said the voice.

'H – hang on,' said Herez, sounding as scared as he looked. 'Katapato is a word I know. We did an operation in Greece once and all around the target villa were signs saying "ochi katapato". It meant no encroaching or trespassing—'

'So,' said Lake, interrupting. 'The planet Gaia is on a red list of no trespassing – so where the hell is Gaia?'

'Gaia is on the system Helios,' said the voice.

'Look up Gaia and Helios in a Greek dictionary,' said Herez.

Lake tried a couple of commands into the ship's computer, but nothing happened.

'I need to access my computer to translate what you're saying,' said Lake, looking at the hovering disc with a hopeful expression.

'Minor access available,' said the voice, after a few seconds.

Lake typed in Gaia and Helios, and asked for a translation.

'Well, that explains a lot,' said Lake 'They're both Greek words, all right. Helios is the sun and Gaia is the Earth.'

'So, Earth is on a no trespassing red list,' said Herez. 'Whatever that is.'

Lake looked at the disc again, adopting his best diplomatic face.

'We are from Gaia – although we call it Earth – and we—'

'This not is true,' boomed the voice, continuing in broken English and interrupting with an impatient tone. 'Gaia is backward still technology, race-aggressive with unkind bias, utilise only fossil fuel ability, no jump drive capability on Helios System.'

'There is now,' said Lake. 'And what do you mean

by an unkind bias?'

'Genocide on selves common, recommended negative for GDA membership,' said the voice. 'You fire fossil fuel weapon at us without provocation – definite unkind bias, as this was first response from emerge.'

'We did not fire on you,' said Lake. 'We have no weapon systems on this ship. You've scanned our ship and slaved into its systems, so you know we have no weaponry. That missile was fired at us by an unidentified ship in the Helios System. We jumped to try and avoid it, only it came with us in the jump—'

'This not is true,' boomed the voice again. 'You to be below arrest on crimes diverse, detention on Katadromiko 37 until Synedrio hearing confirmed at Dasos sitting next. Remain immobile on boarding, noncompliance becomes quickly detrimental to life.'

'Well, that's just dandy,' said Lake, again tapping away at the ship's computer. 'Sit still or be killed. I wonder who we're being arrested by?'

They didn't have to wait long. The flashing, rotating disc zipped back out the door and was replaced by four stocky humanoid figures, dressed in a full grey body-armour and helmets, their faces hidden by curved screens that seemed to have some sort of head-up display, continually flashing information across them. They also had what looked like a weapon system strapped to their forearms. They kept these pointing at Lake and Herez at all times. Two of the soldiers remained covering the prisoners, while the other two disappeared into the back of the ship, shortly to return, as there were only two small cabins and a kitchen area to check.

'Safi?' asked one of the remaining soldiers.

'Safi,' replied one of the returning soldiers.

The first soldier touched an icon on a small screen on the back of his hand.

'Stand and remain subdued,' he said. 'Follow lieutenant into security housing.'

They both stood, looking at each other, knowing there was absolutely nothing they could do but comply.

They were led out of the airlock, down some steps that had been pushed against the hull and across the vast hangar. As Lake looked around, he counted six other ships parked along one wall, all of varying sizes. It looked like a set from a sci-fi movie. He noticed that two of the ships had the tell-tale scorch marks on the underside of Earth like planet insertion and wondered where these planets were and if he'd get to see some of them one day.

They continued through a door and down several, bland, grey passageways until they were ushered into what looked to be a small one-carriage subway train. The doors silently closed and the round tube-like carriage soundlessly swished away from the station. They lost count of how many stations they went through and, at one point, the carriage stopped and went up several decks before continuing again.

Finally, after about twenty minutes it stopped and they were escorted out into an open corridor. One wall was solid and the other was open with a chest high green coloured railing.

It overlooked an enormous cavern that must have been several kilometres long and at least two wide, with trees, parks – even a river flowing between groups of buildings. Birds could be seen flying between the trees. Lake and Herez stared open-mouthed, not quite believing they were still aboard a space ship.

'It seems we're a little behind the eight ball compared to the rest of the galaxy, Mr Herez,' said Lake, glancing across at a very subdued and miserable looking Herez.

'I feel quite ill,' said Herez, obviously becoming more self-conscious of his very damp crotch that was probably beginning to chafe with all the walking.

Lake noticed he was getting unusually fatigued and soon realised it was the artificial gravity on the ship, set slightly higher than that of Earth.

'Have you noticed how short and stocky the majority of people are on the ship?' said Lake. 'Their home planet gravity must be higher than ours.'

'I need a shower and a lie down,' answered Herez, continuing to remain in his sulky funk.

The lead soldier led them into what must be a security wing. They were handed over to some slightly less aggressive-looking security staff, searched, stripped of any possessions and placed in what they thought were side rooms.

They turned out to be cells– very comfortable cells. They each had a bedroom with a couch, a table, a chair and a small bathroom, and some sort of holographic vision system for entertainment.

As the security officers left them in their new homes, the doorways shimmered, similar to the big hangar door their ship had entered through. Lake quickly discovered that the officers could pass through these doors unimpeded, but he couldn't. It was a solid barrier to him that made his skin tingle when he touched it.

The security staff that had taken responsibility for them were not wearing body armour or helmets and, for the first time, Lake could see what his captors really looked like. They were shorter than him at around five and a half feet tall, but they were very powerful in the upper body, with huge arms and shoulders that reminded Lake of professional rugby players. Their heads were almost human, but when you looked closer, they had a slightly more protruding forehead and a squarer jaw.

After about an hour, a trolley motored into his room, followed by a guard, and a meal was placed on the table. The security officer did not seem remotely concerned about being alone with the prisoner or turning his back on him either. Lake concluded that there must be systems within the room that would subdue him if he showed even the smallest degree of aggression.

The officer pulled a small device out of his pocket and scanned Lake as he was sitting on the couch.

'What does that do?' he asked.

The officer looked up at him and touched an icon on a small pad attached to his forearm.

'Please repeat?' he said through the translator.

'What does that scanner do?' repeated Lake.

'Body nutrient gauge,' said the officer. 'Discover nutrient needs, so health maximum achieved.'

'Thank you. My name is Lake. What's your name?'

'Carlon,' said the officer, and smiled. 'Is you from Gaia on system Helios really?'

'Yes, we are, Carlon,' said Lake. 'Although we seem to have offended your people by mistake.'

'Be patient, Lake,' said Carlon. 'If truthful proved, you guest on honour with GDA.'

'What is GDA, Carlon?' asked Lake.

Carlon looked thoughtful for a moment and turned off his translator. 'Gerousia Dipodi Agones,' he said, then turned the translator back on. 'Council for Bipedal Races,' he repeated. 'Is translation understand?'

'Yes, thank you, Carlon,' said Lake, grinning. 'Now, how does this visual entertainment system work?'

The meal was some kind of stew – similar to an Irish stew – served with something resembling pitta bread. Lake had to admit it was quite delicious. The drink was some sort of cordial and tasted faintly of raspberries, which was all right, but he felt a nice bottle of 2046 Puligny Montrachet would have been much better.

'I'll have a word with my new best mate, Carlon, and see if they have any wine,' said Lake, chuckling to himself, as he reclined on the couch and watched a badly-translated holographic history of the GDA.

He could hear Herez next door, snoring.

20

THE CARTELLA SPACEPLANE –
PROXIMA CENTAURI,
CONSTELLATION CENTAURUS

JANUARY 25TH 2050, 1:29 P.M.

'What the hell?' they all shouted in unison.

'Helmets on,' called Linda. They all dived for their helmets which were clipped to the side of their seats. Linda and Andy managed to get theirs on in record time, but Ed was shaking badly and was all fingers and thumbs. He got a bit of help from Andy and was soon safely sealed up.

They all jumped into their seats and belted up before the inner door failed and the cabin depressurised.

Only it didn't.

There were a few clunks and what sounded like a muted voice swearing.

'Was that someone talking?' said Andy, staring at the airlock door, his eyes the size of dinner plates.

'Are we recording this?' said Linda, gripping the sides of her seat.

'I want to go home now,' said Ed, who was the most uncomfortable, being nearest to the door.

The knock at the inner door made them all jump again.

Then a muffled voice said, 'Hello, anyone home?' in perfect English.

Quick as a flash, Andy replied, 'Three Jedi Knights and we're really pissed off.'

Linda stared at Andy as if he was insane.

'I told you he jokes around when he's nervous,' whispered Ed.

'Ah, would that be Andy Skywalker?' said the voice.

They all looked at each other with complete disbelief.

'Please don't activate your light sabre as it'll set off all the weapon proximity alarms and that just creates paperwork,' the voice continued. 'I'm going to open the inner airlock door now, so please don't panic or anything. We wish you no harm.'

'Resistance is futile,' whispered Andy, trying to remain sane.

The airlock door cycled up with a slight hiss into its housing to show an empty doorway. A smiling face peered round the left-hand side of the door.

'Hello. Permission to come aboard?'

'By all means. Come in,' said Ed. 'It's not that we could stop you.'

The other two sat gazing as a young human male of about twenty stepped cautiously into the cockpit. He stood at about six feet tall, had short brown hair, deep blue eyes and wore a Nirvana T-shirt with blue jeans and bright red and gold trainers.

'Good afternoon, Ed, Linda, Andy,' he said, nodding at each as he said their names. 'Or should I call you Head Butt, Slopes and Cactus?' he continued, smiling again. 'My name's Phil, by the way.' He walked over and shook them all by the hand. 'Please take off your helmets; we have the same oxygen-based atmosphere as you. It's quite safe, and sorry for the suddenness of the meeting. We were planning to introduce ourselves with a little more subtlety, but when you attempted to jump into the vicinity of Uskrre, we were forced to intervene. The planetary defence system there would have detected you and probably vaporised your ship in seconds. The Klatt are just a little oversensitive about their territory and security.'

They all removed their helmets slowly, clipping them back next to their seats and sniffing the air suspiciously.

'Err, how is it you speak English?' asked Ed, looking a little puzzled. 'I mean, you speak it better than me and I'm English. And you're from – where exactly?'

'Yes, yes, sorry. You will have a lot of questions and I wish we had a sort of introduction to your local galaxy video I could show you,' said Phil. 'There is an enormous database of information in our ship's core that you will have access to shortly. In the meantime, I'll try to give you a speed-readers tour, so you don't feel quite so lost.'

Phil strolled across the cabin and sat cross-legged on the floor with his back to the bulkhead.

They all rotated their seats to face him.

'Okay, we're Theos. Our home world is on Paradeisos, in the Aspro System. We kinda look out for underdeveloped humanoid worlds that are on our patch, which is where you guys come in.'

'So, we're underdeveloped?' said Ed. 'That's the nicest thing an alien has ever said to me.'

'Ah, sarcasm. I love sarcasm; not a lot of the other races get it. That's why I love coming over to Gaia and sitting in a London or New York pub, joining in with the local banter. It's so refreshing and entertaining.'

'Gaia?' questioned Ed. 'What's that when it's at home?'

'Sorry, yes. Earth is known to us as Gaia – or to everyone really, as we all use the same star maps. Your Sun is called Helios, so when others ask, you come from Gaia in the Helios System.'

'How many times have you come down to Earth?' asked Linda. 'And how, I mean, where do you park?'

'We can cloak our ships very well. This ship stays in a high orbit and we use a smaller atmospheric shuttle that can take the entry. As for how many times, I've lost count.'

'Is that where you got the Nirvana shirt?' asked Andy.

'Yeah, one of the best gigs I saw – apart from Genesis and Pink Floyd. I always visited when they were touring. Jimi Hendrix, as well, although he wasn't originally from Earth.'

'Hang on there, just a minute,' said Ed, looking at Phil suspiciously. 'Kurt Cobain died in the nineties, well over fifty years ago. You're only, what – in your twenties, so how come you're telling us you saw them live – or do you mean on video?'

'We overcame the ageing process a long time ago, so I always look like this,' said Phil, smiling.

'How old are you then?' asked Linda, looking at him strangely.

'In Gaia – sorry, Earth – years, I'm just over three thousand eight hundred or thereabouts,' he answered, giving them a thumbs-up.

There was complete silence for a few moments, which was eventually broken by Andy. 'You don't look a day over two thousand.'

'There it is,' said Phil, laughing. 'That Earth humour, gets me every time.'

He received a row of blank faces glaring back at him.

'Phil,' said Ed. 'How long has your race been in space?'

'Over nine thousand Earth years,' he said, nonchalantly. 'We'll get the hang of it eventually.' He grinned profusely again.

Unfortunately, as before, he got no smiles in return.

'How many human planets are there out here, Phil?' asked Ed, already afraid of the answer.

'We have so far logged over twenty thousand systems in this galaxy, with humanoid life forms in some form of development. But of course, with over four hundred billion systems, we've barely scratched the surface.'

'Twenty thousand,' they all chorused and looked at each other in astonishment.

'Welcome to the club,' said Phil. 'And so that you know, another reason for us dropping you into one of our hangar bays – apart from stopping you getting vaporised – is that all jumps within the galaxy have to be to – and from – designated jump zones in each system and pre-logged with the GDA.'

'Where are all the designated zones and how the hell do we log a jump?' asked Ed.

'You apply to the GDA, by pulse transmission. The zones have been set for thousands of years,' replied Phil. 'And before you say anything, we'll update your navigation system with everything you need. In actual fact, we'll give your ship a full upgrade to bring it into line with all the CTAs.'

They all looked puzzled.

'What's the GDA?' said Ed.

'And what on earth is a CTA?' added Andy.

'Okay,' said Phil. 'This is where I wish I had that introductory video. The Gerousia Dipodi Agones – or in English, The Council of Bipedal Races. They're based on Dasos, a planet in the Prasinos System. A word of advice: do not disagree or pick a fight with them. At the last count, they had one thousand six hundred and seventy-four members, some of whom are almost as advanced as us and they dispose of dissenters, as you would an annoying itch. They have battle cruisers the size of small planets, crewed by officers and soldiers that have – to use a really excellent Earth term – "a complete sense of humour bypass".'

'CTA's?' reminded Andy, looking hopeful.

'Ah, yes,' said Phil. 'Choros Taxidi Apaitiseon or Space Voyaging Requisites. It's the minimum safety design requirements for all spacefaring vessels and is policed by the GDA. I'll get a copy translated into

English for you, but as I said before, we'll ensure your ship complies before you leave.'

Linda looked at Phil suspiciously with her arms crossed. 'Why are you helping us, Phil. Really, what's in it for you guys? I don't want to appear rude, or ungrateful, or anything, but where I come from, there's no such thing as a free lunch. There's always a catch. Can you tell us where we really stand in all of this?'

'It's right for you to be a little suspicious,' said Phil. 'And we would have been surprised if you hadn't been. Look at it from our point of view: every thousand years or so, a previously quarantined immature humanoid planet develops jump technology. Out they come, all wide-eyed and brave, in a contraption that could fail at the drop of a hat. We knew you wouldn't be long, so we left an FTL detection buoy in your system. It detected your first jump out to the ringed planet. We watched and waited to see where you went next and jumped here with you. But getting back to your question: there is no catch. We want humanoid races to flourish in this galaxy and, once you're out here, you might as well have the same as everyone else, otherwise it just leaves you open to be exploited. As you can imagine, there are races out here who – let's just say — aren't as benevolent as we are.'

'How come I didn't detect you when I scanned the

whole system for planets?' said Andy, pointing at his control console.

'Two reasons: one, we have stealth technology; two, your scanning array is thousands of years out of date.'

'How do we fare overall?' asked Ed.

'Let's say, a little better from now on.'

'You little diplomat, you,' laughed Linda, now relaxing a little.

'Talking of diplomacy,' said Phil. 'If you'd like to change out of your EVA suits, I'll give you all a tour of the ship and a rundown of how much technology has moved on in the last few millennia.'

They all filed back to their cabins to change, enjoying the gravity and Ed wondered how he would be able to sleep in a weightless cot under its influence.

Dressed in light NASA flight suits, they emerged and followed Phil out of the airlock and into the hangar. Apart from their space plane, it contained two other small strange-looking ships, both slightly larger than theirs and, judging from the heat scarring on the undersides, they were capable of penetrating a planet's atmosphere.

'Are you hungry?' asked Phil. 'Because, having been on Earth, I think you'll find the food we eat is quite palatable.'

'I'll give it a go,' said Andy. 'What have you got?'

'Two minutes after first contact and you want to

stuff your face,' said Linda, giving him a dubious glance.

'What if we get sick?' said Ed as they all trooped through a door at the rear of the hangar; it just dematerialised as they approached and reappeared again behind them.

'You won't,' said Phil as he led them down pure white corridors with no obvious lighting.

The walls and ceiling all emitted a glow that got brighter as they progressed along and then resumed back to a dulled level once passed. They were ushered into a two-metre cylindrical tube, which sealed as soon as they were all inside and then seemingly moved upwards, completely silently.

'The ship scanned all three of you earlier to ensure you're healthy,' said Phil. 'Part of that informed us of your dietary requirements and any possible vitamin shortfall – plus any toxins in your systems that need addressing.'

'Shit,' said Ed. 'That must be a long list.'

'Actually, you're all in reasonable shape. Although, Andy, we're puzzled as to why you have a high ethanol reading,' said Phil, giving him a sideways glance.

'Ethanol – why would I have a high amount of that?' asked Andy, looking surprised and wrinkling his nose at the thought.

'Antifreeze,' said Linda. 'Wouldn't want you getting all stiff, would we,' she said, punching him in the arm.

'Actually,' said Ed, looking thoughtful. 'I seem to remember a high percentage of Tequila is ethanol.'

'Ah, shit,' said Andy. 'Here we go again. And you can shut up,' he quickly added, pointing at Linda as she opened her mouth.

The cylindrical elevator suddenly popped up into a large round darkened room. The opaque elevator wall surrounding them disappeared and they all stepped out into the middle of the large room. They soon noticed they were standing in amongst a three-dimensional star map. Four reclined couches sat on low pedestals, three of which were occupied by male humans, all seemingly around the same age as Phil. They all wore similar Earth-style clothes to Phil and had very thin headsets, which looked like old-fashioned bicycle helmets. Hanging in the air, directly in front of each couch, were translucent projected consoles, almost like oversized, stand-alone, head-up displays from fighter jets.

'Welcome to the holo bridge,' said Phil, looking immensely proud. 'And the rest of the crew. That's Mike, Steve and Tony,' he said, pointing at each crew member as he named them.

They all waved in return.

'There are only four of you?' questioned Ed.

'We only actually need three,' said Phil. 'But it's

good to have a contingency.'

'And then there were three,' stated Andy and winked at Phil.

'Very good, Mr Faux,' said Phil, pointing at him. 'We took bets, as we didn't think anyone would get that.'

'Get what, exactly?' said Linda, looking perplexed.

'Genesis,' said Andy. 'They're all named after members of Genesis.'

'What about Peter Gabriel?' said Ed smugly.

'We named the ship Gabriel,' said Phil, returning the smug look.

'For heavens sake,' said Linda. 'I've been kidnapped by an alien seventies prog-rock appreciation society. Doesn't anyone out here like The Pretenders?'

'They were excellent at the Heatwave Festival near Toronto in 1980,' said Phil. 'And they were—'

'Bloody hell, is there any classic band you haven't seen?' she said, interrupting.

'Stop your sobbing,' said Andy and got his second punch on the arm.

'Okay, let's sort you guys out with some food,' said Phil and moved back onto the elevator pad.

They all followed along, with Ed wondering whether the food would be seventies-style as well.

'I quite fancy a prawn cocktail,' he said and received some strange looks.

21

THEO STARSHIP GABRIEL – UNKNOWN LOCATION

DAY 416, YEAR 11269, 06:29FC, PCC

Ed woke with a start and was briefly confused as to where he was. Looking up at a pure white ceiling and turning his head to the left, he found a small shelf beside the bed. He noticed a half-empty beer bottle and a couple of pizza crusts, then with the twinges of a headache coming on, he vaguely remembered the previous evening's events.

After the visit to the bridge, Phil had shown them where their cabins were and then taken them up to what the crew called 'the blister'. It was a large, oval lounge room on the highest deck of the ship, with a domed glass ceiling. It probably wasn't glass, but whatever it was made from, the magnificent view of the galaxy could not be disputed. Tony had joined them and helped entertain everyone with stories of their visits to Earth, going back centuries. All this with an unending supply of cold beer, wine and pizza, which the three guests thought was bloody marvellous.

'Good morning, Edward. Did you sleep well?' said somebody in a sultry female voice, giving him a start.

'Bloody hell,' said Ed, glancing around the room. 'You nearly gave me a coronary. Where the hell are you and where did you come from?'

'I'm here all the time,' the female voice answered.

'Where were you last night then?' he asked.

'You'd had a lot of beer and kept bumping into things, so I thought I'd wait until this morning to introduce myself,' she said.

'Yeah, that was probably a wise thing to do.'

'You can request me to be in standby mode, if you wish,' she said. 'Then all you need to do is call me and I'll be right here.'

Ed sat up, swung his legs over and placed them on the floor.

'What do I call you?'

'Anything you desire, Edward.'

'Okay, I'll call you Marilyn,' said Ed, immediately regretting it. *Better not tell the other two, I'll never hear the end of it*, he thought.

'Marilyn it is then,' she said. 'Would you like a coffee? Flat white, one sugar?'

'How did you know that?' questioned Ed, looking

around the room again. 'I don't even know where to look when I'm talking to you.'

A three-dimensional image of Marilyn Monroe in a bikini appeared in the middle of the room.

'Is this the Marilyn you were thinking of, Edward?' said Marilyn, pouting and looking at him seductively.

'Oh – crap – err – yeah. It was, only – I err – I kind of imagined her with some clothes on,' he stammered, his eyes the size of dinner plates.

She reappeared in her trademark billowing low-cut dress.

'Is this more appropriate?' she said, seemingly disappointed.

'Yes, thank you, Marilyn, and, in answer to your question, I would like a coffee. A large one please,' he said, gradually calming down.

'Would you like a bacon sandwich with tomato ketchup too?' she asked, giving him a wink.

'I've just met the most perfect woman in the world.' He grinned. 'It's a shame you're just a hologram.'

'Touch my hand,' she said, stepping closer and offering her right hand to him.

He tentatively raised his right hand. Expecting it to sweep through the image, he was shocked to find himself shaking a very real, warm hand. He could even smell her perfume. Turning her hand over, he placed two fingers on her wrist, just under her thumb and was astounded to find a strong, regular pulse.

'How the hell does that work?' said Ed, letting go of her hand as if it had given him an electric shock and looked up into her eyes. 'I saw you materialise out of thin air and you seem to be a real fully-functioning human being.'

'Biomatter Spacial Reforming is about the closest translation I can give you,' she said. 'So long as we have a data record of the item, and enough stored elements available, we can create anything we need. Your coffee, bacon sandwich, last night's dinner, even the beer and wine.'

Marilyn walked over to a recess in the wall and picked up a large mug of steaming coffee and a plate containing the best looking double-decker toasted bacon sandwich Ed had ever seen. She placed them on the bedside table next to Ed, along with a couple of tablets.

'Something for the headache,' she said and retreated to an armchair in the corner, signalling to him to eat. As Ed tucked into his sandwich, she continued with more information about the ship.

'The Gabriel is a sentient ship. It's partly organic too. It's grown and constructed at the same time. The ship's hull and bulkheads are made from spores that are cultured and manipulated into a kind of skin and, when formed into the right shape, can be left to harden. Just before the hardening, it's married with a semi-organic brain core that, when woken and given its early build programming, can finish its own construction. Once finished, a crew is assigned, they name the starship and give the vessel its final personality, training and deep core programming.'

'So, we're flying around in a sentient living being?' mumbled Ed, through mouthfuls of bacon sandwich.

'Yes, we are. Although it does have defined programmed limits. It can't fly off on a whim; it needs to have a command from one of the crew.'

'What if the crew are asleep and the ship changes its mind, and decides to go on a trip or is attacked?' he asked, taking a sip of his coffee.

'Good question,' said Marilyn. 'It's not a scenario that's likely as there's always at least one crew member, core-connected at all times. But if an attack did happen, then Gabriel would try to run first and defend last. Gabriel is, in every sense of the word, a pacifist and could never initiate an attack on anyone or anything. But don't get me wrong, its defence capabilities are quite purposeful and adequate. If cornered – well – let's say, whoever it was, would most likely never do it again.'

'Changing the subject for a moment,' said Ed, looking around the room for his NASA ship suit. 'What actually moves or drives the ship? I mean, you don't use ancient, steam powered Ion drives like us, do you?'

'No, we don't,' said Marilyn, giggling. 'We have what's called a Skotadi Chamber. The only way I can explain it in your language is that it's similar to a nuclear power cell, only incorporating dark energy. It's about the size of a basketball, situated in the centre of the brain core and the most heavily-shielded part of the ship.'

'What would happen if it was damaged?'

'A Skotadi Chamber has, as yet, never been breached, but if one was, you wouldn't want to be within a light year of that. Not unless you had ambitions to be part of a new star. But don't let that scare you; we'll be giving all three of you training and a full run-down on all this for your ship.'

'You're putting a bloody nuclear bomb in my ship?' said Ed, looking at Marilyn aghast.

'I wish I hadn't used that simile,' groaned Marilyn. 'It's not a bomb. Just think of it as a high-powered battery. It's a necessity to power all your new sexy systems.'

'New systems?' repeated Ed, looking puzzled. 'I thought we were getting a bit of an overhaul to bring us up to date with regulations.'

'Well, we couldn't really do that with the old clunker you turned up in, could we? I mean, it's like entering Formula One with a Model T. Sorry, there I go again using annoying similes,' she said, cringing.

'No, I think that sums it up pretty well,' said Ed, still trying to find his ship suit.

'It's in the bathroom, hanging behind the door. There's two more in that cabinet over there,' she said, pointing at a row of drawers built into the wall.

'But I only have one ship suit with me,' said Ed, looking puzzled.

'I made you two more,' she said. 'Also a pair of jeans, trainers and a Pink Floyd T-shirt.'

'What year?' he asked, walking over to the drawers to have a look.

'1977, In the Flesh Tour. All of the boys went and raved about it.'

'Cool,' said Ed as he pulled the T-shirt out of the drawer and admired the pig over Battersea Power Station design. 'I've never been able to find one of these, but, hang on, I thought you said there's always one of the crew core connected at all times?'

'They went to every show and took it in turns to man the bridge,' she said, smiling.

'Lucky buggers. I'd give my right arm to have witnessed just one show, and they've seen them all,' said Ed, looking at the floor with a faraway expression.

'Put a core helmet on and watch the show,' she said. 'We have all the tours recorded.'

'I've seen all the videos a hundred times.'

'Not like this you haven't,' she said and walked across the room, opened a drawer, grabbed one of the core helmets and gave it to Ed. 'Put this on, lie back on the bed and shut your eyes.'

Ed did as he was told.

'Madison Square Garden, second night of four,' she said.

Ed nearly levitated off the bed.

It was the intro to 'Sheep'. He was there in the third row; he could see and feel the crowd around him, smell the sweat and marijuana. David Gilmour was only meters away, the deep bass moving his bacon sandwich around in his stomach. He opened his eyes and sat up, grabbing the helmet off his head and stared at it, as if it was venomous.

'How the fuck is that possible?' he stammered, looking up at Marilyn, who was grinning from ear to ear.

'One of the boys had a helmet on under a baseball cap at all the shows they went to, which was, as you know, an awful lot. Everything they saw was transmitted back to the core and recorded, so even the crew member back on the ship that night could watch the show from the comfort of the bridge couch.'

'That's – that's – just spectacular. Can I have all these recordings on my ship?'

'The brain core on your ship will be an exact copy of ours,' she said. 'Minus the crew's personal files. You really don't want to see some of the private things they got up to over the last three thousand years,' she added, looking a little shamefaced. 'Everything else will be there and – I must admit – between the four of them, they personally witnessed an awful lot of major events in Gaia's – sorry, Earth's – history.'

'A small point,' said Ed, looking at Marilyn, pensively. 'If your programming is so more advanced than ours, then why do you keep forgetting to call our planet Earth? Surely, when you've been told once, you wouldn't make that error again.'

'Excellent point, Edward,' she said. 'Our programming is designed that way, to make us appear more human. Not to a point where we could make a critical error and endanger the ship or anything, but enough to make tiny *faux pas* occasionally to make you feel comfortable.'

'Isn't there anything you guys haven't thought of?' he said, suddenly realising he was still in his underpants and that it might be a good idea to have a shower. He stood up and wandered over to the flush-mounted drawers again.

'Third drawer down,' she said. 'I took the liberty of providing underwear too.'

'Thanks, Marilyn,' he said, grabbing a clean pair of

jockey shorts, jeans and the seventies tour shirt. 'I won't be long,' he said and padded off to the bathroom.

After closing the bathroom door, he stripped and turned to check out the shower controls.

That's odd, he thought, finding nothing that seemed remotely familiar.

Opening the bedroom door a crack, he asked Marilyn how to operate the shower. He almost jumped out of his skin when she answered from behind him. Spinning round and, immediately covering himself with his hands, he found her standing naked in the cubical.

'I'll show you,' she said, putting her hands up above her head. 'Shower please.'

A bright red light flickered over her body as she slowly turned a complete circle; it was over in about twenty seconds.

'Before you ask, Mr Scientist,' she said. 'We call it an acoustic shower.'

'Th – thank you,' he stammered, feeling his cheeks burning. 'I was kind of hoping you'd shout instructions through the door.'

'Why?' she asked. 'Don't you like naked girls – are you—'

'No – no – nothing like that. I'm definitely heterosexual – not sure I could play around that way with a computer programme and I've never had the need to use a sex toy,' he said, immediately regretting saying something so unkind.

'That may be,' she said, looking down at his hands, 'but I believe your body has other ideas.'

He looked down and realised his dick was completely contradicting everything he'd just said. He looked up again to find her standing right in front of him. She leaned in and kissed him on the mouth.

'Anything that happens in this cabin, stays in this cabin,' she whispered.

22

GDA CRUISER KATADROMIKO 37 – EN ROUTE TO DASOS

DAY 416, YEAR 11269, 07:46FC, PCC

Captain Fleoha Utz stood in her bridge office, staring at her infoportal, trying to make sense of where the small, primitive vessel sitting in one of her pilot hangars had come from.

The bipedal crew of two had insisted they were from Gaia in the Helios System, although they seemed to call it something else when they first arrived.

Utz knew the Helios System was off-limits and Gaia, the only inhabited planet, was several millennia behind in spacefaring technology. But here they were, in a very basic unrecognisable, electricity-powered ship, one hundred and twenty-six light years away from Helios – and with the affront to actually open fire on her battle cruiser with a ridiculously-ancient chemically-propelled weapon.

'Lieutenant Siintu, attend my office please,' she

announced into the bridge audio and sat down behind the large desk, transferring the infoportal data from the wall screen to the desktop portal so only she could read it.

Siintu entered and stood formally in front of the desk, appearing a little uneasy.

'Stand easy, Lieutenant,' said Utz, not looking up and continuing to read from the portal.

Siintu visibly relaxed her demeanour, but knew better than to say anything.

'Do we have anything to suggest where that alien vessel really came from?' Utz asked finally.

'No, Captain. But, as I first concluded from the initial scans, the design and materials used in construction are identical to a local Gaian re-entry vehicle. Only this one has a very primitive unshielded jump drive – it's so loud, you could detect it from two galaxies away.'

'And the weapon systems?'

'None at all. They don't even have any shielding. If they hit even the smallest debris, it would go through them like an astrapi bolt.'

'So, if they didn't discharge the weapon, who the hell did?'

'As you know, Captain, they insist most fervently that the weapon was fired at them in the Helios System and they had to initiate an emergency jump to avoid it, except the weapon was so close when the jump was made, it was involved in the envelope and on emergence it had passed them.'

'Do you believe this could actually occur, Lieutenant?' asked Utz, staring straight at her security officer.

'I have tried over a hundred computer simulations and not once has a close-to-strike weapon seemingly passed by, mid-jump. I'm not saying it's impossible, but how many ships have jumped to avoid attacks or weapon strikes over the last few thousand years and have ever reported the weapon jumping with them?'

'Thank you, Lieutenant. I think I need to talk to them personally before making my report to the Gerousia. Would you have them sent up to me and make sure they're collared.'

'Yes, Captain, they'll be on the next available tube,' answered Siintu, quickly leaving the Captain's office and going to speak to the duty officer in the security station.

XAVIER LAKE HAD JUST STARTED his breakfast when Carlon entered his room again, which he thought was odd because he'd only been gone two minutes having brought in his food.

'Are you joining me for breakfast, Carlon? People will talk, you know, if we keep meeting like this,' he mumbled through a mouthful of what resembled toast.

'No, Lake. You are joining the Captain right now. Could you stand up please?' said a rather harried Carlon.

Lake did as he was told and had a thin, metallic collar clipped around his neck.

'What does that do?' asked Lake, following Carlon as he beckoned him towards the door.

'Stops you from endangering either the ship or its crew. Do what everyone tells you to do because I don't want to be standing next to you if that collar goes off,' said Carlon, waiting outside Herez's door.

'Your translator machine is getting better,' said Lake. 'I take it that it has some sort of adaptive learning capability?'

'Yes, it listens to you and copies your colloquialisms, dialect and even slang. I understand you better too.'

'Morning, boss,' said Herez as he followed his escort out of his room.

'Mr Herez,' said Lake. 'I trust you had a pleasant sleep –the rest of us had to put up with your snoring rattling the bulkheads.'

Carlon and his colleague both chuckled and signalled them to follow.

They were taken back the way they had come the previous night, to the little tube carriage. Again, it whisked away silently, continuing along the length of the ship, only stopping once and going up a long way this time.

When they emerged, it was into a much narrower corridor with armed guards manning bulkhead airlocks every twenty metres. Finally they reached a closed door. Armed personnel barred their way and went through a series of checks before finally opening the airlock doorway into the bridge.

The bridge itself was large with at least one hundred people all sitting on recliner couches, which faced into the centre of the room, where a giant holographic display of the ship's location rotated.

The display was incredibly detailed and showed the local stars with all their relevant planetary systems rotating around them, comets and even space debris.

Lake and Herez moved slowly around the outside of the room on a slightly raised walkway, trying to take it all in.

On the far side of the bridge, the escorts stopped and waited outside a small door. After only a few seconds, the door seemed to disappear. They were ushered inside and ordered to stand in front of a large desk.

'Good morning, I'm sorry to disturb your breakfast, gentlemen,' said Captain Utz, talking to them through

Officer Carlon's translator and eyeing the two tall, stooping humans with a slight look of disdain. 'But I need you to explain exactly where you came from and why my vessel was fired upon.'

Lake looked at Utz. He was surprised the Captain was a woman, although he certainly wasn't going to show it. He cleared his throat and started to explain. 'I apologise, Captain, for the misunderstanding. We are genuinely from Gaia. We've recently developed our first jump drive and were preparing for our first jump test. It appears someone from my planet didn't want the tests to go ahead and, as we approached our jump point, they fired a missile at us from a cloaked ship. We have no weapons or shields on the test ship, so our only option was to initiate an emergency jump, which is programmed to emerge into a randomly selected clear zone of space. When I initiated the jump, the missile was only a fraction of a second away from impact and, during the jump, it seems the weapon, being so close to our envelope, somehow got involved and initiated its own envelope, coming with us. When we emerged, we thought we had jumped away from it just in time. I'm sure you were as surprised as us when it appeared in front of our ship and started hunting for a new target. We believed it was going to turn back on us and re-engage. The rest you know,' said Lake, taking a breath and trying very hard to look contrite.

'And what about you?' she said, looking at Herez. 'Do you have anything to add to this rather convenient story?'

'No, Captain,' said Herez. 'Mr Lake told you everything we know. Before we met your ship, we had no idea there were other races out here. It's all been quite a shock for us.'

'I see,' said Utz, staring at them both. 'Well, unfortunately, my hands are tied in a matter such as this. Firing on a GDA vessel is a serious offence and is only dealt with by the Gerousia on Dasos. So, I'm duty bound to keep you on the ship until we get back there. You're in luck, though, as we are only a few days away from Dasos, so it won't be a long wait.'

'I hope we don't have to wear these all that time,' said Lake, indicating the collars around their necks.

The captain stared at the two of them for several seconds before replying. 'I'll give the two of you the benefit of the doubt. During SC periods you remain secure in your rooms and during FC periods you can have the use of the recreational areas. Security personnel will show you where these areas are. You'll be given a wristlet that gives you access and lets us know where you are at all times. Abuse this trust once and you're locked up full time with the collars. Is this clear, gentlemen?' she growled, again glowering at them both.

'Yes, Captain,' they said in unison.

'Thank you. Mr Carlon, you may return them now.'

On the way back, Herez was looking noticeably puzzled.

'You don't know what FC and SC are, do you?' said Lake, looking at him with a smile.

'No, not a clue, boss,' answered Herez, looking annoyed.

'The GDA have a consolidated planetary space time – based on Dasos time, surprisingly enough. All the ships in space can run on the same clock – despite whichever planet you're from. As soon as you're in space, you operate on FCC time. It makes booking a jump zone a lot safer and stops ships trying to emerge into each other. Within this there are two periods: FC is space day time and SC is space night time.'

'How do you know all this stuff?' Herez asked.

'Well, while you were rattling the walls with your snoring, I was watching GDA instructional videos.'

'Oh,' he said, sheepishly and remained quiet all the way back to his room.

23

THEO STARSHIP GABRIEL – TRELORUS SYSTEM,

ORBITING THE PLANET PANEMORFI

Day 416, Year 11269, 10:46FC, PCC

Steve and Tony had jumped the Gabriel into the Trelorus System overnight. It was going to take a few more days to finalise the rebuild on the Cartella. The new hull and interior bulkheads had to be grown in a hard vacuum, which made shuttle bay 2, where the Cartella was being improved, off limits until this was completed.

In the meantime, Phil had decided to show their guests the highlights of the region. This was why he was up in the blister, showing Linda the planet Panemorfi. The Gabriel was in a low orbit so the most beautiful planet Linda had ever seen filled most of the glass dome.

'That's just spectacular,' said Linda. 'How far from Earth are we?'

'Five hundred and seventy-seven light years,' he replied. 'Give or take a few million kilometres.'

'Wow, this ship can jump that far?' she said, looking back at Phil and then lying down on a couch to get a better view of the planet above.

'The Gabriel can jump up to one thousand light years, although you really need to have your emergence co-ordinates spot on when you start doing the big numbers and don't try to be too close to anything either. As with most things, the longer the range, the less accurate. It's best to head for the large open spaces.'

'Are we playing cricket?' said Ed, bounding into the blister with a grin from ear to ear. 'That's what I do in a large open space.'

'We were talking about jump co-ordi—' Linda stopped mid-sentence and stared at Ed. 'Where did you get that shirt? And jeans? And trainers?' she said as she looked him over.

'The computer made them for me. Cool, eh?'

'I want some.' She pouted, putting her hands on her hips and staring expectantly at Phil.

'What would you like?' said Phil.

'Something similar please – with a—'

'Pretenders T-shirt?' he interrupted.

'Err, yeah.'

'Which tour?'

'Bloody hell, I don't know,' she said, holding her arms out questioningly. 'I'm not as nerdy as you lot.'

'Gabriel,' Phil called. 'Can you form a pair of jeans, trainers and a 1979 Pretenders T-shirt for Linda?'

'There are three different designs,' said Gabriel.

'Pick one,' said Phil, rolling his eyes at the other two.

Seconds later, the clothing materialised on the couch next to Linda, making her jump. She snatched up the clothes and disappeared off to her room, saying a faint 'thanks, Phil' halfway up the corridor.

'WOW, WHERE'S THAT?' said Ed, looking up at the huge blue planet revolving slowly past the glass dome.

'Panemorfi,' said Phil. 'In the Trelorus System. It's a vacation planet, which the local spacefaring races use from time to time. Being ninety percent ocean, there's only islands on the entire planet, so you need to book as they're trying to keep it uncrowded and exclusive. Saying this place is beautiful is the understatement of the year; it's like a planet version of the Maldives.'

'Shame we don't have a reservation then,' said Ed, looking forlornly up at the view.

'Who said we don't?'

'How can we?' said Ed. 'We've only just got here and you said it's exclusive.'

'I did, and it is,' said Phil. 'But you don't need a reservation when you own one of the islands. There are just over five thousand islands on Panemorfi; the biggest ones are around forty square kilometres and are dormant volcanoes. The rest are all gathered in archipelagos here and there. No moons, so no tides. The planet is in a very slight elliptical orbit, so only two seasons: very warm and warmer still. The gravity is eighty-five percent that of Earth.'

'Sounds awful,' said Ed, smiling broadly. 'When are we going down there?'

'Going where?' said Andy, striding into the blister, dressed in shorts, a Hawaiian shirt and flip flops.

'I think someone already knows exactly where we're going,' laughed Phil. 'Have you been chatting with your room computer?'

'Yeah, she's awesome,' said Andy.

'Ah, that reminds me,' said Phil. 'Don't –whatever you do – let your room computers talk you into having sex; the sexually transmitted diseases they carry are completely incurable.'

'What?' said Ed – and Andy in stereo – staring at

Phil, then at each other and then back at Phil again, a look of horror on their faces.

'Just look at your faces: gotcha! Ha,' laughed Phil, backing away quickly from them. 'I'll meet you in shuttle bay 1 in ten minutes. Grab Linda on the way.'

'Little shit,' said Ed as Phil headed for the door, throwing one of the sofa cushions at his retreating figure.

'He's a very big shit,' said Andy.

'Who is your roommate then?' asked Ed, looking at Andy with a grin.

'Samantha Caine.'

'What, the supermodel?'

'Yep, who's yours then?' asked Andy, eagerly.

'Err…'

'Come on, Edward. Who was it?'

'Marilyn Monroe,' he said, with a guilty expression.

'Shit, yes. I never thought of her. Good choice, though. I might give her a go tonight.'

'Hey, she's my girl,' said Ed, bristling.

They both stood silently, staring at each other for a second and then fell about laughing.

'What are you two giggling about now?' said Linda, strolling in, wearing her new clothes.

'We're going on holiday,' said Andy.

'Have you got your bucket and spade?' said Ed.

They spun Linda around, and explained what was happening on the way to the shuttle bay.

SHUTTLE BAY 1 was a mirror image of bay 2 as it was on the opposite side of the ship. Again, there were two Theo shuttles sitting against the far bulkhead, both, as with the other two, showing heat scarring from many atmospheric insertions.

Phil was already there and asked Gabriel to open up his shuttle.

Immediately an airlock opened and steps appeared that didn't seem to have any visible means of support.

Steve had told Ed earlier that the four crew members each had their own shuttles, which were capable of three hundred light year jumps as well as planetary insertion.

Phil beckoned the small party into the main control cabin.

'Three additional passengers, Gabriel,' he informed the computer and, even before he finished speaking, three extra couches formed in a semi-circle around the pilot's seat.

Once he powered up all the systems, Phil actually had very little to do. The shuttle lifted off the deck, with only a slight whining noise, and exited out into space through a shimmering energy field – all seemingly without any input from him at all – and continued to fly on a predetermined flight path down towards the planet. The almost-silent and smooth flight ended as they hit the upper atmosphere with an ever-increasing roar, along with some mild vibrations and buffeting.

'I didn't bring any sunglasses,' shouted Linda, squinting through the front screen as they plunged lower and lower into the ever-thickening atmosphere.

'There are plenty of things like that on the island,' Phil replied. 'Everything you could ever need, and more.'

Ed looked across at Andy, who returned his gaze. He knew they were both thinking the same thing.

'Err, Phil?' said Ed, questioningly, watching the ocean coming towards them at what seemed like a suicidal velocity.

'Yeah,' he replied, leaning back and putting his hands behind his head.

'Are we going to start some braking turns or something soon? That ocean is getting really close and we're still doing Mach fifty, straight down,' he shouted, as his knuckles turned white from gripping the sides of his couch.

'This ship's about as aerodynamic as an elephant so braking turns are no use but, with our artificial gravity system, we can adopt super high G turns without spilling your beer and stop on a dime.'

Almost as Phil finished speaking, the ship stopped its mad descent and was suddenly racing across the ocean.

'Whoa,' cried Linda. 'That's freaky; there's absolutely no sensation at all. We should've been squished into the floor.'

'Outstanding,' said Ed. 'I'd love to see the math behind that chicanery.'

A rotating holo-projection of an enormous mathematical equation lit up in the centre of the cabin.

'Stop showing off, Gabriel,' said Phil. 'Concentrate on landing my ship.'

'I could land a thousand ships standing on my head,' said Gabriel, its condescending voice coming from all around them.

'Does your computer have an attitude setting that can be adjusted?' asked Andy.

Phil smiled and said, 'Gabriel, please re-orientate your imperious inclinations to diminish the likelihood of our guests feeling impuissant.'

'Imperious inclinations re-orientated. I ask forgiveness for any unintended previous impetuousness,' said Gabriel, in an overly apologetic tone.

'Bloody hell,' said Linda. 'It was bad enough with you two constantly pissing around. Now I've got an annoying computer that does it as well.'

'Are we there yet?' said Andy, in a childish voice.

'Sit still and be quiet, Andrew, or you'll be sent straight to bed with no dinner,' said Gabriel.

'Phil, can you drop me off at a different island?' said Linda in a pleading tone. 'Preferably one with a large wall I can bang my head against.'

———————

A GROUP of islands grew on the horizon, rapidly increasing in size. The shuttle turned towards the outermost island and slowed dramatically, lowered its landing struts with a faint hissing noise, turned one hundred and eighty degrees to face back out to sea and landed softly on the sand amongst an orchard of palm trees.

Phil powered down the shuttle's systems and opened the airlock doors.

Ed, Andy and Linda all crowded at the door, peering out at the idyllic view.

The sea had appeared a deep blue from up in the shuttle, but here, in the shallows around the islands, it was a crystal-clear aquamarine with multi-coloured fish of all sizes, swimming slowly amongst the rocks and coral.

'This is pretty cool,' said Ed. 'Who wants to go first then?'

'It's your show, boss,' said Andy.

'And I'm just crew,' said Linda.

'How about we all go together?' said Ed. 'Phil, is there any way to record this moment? It's the first time a human from Earth has stepped on a planet in another solar system.'

'All the ship's optical systems are recording at all times, Ed, so I can give you photographs, videos – even holographic images of whatever you want,' he said.

'Okay,' said Ed. 'Everyone on the bottom step, turn around, hold hands, smile at the cameras – and one, two, three: jump!'

They all jumped backward onto the sand together, surprised at how high they went in the slightly lower gravity

'Hurrah,' they all shouted.

'Hurrah,' called Phil, from the shuttle door.

'Hurrah,' they heard Gabriel say, faintly, from inside the shuttle.

'Right, now that craps over with, can I show you guys around?' said Phil, bounding down the steps that then dematerialised, followed by the outer airlock sealing itself.

'By all means,' said Ed, scooping up a handful of sand and inspecting it closely. The grasses were reasonably familiar too – even the palm trees reminded him of Florida, except they had a blue tinge to the trunks and the tips of the leaf ferns.

There seemed to be around a dozen low cottages on the island, all beachside, although it was hard not to be beachside when it was possible to walk across to the other side of the island in about three minutes.

'We all get a cottage each,' said Phil. 'But before that, I'll show you the communal areas. I'm kinda hoping everything's okay here because we leased the island to a GDA ship for some crew leave last week, which is something we never do. They had a double-booking problem on the adjacent archipelago and needed the extra accommodation. When we get to the entrance, I'll ask you to say your name and the computer will remember your voice pattern. This will give you access to everything during your stay.'

Phil led them up to a single-storey building in the centre of the island with a small doorway set into one side. It didn't look much at all and Ed, Andy and Linda all looked at each other with bemused expressions.

'*Nisi anagnorizo foni*,' said Phil to the building.

'Good morning, Phil,' said a voice, seemingly from all around them. 'It's wonderful to see you again. Would your guests like to state their names please?'

Phil nodded at them in turn and they said their names.

'Thank you, your cottages have been allocated.

Welcome to Theo Island. Anything you desire I can provide; just ask.'

There was a slight rumble and the whole building began to rise up from the sand. The walls opened, hinging slowly upwards to provide sun shade around the entire premises. Inside was a beautiful self-contained holiday resort with a small eating area, a bar with an array of bottles to rival any beach bar Ed had ever seen and lounge areas with a multitude of furniture styles.

'Don't bother fixing up our ship, Phil,' said Andy. 'I'll be fine right here for the next hundred years.'

'Me too,' said Linda as she noticed the half-naked Adonis of a barman materialise behind the bar.

'Doesn't do anything for me,' said Ed, looking at Linda with a grimace.

Immediately a beautiful, brunette barmaid in a bikini appeared and beckoned Ed to the bar.

'Anything you desire – just ask,' said the building again.

'Now, that's more like it,' Ed said, sprinting forward and only just beating Andy to order his drink.

'Must be your round, Virr,' said Andy, grinning at the barmaid.

'Both rounds, Mr Faux,' he said, looking at the girl's ample figure.

'You're disgusting, the both of you,' scolded Linda,

but ogled the woman's body just the same. 'Now, what's your name?' she asked the barmaid.

'Ample,' she said, beaming with a smile of perfect teeth.

The two boys doubled up with laughter.

'Why couldn't it be Carol or Jane?' she whined and quickly submitted to giggling.

Phil strolled over and stared at the three of them sniggering uncontrollably.

'How much have you had already? We've only been here two minutes,' he asked, looking at the bar staff, who were both grinning like Cheshire cats. 'Are you two really the smartest scientists on your planet?' he asked, shaking his head and walking off across the sand to check the cottages had been left clean and tidy.

24

GDA CRUISER KATADROMIKO 37 – EN ROUTE TO DASOS

DAY 416, YEAR 11269, 22:28SC, PCC

Gardlin Habbs, the Chief Medical Officer on board Katadromiko 37, was baffled and quite alarmed.

Never before had he seen so many of the crew get sick at one time. It was unheard of and the computer had run and rerun the tissue samples and found no match on the GDA database. He was concerned with almost all of the cases; his crew had developed a rash of red bumps on the skin and they were getting worse.

He had informed the Captain of his worries.

She had asked if he had any idea of when or where the virus came aboard. He didn't, as they had stopped at fifty-seven planets or space stations on this voyage, and it could have been any one of them.

The two prisoners had been discounted as they had both been scanned before they left their vessel, so she had agreed to place all cases in isolation. Anyone showing symptoms was to alert their nearest medical station and stay in their quarters – which was fine four hours ago when there was only a handful of cases. Now, he had five hundred and sixty-four and this was rising by dozens per hour. All eight medical satellite stations and the main medical suite were all over capacity. Before long, he'd have to commandeer a hangar.

He opened the outer door to the research laboratory, entered and waited while he was scanned, something he had done a hundred times over the last couple of months and this time it was no different: he stood and waited for the inner door to open.

Only it didn't.

He glanced down at the control screen, already knowing what he was going to read and he wasn't disappointed.

'Unlisted Virus Detected,' was written in red and flashing. He walked back to his office and called his colleague inside the laboratory.

'Anything new for me, Dric'is?' Habbs asked.

'Well, the re-adaptation is amazing,' she replied. 'I've thrown every anti-virus we have at it: it stalls it for about an hour and then it develops a workaround and comes back at you harder than ever. I really don't know what to do. I mean, we're the GDA; we're supposed to guard the human-populated galaxy from just this sort of threat. It's almost as if—'

'If what?' said Habbs.

'As if the virus were deliberately manipulated, even weaponised to defeat everything we have,' Dric'is said, staring straight at him through the glass.

'That's a big call, Dric'is.'

'Have you ever known me to be wrong with a diagnosis before?'

'No,' said Habbs. 'I hope you're wrong, but from what I've seen so far, I don't believe you are.'

'What are you going to do?'

'Are you showing any symptoms?'

'I don't think so,' she replied.

'Then you stay sealed in there and don't contaminate yourself. You can sleep in the auto-nurse and make sure you scan any food and drinks the computer synthesises for you, just in case.'

'What about you?'

'Check the entry airlock panel,' he said. He heard her walk across the room and then a faint, 'Ah shit' as she read the warning. The footsteps returned.

'Now I'm really scared,' she said, sounding on the verge of tears.

'Get some sleep, call me when you wake and we'll have another crack at it.'

'I'm setting the computer to run while I rest. I don't understand why we can't solve this. We have the most powerful computers in the galaxy and we're getting nowhere,' she said and yawned widely.

'Goodnight, Dric'is.'

'Night, Habbs.'

LAKE WAS GETTING IRRITATED. He'd been up now for almost two hours and he hadn't had his breakfast. He walked over to the entrance door and peered out to see no one at the security desk. He pushed his hand against the invisible door beam to find it was still operational and, snatching his tingling hand back, he swore under his breath.

'Herez, are you awake?' he called in the direction of the next room.

'Yes, what's happened to breakfast?' came the abrupt reply.

'I don't know. It's very quiet out there and there's nobody at the desk.'

'The door beams deactivated at 02:00FC yesterday,' said Herez. 'They might again today, as everything on this ship seems to be automated.'

'Okay, that's not long. We'll wait and – what was that?'

'What was what?' said Herez.

'Did you make a knocking noise?'

'No.'

'Carlon, is that you?' said Lake.

There was a scraping noise, the location of which Lake couldn't pinpoint, but it was definitely coming from somewhere near the security desk.

'Carlon, stop messing about out there and get us some breakfast.'

A shaking hand appeared around the bottom left-hand side of the desk. It stopped moving for a few seconds and suddenly jumped back into motion again.

Lake stared at the struggling hand in complete puzzlement. It grabbed the side of the desk and seemed to be pulling. An arm appeared, shortly followed by a head. Lake could see that all the exposed skin on the hand, arm and head was covered in sores.

'Are you seeing this, Herez?' said Lake as the body stopped moving and lay still.

'I am. What the hell?'

It wasn't Carlon; it was the night guard. His eyes fluttered open again, he tried to reach out towards them and collapsed, his eyes remaining open this time, staring blankly across the room.

'That doesn't look good, boss,' shouted Herez.

'Is there anybody there?' said Lake. 'Man down – we need help here – anybody.'

The reply was silence, apart from the faint whirring of the life-support systems in the background.

'Hello? Hello? Can anyone hear me?' called Herez.

They both continued shouting for another few minutes, again with similar negative results.

'Shit,' muttered Lake as he searched around the lounge room for something he could use to make a noise that might attract attention. As he moved into the bedroom, he noticed the clock time projected on the wall tick over to 02:00FC.

Behind him, in the lounge, he heard the slightest noise: a faint *click*. He turned and stared at the door. Picking up one of his shoes from beside the bed, he threw it towards the entry door. It bounced once, skidded through the door and out into the security office.

Lake bounded over to the door, stopped and stuck out his hand, still not trusting that the beam was off. His hand went through unimpeded. He looked at the security officer's body lying only a few metres away and suddenly wondered if the door beam had been protecting him from whatever that virus was. It was too late now if it was airborne.

He kept close to the wall and stepped around to Herez's door, checked that it had also opened, and strolled in to find Herez tying a triangle of bed linen around his nose and mouth.

'I don't think that'll do much, Mr Herez,' said Lake.

'We need full hazmat suits, but if it's airborne, we're already too late.'

'Surely their medical advances have followed along with everything else, boss,' said a muffled Herez, now looking like a bandit.

'I'm sure it has, but whatever that is,' he said, pointing at the body, 'they're not immunised against it. Let's hope it's an isolated case and let's also hope that we're not the source.'

'Us?' said Herez, looking at Lake with wide eyes. 'They scanned us so many times. You'd think that if we had anything, it would have shown up.'

Lake fired up Herez's holo projector and found a schematic, which showed a plan of the ship; their location was flashing. He requested the location of the medical centre and discovered there were eight medical satellite stations dotted around the ship and the main medical suite was on deck 307, adjacent to tube stop 23.

'Come on,' said Lake. 'Let's go get some help.'

They both filed out of Herez's room and, keeping as far away from the body as possible, crossed to the entrance of the security suite. Outside, they retraced their steps to the nearest tube stop without meeting anyone and Lake touched the request tube icon which was set into the wall. Seconds later, the door opened, they entered and, as they had observed the security officers doing before, Herez tapped in 307-23 and hit the 'go' arrow. Neither of them spoke during the five-minute journey and, when the door finally whisked open, they were greeted by another body, again with the same sores covering all its exposed skin.

'Oh, shit,' said Lake and peered around the door towards the medical centre. The line of bodies stretched for at least a hundred metres and, again, the silence was complete.

Lake stepped out, closely followed by a shocked Herez, who was frantically holding his mask tight against his face. They tiptoed their way towards the medical suite, trying desperately not to touch any of the bodies, which was more difficult the nearer they got to the suite. They saw individuals, couples and families still lying in each other's arms. Soldiers, civilians and senior officers all either sitting or lying, waiting in line for treatment that would never come.

'It must have been so fast,' mumbled Herez through his mask. 'This is so sad. D'you think we'll get blamed for this as well?'

'How can we?' said Lake. 'The security logs will show that we were asleep the whole time and we've not released any aerosols or had any opportunity to tamper with either the air or water supply – because that's what it would take to wipe out a whole starship on this scale, and this quickly.'

They entered the medical suite through the main

doors, which were blocked open by bodies. The scene was worse here: hundreds lay, all with staring eyes and skin covered in open sores. The medical suite was the size of a general hospital on Earth. Department after department, with the same tragedy laid out on every seat and floor. Lake and Herez searched room after room with increasing depression setting in.

As Lake was about to suggest trying elsewhere, they both heard a knocking. It was faint at first, but got louder as they followed the sound to what seemed to be a research area. Right at the back, they heard someone banging on a wall and, as they approached, they could hear a girl talking to herself. She was sitting on the floor with her back to them in what looked like a sealed laboratory, banging a tray against the airlock door.

'Hello,' said Lake, softly, trying not to make her jump. It wasn't successful; she nearly levitated off the floor.

She jumped up and stared at them, putting both hands on the glass window as she garbled away in an alien language.

'We can't understand your language,' said Herez, pointing at his ears.

She seemed to get the idea and pointed at the computer pad over at the desk in the corner of their room. Lake sat at the pad terminal on their side of the wall and looked up to see her frantically typing at hers.

She looked up at him a few seconds later and a chime announced something had come through to his pad.

He clicked the flashing icon and a message appeared on the screen, still in the alien language. He looked up at her, puzzled, and she indicated for him to watch the screen.

She again started typing on her pad.

Suddenly, Lake's pointer started moving of its own accord and he realised she had remotely taken control of his unit.

The pointer moved up to the right-hand corner and clicked to bring a drop-down menu into view. She then selected one of the choices, which opened another larger menu. She stopped and looked at Lake, indicating for him to make the next selection.

'How the hell do I know which is the one I want?' moaned Lake, staring at the menu in complete bewilderment.

'It's got to be something to do with language,' said Herez. 'Scroll down and see if we see anything familiar.'

Lake scrolled slowly down the list of words, until suddenly Herez said, 'There,' pointing at a word they knew. *Gaia*. Clicking on the word brought down another sub-menu with a dozen choices. They both saw the one they wanted at the same time: the tenth name down was Anglika. As soon as Lake clicked on the icon, the text in the message changed to 'Why you not affect.'

'Ah, okay,' said Lake and began typing his response. 'We do not know. We woke up this morning and everyone is dead.'

He looked up at her again and she moved his pointer over to what must be the reply icon and clicked it.

The scream made them both jump and they looked up to see her holding her head in her hands, repeating the same word over and over. 'Ochi – ochi – ochi...'

'Oh shit,' said Lake. 'She didn't know.'

'I'm so sorry. We did not realise you did not know,' he typed and hit the reply icon himself.

She read the message, looked up and nodded, then started typing again.

'Are you two in the vessel from Gaia?'

'Yes, we are.'

'I don't believe you are responsible for virus. It arrive from elsewhere.'

'Thank you, we were frightened that we had caused this. My name is Lake and my partner is Herez. What is your name?'

'Dric'is. I scanned you before came aboard, so I know you not the source of infection.'

'That's good. Is there anything you need?'

'As you not seem to be affected, I need blood samples from both.'

'I thought you might say that.'

'There is blood siphon in drawer next by you.'

Lake opened all the drawers and kept holding things up so she could see. Finally she nodded.

'You need press the green icon, wait for to flash, push unit against underside of arm and press green icon secondly.'

He did as he was told, up to the last bit. He had it pressed on his left arm but just stopped and stared at it.

'I'm not very good with blood, Mr Herez. Would you do the honours and press the button when I'm not looking?'

'Look away, boss,' said Herez and touched the green flashing icon.

Lake felt a slight pressure for a few seconds, then a beep. When he looked down, the little glass container was full. He picked the unit off his arm to find only the smallest of marks and no dripping blood.

'Well, that's an improvement,' he said. 'Now your turn.'

He replaced the blood container with a fresh one from the drawer.

When they had both provided samples, Herez put both in the airlock chamber. The air was purged and Dric'is retrieved them from her side.

'Do you need anything else?' Lake typed.

'No. Search ship. If you find alive, make sure stay sealed up until can manufacture a cure.'

'Yes, good idea. We will see you tomorrow, Dric'is.'

Both Lake and Herez waved as they left the laboratory to continue their search.

25

THEO ISLAND – THE PLANET PANEMORFI

DAY 417, YEAR 11269, 00:45FC, PCC

Was that a scream? thought Linda, as she woke on the second day in paradise.

She jumped out of bed and peered through the blinds, and across the beach, to see Andy chasing a semi-naked, giggling barmaid across the shore with a canoe paddle in one hand and her bikini top in the other.

'Stupid oversexed scientists,' she said under her breath.

A little snort came from underneath the bed cover.

'Be quiet, you,' said Linda. 'It's about time you disappeared – literally.'

'Pot calling the kettle black,' said a beautiful, female brunette, crawling out from the covers with a big smile on her face.

Linda looked at her with a puzzled expression.

'Calling them oversexed,' she said. 'After what you

did to me last night,' she added, licking her lips suggestively.

Linda looked at the girl, putting on an expression that wouldn't have looked out of place on the face of a nun.

'Don't know what you mean and what are you doing in my bed, strange girl? Be gone,' she said, laughing.

'Are you going to tell them?' the young girl asked.

'When I'm ready. They're on a need-to-know basis and, at the present time, they don't need to know.'

'It's Andrew, isn't it,' said the girl, nodding and winking at Linda.

'How could you possibly know that?' said Linda, staring.

'I'm a computer, I know everything,' she said and promptly disappeared as a knock on the door broke the moment.

'Linda,' called Ed. 'Breakfast in five minutes. Steve's done mango crêpes with Buck's Fizz.'

'On my way,' she called, and ran for the shower.

'It's good to see all of you getting down here,' said Linda.

'Yep, I drew the short straw yesterday, but I get the next two days down here to play,' said Steve, smiling and loading another crêpe with fresh mango and cream.

'These are awesome,' mumbled Andy, with a mouthful of crêpe and a smear of cream on his nose.

'Please excuse my pet,' said Ed and pretended to slap Andy on the back of the head. 'He doesn't get fed very often.'

'Make sure you all get a good breakfast,' said Phil. 'And not too much Buck's Fizz. You're all getting flying lessons today.'

'I've been a pilot for nine years,' said Linda. 'Why do I need any lessons?'

'Because your ship will have our tech in it, which means using the power of thought to fly it. You will need some brain training to literally get your head around that aspect. It's very different to what you're used to and will surprise you with its capabilities.'

An hour later, Phil, Ed, Andy and Linda were all sitting in Phil's shuttle, with Linda wearing the funny cloth cycling helmet and looking a little pensive.

'You mean, I've got to fly the ship with my eyes permanently closed?' she said, appearing less confident by the second.

'Just relax, close your eyes and feel the ship around

you. Feel its power; it can do whatever you imagine,' said Phil, calmly.

Linda closed her eyes and Gabriel slowly released control over to the pilot.

'Oh crap,' shouted Linda, her head moving rapidly around and her arms flailing about.

'Think calm thoughts, Linda,' said Phil. 'Get used to the complete vision you now have.'

Linda settled down and became still.

'This is something else,' said Linda. 'It's like being everywhere at once and the ship is part of you.'

'Imagine the ship rising slowly into the air and cruising out over the ocean,' said Phil. 'Don't let your mind wander, otherwise the ship will too.'

'Okay, wow, that's just freaky,' said Linda, with a big grin on her face.

Ed was watching her and Phil when he suddenly realised the shuttle had lifted off the island and was currently travelling at Mach 2, about a hundred metres above the ocean. He gazed out the front screen, then back at Linda, who was now officially the first human from Earth to fly an alien spacecraft.

'One hundred thousand feet please, Linda,' said Phil.

The shuttle soared upward and, in a matter of seconds, was at the required altitude.

'How do you know when it's at the correct height?'

said Andy, trying to see a gauge or something that informed her of the fact.

'You just feel it,' said Linda. 'You're the ship; you just know everything that's going on – all the time, all around you.'

'Can you feel the Gabriel up in orbit?' said Phil, smiling.

'Yes,' said Linda. 'Wow, yes I can.'

'Take us there and dock in the port hangar,' he said.

Again, the little shuttle quickly gained altitude and was in space in a matter of minutes. The Gabriel appeared a few minutes later, first of all appearing as a speck of light and quickly growing into the starship.

'She's beautiful,' said Ed. 'This is the first time we've seen the Gabriel from outside.'

The Gabriel hung above the ocean planet and was indeed a graceful looking ship. The organic nature of the design was acutely evident – she didn't appear to have a straight line or corner anywhere on the outer hull. She was pure gleaming white and seemed to flow in every direction.

'Can you hold here for a moment please, Linda,' said Phil. 'Now, you remember I told you about our cloaking technology; I thought it would be a good opportunity to show you how effective it is. Gabriel, can you cloak the mother ship?'

The starship vanished.

'Whoa, that's weird,' said Linda. 'I can't even feel it anymore.'

'Open the hangar door please, Gabriel,' said Phil.

The hangar doorway appeared in the middle of clear space. It looked like a portal into another universe.

'I'm seriously impressed, Phil. That's the best trick I've seen yet,' said Andy.

'Cool, eh?' said Phil. 'Okay, think her in, Linda.'

The shuttle crept into the landing bay with its landing struts extended, turned back to face the door and settled in the corner with a clump.

A spontaneous round of applause greeted Linda as she opened her eyes and removed the helmet. Grinning from ear to ear, she stood and took a bow.

'Thank you, thank you,' she gushed. 'I'm here all week and my book is available in the foyer at a very reasonable price.'

'Very good, Linda. Excellent,' said Phil. 'Your previous piloting skills held you in good stead. Not everyone makes it look that easy the first time.'

Several hours later, both Ed and Andy had had their turns wearing the helmet. Neither had shown a natural flair for piloting, but they could both get the ship from A to B with little risk of injury.

Phil had relieved Tony on the bridge of the Gabriel and Linda was piloting the shuttle back down to the island.

Gabriel could have done this for them, as he did the first time, but Linda was really keen to practice her newfound skill. She wanted to undertake an atmosphere insertion, which took a bit more concentration as she had to take the hull temperature into account and adjust the velocity and attitude accordingly.

It was dusk as they approached Theo Island, the lights from the little cottages reflecting in the mill pond flat ocean and, with Panemorfi's star sinking into the ocean behind, it made the last few minutes of the flight quite memorable.

Linda brought the shuttle's speed down so they could all enjoy the beautiful vista for a little while longer.

The shuttle touched down adjacent to Mike's ship and powered down.

They all emerged to discover Steve and Mike had prepared a barbecue: a selection of meats, burgers, sausages and delicious looking salads. It was all so decoratively presented it seemed a shame to disturb such a work of art. The island computer had generated an all-female reggae band, playing a selection of recognisable songs from Earth. Andy said he recognised the girls in the band, which Ed and Linda decided was the beer talking. But he insisted they were the girls from a Robert Palmer video his dad used to put on a lot when he was a kid.

Later in the evening, Ed sat down on one of the loungers and sipped at a glass of a very acceptable Sancerre. Andy had insisted they all dance to give the band some encouragement. Not even the three Theos or the bar staff had escaped his enthusiasm. Even now, he hadn't stopped; he'd persuaded the drummer to let him have a go and the rest of the band were now scowling at him as he failed, yet again, to keep a constant tempo.

Linda plonked herself down on the lounger next to Ed and turned her head so the light breeze blew her hair out of her eyes.

'He can't help himself, can he?' said Linda, glancing over at the band to see that Andy now had the drummer sitting on his lap and was being taught the basic reggae rhythm, much to the band's approval.

'He just loves his girls. He's been the same all the years I've known him,' said Ed.

'Haven't you had a bit of fun with Gabriel's little creations?' said Linda, easing back into the lounger and putting her feet up.

Ed looked over at Linda, trying to gauge which direction her question was coming from.

'I have,' he finally said. 'I'm just not as public with my relationships as some,' he said, purposely looking across at Andy. 'What about you?'

'What about me?' she answered, just a little bit quickly, which didn't go unnoticed.

'Trying to hide the fact you're gay,' he said very casually and continuing to watch Andy.

'You know?'

'I had an inkling,' he said, looking back at her and meeting her gaze. 'When I heard two female voices coming from your cottage this morning, it kinda confirmed it.'

'You okay with that?' she asked, continuing the eye contact.

Ed reached over, took Linda's hand and kissed it.

'Of course, I'm okay with that,' he said, 'and so too will Andy.'

'Oh shit, Ed,' said Linda, a tear running down her cheek. 'I've been so worried. Thank you. I can relax now.' She downed her glass of wine in one gulp, sat back on the lounger again and exhaled loudly. She glanced over at Ed again with a big grin on her face. 'Can I introduce Sandy?' she said.

'Of course, but beware the Andy,' he said. 'He'll be over in heartbeat.'

A beautiful young girl appeared, wearing just a swimsuit and sat on the lounger next to Linda.

'Hello, Ed,' said Sandy, offering her hand.

'Well, hi,' said Ed, shaking the proffered hand. 'I'm extremely pleased to meet you and, if we're all putting our cards on the table, can I introduce Marilyn?' Ed drew a sigh of relief as Marilyn appeared, also wearing a swimsuit.

'Marilyn Monroe,' gasped Linda and looked over at Ed with both thumbs up. 'Wow, I hadn't thought of her.'

'That's what Andy said,' laughed Ed. 'And talk of the devil. Surprise, surprise – here he comes now.'

'New girls in the camp,' called Andy, as he almost tripped over, running across from the stage.

'Andy,' said Ed. 'This is Linda's girlfriend, Sandy.'

'Ah, indeed. Wow, cool,' Andy said, shaking Sandy's hand. 'Linda, I always thought there was something really cool about you,' as he bent down and kissed her on the forehead. 'And you're Marilyn,' he said, grinning and shaking her hand too. 'I've heard lots about you.'

'Not everything, though,' she said, smiling at him. 'There are some things about me that I'll just leave up to your imagination.'

'Indeed you can, right, bar's open and it's my round,' he said, as he trotted off to play with his favourite barmaid.

'Told you he'd be okay with it,' said Ed, looking over at Linda.

'I wonder if the Theos understand the concept of same-sex relationships,' said Linda, looking around for either Tony, Steve or Mike.

'Steve went back to his cottage a while ago,

complaining of nausea,' said Ed. 'I think our Earth food is a bit rich for them.'

'I think you're probably right,' said Linda. 'I know, I've put on a couple of kilos since we met them.'

'Shall we get some exercise then?' said Ed, grinning. 'I'll race you to the bar.'

———

'ED – ED – WAKE UP,' called Marilyn, shaking him roughly.

'Wha – what – what is it?' he mumbled, wiping the sleep from his eyes. 'What time is it?'

'It's still the middle of the night,' said Marilyn.

'Marilyn, we did it three times and—'

'No, not that,' she said, with a look of real concern in her eyes. 'Gabriel is very agitated. Phil got sick and put himself in the auto-nurse to have himself diagnosed. The machine put him immediately into an induced coma. Gabriel then tried to contact either Mike, Tony or Steve but they're not responding. Please, Ed, this has never happened before, not in many millennia.'

'Okay, okay, I'm awake. Why haven't you gone over to check?' he asked, struggling to get into his underwear.

'Their cottages are at the far end of the island, out of range of our holo reflectors,' she said.

'Don't they have reflectors inside?'

'Yes, but they're private, and I need their authorisation before I can access the zones,' she said.

Ed slipped on his trainers and opened the door, looking back at Marilyn. 'Tell Gabriel to give me as much light as he can to show me the way.' He disappeared out into the dark, crossed the beach and headed up past the bar and restaurant building, underneath the two shuttles and off into the darkness.

Suddenly, beams of laser light coming from above pinpointed three cottages about two hundred metres ahead. Gabriel was showing him the way from his orbit. He reached the first cottage and banged on the door, but got no response. After three attempts, he tried the door and found it locked.

'Authorised entry is not permitted,' said the cottage.

'Bloody hell,' shouted Ed, jumping back. 'I nearly gave birth. Are you a sentient security system?'

'Semi-sentient,' said the cottage.

'Can you contact Gabriel up in orbit please, he's concerned for the safety of Mike, Tony and Steve. We want to check they're all right,' said Ed, feeling an idiot for talking to a door in his underpants in the middle of the night.

It only took a few seconds before all the lights came on and the door clicked.

'Entry authorised for Edward Virr,' said the cottage.

Ed soon found Tony. He was dead and on the floor next to the bed, staring blankly up at the ceiling and covered in an ugly rash of sores.

'Ah, shit no,' said Ed. 'Tony, what have you done? What the hell is this?' He turned and ran out the front door, across to the next illuminated cottage and shouted his name at the front door. Immediately, the lights came on and the door clicked.

'Entry authorised for Edward Virr.'

He crashed through the front door and nearly fell over Mike. He'd made it into the lounge, where he lay face down, three metres from the door and just as dead.

'What the hell happened?' said Andy as he sprinted into Mike's cottage, only just avoiding the body on the floor.

'It seems to be some sort of virulent virus,' said Ed. 'Must be very fast-acting,'

'I'll check on Tony and Steve,' said Andy.

'Don't bother with Tony,' said Ed, shaking his head. 'Let's both check on Steve.'

They walked over to Steve's cottage together, knowing it was pointless to run. Ed went through the now-familiar routine with the security system and when the lights came on and the door clicked, they entered slowly this time.

They needn't have worried. Steve was still in bed, staring blankly at the ceiling and dead too.

'Fuck,' said Andy.

'My sentiments exactly,' said Ed.

'What about Phil?'

'He's in a coma – in the auto-nurse,' replied Ed. 'I'm kinda hoping that will hold off the virus until we can find a cure.'

'What the hell can we do? We're a physicist and a mechanical engineer not biologists, and we might be infected too.'

'Well, if we are, we're going to find out about it pretty soon,' said Ed. 'Come on, there's nothing we can do here tonight. We need to let Linda know what's happened and sober up.'

Linda met them as they walked into the bar area and, as they explained, a look of horror appeared on her face. They both grabbed her as she collapsed and dissolved into floods of tears.

Ed and Andy's eyes met, before they quickly looked away and stared out to sea, tears running down their faces too.

26

GDA CRUISER KATADROMIKO 37 – STATIONARY, POLEMISTIS SYSTEM

DAY 417, YEAR 11269, 03:47FC, PCC

It was obvious from the start: with only two people, trying to search a ship of approximately eighty-four cubic kilometres was a completely impossible task.

Lake and Herez had decided to begin with the bridge; firstly, because they had been there before so they knew the way and, secondly, because they might be able to see where the ship was on the big holo map.

The information holos that Lake had watched in his room on that first night had told him that the Katadromiko 37 had a crew complement of over forty-seven thousand. He wondered, as he walked, if all of them – except one – had perished.

Corridors after corridors leading to the bridge had been scattered with the dead and it seemed ridiculous that a race of humans this advanced could succumb so absolutely to a virus in such a short time frame.

Unsurprisingly, the bridge doors were closed, the security guards lying dead at their posts.

Lake noticed that their wrist control panels were still active and they both, very carefully, helped themselves to one each.

'Don't press anything with it pointing in my direction,' said Lake. 'You remember how they had these things pointed at us when we arrived.'

'I'm quite happy for you to press something first,' said Herez, looking nervously at his newly acquired wristlet full of winking icons. 'How do we know that one of these flashing thingies isn't the self-destruct button?'

'We need Dric'is to decipher them.'

'Hang on, what are those?' said Herez, pointing at the two guards.

'Those what?'

'The lanyards around their necks. They have a single icon in the middle.' Before Lake could stop him, Herez picked one off the guard's chest and pressed the icon.

'No – don't—'

The bridge doors opened.

'—press that,' said Lake, glaring at his employee.

'Don't give me that look. It worked, didn't it?'

'It could've been a panic button that seals the whole deck or activates ray guns or poison darts or fucking anything,' said Lake, continuing to scowl at Herez. 'Don't press anything else; is that clear?'

'Yes, boss,' said Herez, hanging his new lanyard around his neck and entering the bridge.

The room was almost deserted. It must have been the night shift as only a few of the couches were occupied by dead bodies. The large holo map was on and the little ship icon was flashing, from where it sat right in the middle of a small system; but it appeared to be stationary. A single star was a way off on the starboard side and two planets were quite close to port.

'Well, at least we're not heading for a black hole at warp factor 9,' said Lake. 'I'm quite happy with stationary.'

'Just as well,' said Herez, looking around the room. 'The control systems for this monster are way over my head.'

Lake sat down on one the recliner couches.

Immediately he was surrounded by holo icons, some flashing, some not, and a rainbow of different colours. Text started appearing in the air, right in front of his face. Lake just sat and watched, wondering how the hell all this worked and what the ship was trying to tell him.

'I wish we could talk to the computer,' said Lake.

'You can,' said Dric'is, strolling onto the bridge, a haunted look on her face.

Herez, who had his back to the main entrance, jumped out of his skin.

'Damn,' he said, swivelling round and instinctively ducking. When he recognised it was Dric'is and realised that she was talking through a translator, he relaxed a little. 'How can you be out here?'

'And so quickly,' said Lake, suspiciously.

'Your blood samples contained the anti-virus; that's why you're not affected. My computer was able to quickly recognise, isolate and synthesise more of the same for myself. I therefore ask the question: why were you immune? Was that part of your plan?'

'Our plan?' said Lake. 'We had no plan. It was you that dragged our ship aboard.'

'You fired a primitive weapon that you knew would have no effect on us, but it ensured you got our attention and we were compelled to arrest you and bring you on board. That's how you got the virus onto the ship and now, the first place you go to, after wiping out the crew, is the bridge so you can commandeer the vessel. How do you think that looks from my point of view?'

'It's all complete rubbish,' said Herez. 'Earlier you said the virus had nothing to do with us. Why are you now suddenly accusing us of deliberately causing this?' He stepped around the couch between them and closed in on Dric'is. He suddenly realised she was wearing one of the armlet weapons and was bringing it up towards him. He made a last second lunge.

'No!' shouted Lake.

The lightning bolt struck Herez in the upper chest, flinging him back over the couch he'd stepped around. He landed heavily in a tangle of arms and legs and remained still, a small puff of smoke rising from his clothing where the lightning bolt had impacted.

'Shit,' shouted Lake, staring at the crumpled form. 'Is he still alive?'

'Unfortunately, he probably is,' said Dric'is, glaring at Lake. 'Take that weapon off slowly and drop it on the floor.'

Lake did as he was told and remained sitting on the couch with his hands in full view.

'We're really not responsible for any of this,' he said. 'I realise it doesn't look particularly auspicious, but—'

'Shut up, Lake. You left the medical station, armed yourselves and came straight for the bridge. What were the arm weapons for, eh? To dispose of anyone alive on the bridge? As far as I'm concerned, you've murdered all my friends and colleagues, all forty-seven thousand of them, people from hundreds of systems and planets. You will be the most wanted human being in the galaxy when this news gets out and I'm going to be the one who brings you in.' She glared at him and indicated to Herez. 'Now pick him up.'

Lake slowly got up off the couch and stepped over to where Herez's unconscious form was slumped.

'I don't know if I can lift him in this heavy gravity,' he said.

'Just do it,' she said. 'Or I'll stun you too and drag you both down to security in a freight cart.'

Lake got down on one knee, grabbed Herez's arm and heaved his torso up onto his shoulders, shuffled him around a little until he was reasonably balanced and slowly stood up, pushing against the couch for leverage.

'Into the corridor and down to the tube,' she said, indicating the way with her arm weapon.

Lake staggered out of the bridge and down the corridor.

The extra gravity was bad enough with his own weight, but carrying ninety kilos of additional dead weight made it exhausting.

The tube carriage Dric'is had used was still waiting, so they filed in.

He set Herez down on one of the seats while she stood at the far end of the car, watching him closely.

Neither said a word during the journey.

On arrival at the stop nearest the security office, Lake picked up Herez once more, although it was easier this time getting him up off a seat instead of the floor.

Dric'is indicated for Lake to go first and, as he squeezed the two of them through the door, he watched their reflection in the glass opposite. Stopping to reposition Herez on his shoulders, he waited until he saw she was directly behind him. Then he threw himself and Herez backward through the door and across the carriage, crushing Dric'is against the far wall.

Her arm weapon discharged on impact and the lightning bolt hit the door frame.

Dropping Herez, Lake turned and, remembering his boyhood karate lessons, he parried the arm that contained the weapon and initiated a textbook solar plexus palm strike.

She exhaled loudly but, before she could recover, an old-fashioned uppercut snapped her head back and she was unconscious before she hit the floor.

Lake quickly removed her arm weapon and hurried down the corridor with her over his shoulder. He deposited her in Herez's room and dashed over to the security office's computer terminal. He kicked the dead guard away from the seat and, sitting at the terminal, he remembered the routine to change the language to English and proceeded to find the correct menu for the door locks, setting them to permanently secure.

When he returned to the tube, Herez was sitting up, staring at him.

'How the hell did I get here?' he said, rubbing his chest where the bolt had hit him.

'I carried your fat arse here,' said Lake. 'Now get up. We've got to get off this ship, fast, before reinforcements arrive.'

'Where's Dric'is?' said Herez, struggling to regain his balance.

'Having a little lie down. Now hurry up and sort your shit out.'

Returning to the security office, Lake sat at the computer terminal and brought up the ship schematic.

He requested the shuttle bays first, of which there were fourteen. He then asked for shuttle bays below his present position as he knew they had come up several floors when they first arrived. That reduced the number to eight. Then he cut that to bays in the rear half of the ship on the starboard side. The list was now three. He found a marker pen in one of the drawers and proceeded to write the numbers of the nearest tube stops on the back of his hand.

'You'll never escape,' said Dric'is, glaring at Lake and Herez through the beam lock. 'They'll hunt you down across a thousand galaxies if need be.'

'Ah, the treacherous, trigger-happy bitch awakes,' said Herez.

'And I thought you two were engaged,' said Lake,

with a smirk. 'After all, she did give you that nice red medallion in the middle of your chest.'

'It would've been a bloody great hole if I'd known any better,' howled Dric'is.

'Do you want me to tidy up, boss?' said Herez, indicating to Dric'is, who was testing the beam lock with a chair leg.

'No, we've not committed any crime here. It'll only give them a real reason to pursue us.' Lake turned his attention to Dric'is. 'When your friends arrive and the truth of what really happened here comes out, I want a full apology and compensation for the trauma you've caused to myself and especially my colleague here.'

'Never going to happen, you murdering bastards,' she shouted as Lake and Herez strolled out into the corridor.

They made their way down to the tube, where the scorch mark was still on the door frame. Lake entered the first destination into the control panel and off they went. It didn't seem familiar when they arrived, but they had a quick look in the hangar anyway. It contained twenty single-seater fighter spaceplanes. They were black and sleek and armed to the teeth.

'Just think what we could get for just one of these back home, boss,' said Herez, running his fingers down the fuselage of the nearest one.

'I think I would go for that one,' said Lake, pointing at a large shuttle, sitting back in the corner. It had once been white, but had greyed at the edges with age and had the tell-tale scorch marks of planetary insertion. It could obviously carry a reasonable cargo and seemed to be armed as there were sinister-looking pods and attachments hanging off it. 'Anyway, it's not our hangar. Let's check out the next one.'

They knew they had the right one as soon as they emerged from the tube; the corridor leading down to the hangar was familiar, although the sight that beheld them as they entered the large space was most definitely not what they were expecting.

Their space plane was in pieces.

'Oh, shit,' said Lake as he surveyed the parts of his ship lying around the floor and under the main body. 'What the fuck have they done?'

'Probably looking for the missile system that wasn't there,' said Herez. He climbed the steps and poked his head into the cabin. It was trashed. 'Don't even think of looking in here,' he said, quickly jumping back down.

Lake looked around the hangar.

The small shuttles were still there against the far wall and he walked across to inspect them. The nearest one was open and had its steps extended.

Lake jumped up and stuck his head inside. He soon found what he was looking for: past the airlock and set into the wall was the now familiar computer keypad. He went through the convert language routine and hunted around in the menu for the flight prep instructions and soon found the flight checklist.

Herez had followed Lake up into the shuttle and began to check what else would be helpful to make it flight-ready.

'Come on,' said Lake as he went out the airlock and jumped down from the ship.

'Where are we going now? I thought we had to get off this ship?'

'If you're going to steal a spaceship,' said Lake, heading back out the door towards the tube, 'steal the most powerful one.' He headed out the door towards the tube.

Herez caught him up and they both got back on the tube car.

Lake led them back to the previous hangar and walked over to the far side where the big freighter was.

'This is the one,' he said with a grin. 'Shall we play?'

The loading ramps were extended so they could walk straight in. They found the control cabin up a set of stairs and past four crew cabins.

Lake again changed the language on the computer terminal and brought up the flight prep lists. Soon he had the ship powered up and started closing the cargo doors. When he got to the last door, he looked out the front screen at the hangar below and thought for a moment.

'Come,' he said, beckoning to Herez.

Each of the twenty fighter ships was sitting on its own motorized trolley.

Lake started pressing icons on the control pad of the nearest one until it lit up. Two minutes later he, with the help of Herez, motored one of the tiny fighters up into the freighter's cargo bay, shut it down and smiled to himself.

'As for compensation, I'll take this with me,' he said, patting Herez on the back. 'Come on, let's fly this bitch,' he said before running up the stairs to the control cabin and over to one of the two pilot's couches.

Herez sat in the one on the right as Lake planted himself down in the left and started reading the pre-flight checklist. Lake was able to identify most of the floating icons around him as the checklist lit them in sequence. When it came to donning the flight helmet and engaging brain-thought interfacing with the flight computer, he stopped and looked around the cabin for something that resembled a helmet.

'Can you see a helmet anywhere?'

'No, but there's one of these in the seat pocket to your left,' said Herez, holding up what looked like a wool beanie hat in the design of an old cycling helmet. Lake pulled his out and gave it a strange look.

'This can't be what they mean, surely?' said Lake and slipped the cloth helmet on. Nothing happened for a second or two until he blinked and, for a millisecond, saw the outside of the ship.

'That's weird,' he said and blinked again, getting the same strange result. Then it dawned on him what he was supposed to be doing. He shut his eyes.

'Wow, well I'll be damned,' he said and started moving his head around, grinning.

'Do I need to put mine on?' asked Herez.

'No, I think it would confuse the system. We'll try it when we've got a bit more space.'

All of a sudden, the ship jerked to starboard and clunked back down on the deck.

'Oops,' said Lake. 'It's a little twitchy.'

He concentrated on the ship again and imagined it rising up in the hangar. As soon as the ship jumped up off the deck Herez grabbed the sides of his couch. Lake turned the freighter towards the bay door and imagined it open; a split second later it shimmered and became space and stars.

'Oh, wow,' said Herez. 'Are you doing all this with just thought?'

Lake held up a hand to silence him; he was concentrating hard so as to not bump the doors on the way out.

When the freighter was clear of the hangar, he

imagined the struts were up, and a reassuring whining from below confirmed the landing struts were retracting. He took the ship out to two hundred kilometres and asked the computer if the ship had any stealth settings. Two icons appeared in his thought vision: one labelled electronic and the other visual. He imagined both being touched and immediately the white lighting in the cabin turned a subdued blue.

'Okay,' said Lake. 'Shall we go somewhere a little more familiar?'

'Can we adjust the gravity first?' asked Herez.

Lake closed his eyes again and thought about gravity controls. He found several and soon found the right icon and reduced the gravity weight percentage from one hundred percent down to seventy-five.

They both noticed the difference immediately and Herez emitted a sigh of relief.

Lake thought the jump co-ordinates into the computer and the freighter vanished from the Dyo system.

27

THEO ISLAND – THE PLANET PANEMORFI

DAY 417, YEAR 11269, 09:20FC, PCC

Ed sat in the pilot's seat of one of the shuttles, talking to Gabriel.

Earlier, they'd carefully brought the three bodies out of their cottages, taken tissue samples and placed the three Theos on the beach, well away from any buildings and palm trees.

Gabriel had scanned Tony, Steve and Mike from orbit to confirm they were deceased.

Ed, Andy and Linda had stood some distance away with their heads bowed as Gabriel had cremated the bodies using the ship's Asteri Beam – it formed part of the starship's defensive systems and translated to 'star beam' or 'sun beam.' Within a split second, the bodies had vaporised and the two-metre circle of beach where their bodies had lain became molten glass.

'I'm going to bring the food and water samples up,'

said Ed. 'Is there anything else you think you might need to find the source of this?'

'No, Edward. I believe that will be sufficient,' said Gabriel. 'Please close the island down before you depart. I have added yours, Andy's and Linda's voice commands into the island's security system, so you are now authorised to use this facility whenever you wish. Let me know when you're ready to depart and I will autopilot the shuttles back here.'

'Thank you,' said Ed and they made their way back to the main building.

He sat on the loungers for a while with Andy and Linda, staring out to sea.

'Why are we immune?' asked Linda. 'What's so different about us?'

'With Gabriel's help, I'm hoping to solve that problem,' said Ed. 'Come on, you two. Phil's not going to get better while we're all moping about down here.'

They all stood, gathered their belongings from their respective cottages, instructed the island to close down and boarded one of the shuttles. It immediately took off, closely followed by the second empty one.

IT MADE them feel a little better when they saw Phil lying in the auto-nurse.

He didn't have the ugly rash that the other three had had.

He must have activated the auto-nurse very quickly, thought Ed.

Under instruction from Gabriel, he placed the samples one at a time into the analyser and had the results within a few minutes.

'The virus is a variant of what you would know as smallpox,' said Gabriel. 'Instead of the usual sixty percent fatality rate, this has been engineered to one hundred percent – and to be especially virulent to Theos.'

'You mean that this is a targeted biological weapon attack?' asked Andy.

'It would appear so. The virus strain had been added to the water supply on the island, most likely at the desalination unit.'

'So, it's murder!' said Linda and stared at Phil. 'Who'd want to kill these guys? They're so … friendly.'

'Gabriel, why are we immune?' said Ed.

'You were all inoculated in 2029 after the outbreak in central Africa.'

'I remember that,' said Andy. 'I was about twelve or thirteen then. That's a good anti-virus if it's still active.'

'I need some of that anti-virus for Phil as soon as possible.'

'Can't you refine some from our blood samples?' said Ed.

'If Phil hadn't been affected, then that would work. But as the virus has got a hold in his system, I need the anti-virus in its pure form. You need to go back to Earth and get some.'

'Okay, is our ship ready?'

'No, not for another three days.'

'Then how the hell do we get the vaccine?'

'Before Phil got in the auto-nurse, he authorised the three of you to command this starship, so I need one of you on the bridge at all times.'

'I'm there,' said Linda, diving out the door and running for the lift tube.

'Gabriel,' said Ed. 'Phil told us that a GDA ship used the island recently and it was very unusual for them to do so.'

'That is correct.'

'Are the Theos in any dispute with the GDA?'

'Not to my knowledge.'

'What was the name of that visiting ship?'

'The Katadromiko 37. It's a large battle cruiser.'

'And where is it now?'

'Last recorded jump was into the Dyo System two days ago.'

'Are there video logs from the island during their visit?'

'There is data available.'

'When you say "data", does that include visual feeds?'

'Yes, from receptors around the main building and from the stationary satellite.'

'Can you scan through the feeds of the GDA visit and show me any that involve movement around the desalination plant during that period?'

'No movement detected.'

'So, nobody went near the plant during their visit?'

'Correct.'

'Try the period from then until we arrived.'

'No movement detected.'

'Okay, now go back from the GDA visit until you find movement.'

'Movement detected. Displaying holo playback.'

An image from above the island appeared of the small desalination unit and a large dark shadow swept up and stopped on top, but before they started to get excited, it flapped its wings.

'Shit, it's a bird,' said Andy.

'It's an Alieia bird. A large sea fishing bird that spends weeks over the oceans hunting for—'

'Yes, thank you, David Attenborough,' said Ed. 'I really don't think that's our man. Keep going back please.'

They saw another two birds and something

resembling a turtle. On day 395, what looked like a small boat pulled up on the beach, adjacent to the plant. It was dark, but Gabriel was able to enhance the quality using the faint amount of light bleeding over from the security lights around the cottages nearby.

Four figures fanned out across the beach from the boat. Three took up defensive positions in a semi-circle around the plant and one approached, spending about two minutes at the desalination plant.

'Gotcha,' said Ed as they watched the group re-form at the boat and motor away from the island.

'Can we follow that boat, Gabriel?'

'For a while, yes. The satellite has a footprint of about forty kilometres.'

'How far to the nearest island?'

'Thirty-two kilometres. I will speed up the feed.'

The little boat suddenly flew across the ocean and, sure enough, it pulled up at the next island under a small jetty next to a large resort complex. Gabriel slowed the feed again and as they watched, four little shadows, one at a time, popped up out from under the jetty and sauntered back to the main building.

'What's the name of that resort, Gabriel?'

'The Okeanos Resort, and it's open to anyone who can afford it.'

'Are you able to check out the guest list for any groups of four adults?'

'Hacker is my middle name, Edward.'

'Oh, shit. We're teaching an alien computer how to take the piss,' said Andy.

'You forget, Andrew. I've been hanging around Earth for several millennia so I don't imagine there's an awful lot you can teach me about taking the piss.'

'Ignore him, Gabriel,' said Ed. 'I just need to know how many—'

'Two groups of four. One a group of women who won the trip in a competition and a freighter ship's crew, from a ship called the Metaforeas. They're your best bet as they stayed for one night after dropping some cargo off at the resort.'

'Why would that be something of interest?'

'Because it's never happened before. That freighter has dropped goods here regularly for years and never stopped overnight. The captain paid with his own funds for four of his crew to stay at the resort for one night. He has seven in his crew, eight counting himself. So why only four on that particular night?'

'It has to be them. Where is that freighter now?'

'Gone.'

'Yes, I know it's gone now—'

'No, destroyed, four days ago.'

'How was it destroyed?'

'It was approaching its home planet of Krix'ir and it exploded. The GDA investigators have not been able to determine exactly why, but they did discover explosive residue on some of the recovered wreckage and the scan logs from the nearby space station show just one of its twelve lifeboats ejected four minutes before the explosion. They report that the lifeboat was then caught in the explosion and burned up in the atmosphere, along with all the other falling wreckage.'

'Or was that the way it was supposed to look?' said Ed, thinking hard. 'Why was there only one lifeboat ejecting? If a bomb had been found on board, there would be mass panic to get off that ship and lifeboats going in all directions.'

'So, you think the bomber was on the single lifeboat?' said Andy.

'Yep. Position the lifeboat in front of the freighter and press the remote detonator. Then tumble into the upper atmosphere with all the other junk. Gabriel, how many ships have left Krix'ir in the last four days?'

'None. All space travel on and off Krix'ir was suspended until the completion of the investigation.'

'He's still there. Our killer is still on Krix'ir,' said Ed, clapping his hands together and staring at Andy.

'We have to get the anti-virus first for Phil, though, yeah?'

'Absolutely, Phil's our first priority. Let's go and tell Linda the news.'

'She knows,' said Gabriel. 'She's one with the ship; everything I know, she knows.'

'I can see you and even talk to you,' said Linda. 'That was a pretty cool bit of deduction back there, Edward. Are you sure your surname isn't Holmes?'

'You keep your eyes on the road, Slopes,' said Ed, grinning. 'Remember, you only have a shuttle licence. You're still on learner plates for this intergalactic hauler.'

28

GDA FREIGHTER – EN ROUTE TO GAIA

DAY 417, YEAR 11269, 01:19FC, PCC

After three jumps and over five hundred light years travelled, Xavier Lake had relaxed a little.

It had taken him longer than he'd liked to learn about the new ship. Plotting jump and emergence points with the power of thought was not easy, though the computer always checked the validity of any input to avoid miscalculations. It displayed the jump in a holo map which was projected both within the pilot's omniscient vision and physically in the middle of the control cabin.

He still lacked finesse but, as with anything, practice makes perfect. The helmets he had discovered were called Pantognostis Orama Kranos – or POKs – which translated to Omniscient Vision Helmet. He had also learned that the ship wasn't a shuttle or a freighter at all; it was an armed military troop carrier, designed to look like a freighter so it could rapidly deploy a squadron of soldiers with all their equipment at any given location.

Once Lake was satisfied that nobody had either followed them or was anywhere near them, he had put the ship into an orbit around a small, uninhabited planet in a system the computer had called Ipios. The ship was put into hide and detect mode and remained completely cloaked. He finally attempted to get some food, which was an adventure of its own, given the peculiar culinary delights of the GDA.

Herez returned, having spent some time rummaging around in the bowels of the ship, and was very excited to show Lake a hatch in the floor of the main troop cabin. It led down to a small stairway into an armoury, which was stacked from floor to ceiling with weaponry of all shapes and sizes – enough to start an interplanetary war. No matter how much they wanted to check out each and every rifle, hand gun, grenade and cannon, they wisely decided to leave them well alone. It wouldn't be very prudent to blow a hole in the side of the ship with a negligent discharge.

'I'll have a look on the computer menus to see if there's any instructions on the use of our newfound arsenal. But, first, we must decide where on Earth we can hide this beast.' Lake laughed at his own joke before realising Herez hadn't understood and was staring at him blankly.

'What about DeLand in Florida?' Herez said, after thinking for a moment. 'The hangar there should be big enough and you own the holiday ranch at Lake Beresford. We could hide there for a while.'

'That's not a bad idea at all, Mr Herez,' said Lake and, the more he thought about it, the more ideal he realised it was.

DeLand Municipal Airport was on the north side of DeLand, Florida. Lake Aerospace had built the hangar there in the early forties as an emergency service area for any of their scram-jet space planes that needed to come down in the northern hemisphere. The facility was very rarely used; it had state-of-the-art security and was surrounded by industrial units – so, at night, the area was completely deserted.

'Do you know the entry security codes?' asked Lake.

'Yes, as soon as the ship is in there, I'll change the codes so only we can enter. If we leave the ship in stealth mode, nobody will know and, even if someone climbs up to peer in a window, the hangar will appear empty.'

'Remind me to give you a bonus,' said Lake, chewing on something vaguely edible from the GDA's food replicator.

'A bonus?' said Herez, sounding thoroughly underwhelmed. 'Remind me to go "hip hip hooray".'

'Sometimes you can be very unappreciative of your honoured position,' said Lake, glowering at his underling.

'An international arrest warrant on Earth; wanted for warmongering, mass murder and theft in the rest of the galaxy... "Honoured position" isn't exactly the place I consider myself at the present time,' said Herez, sitting on the other pilot's couch and crossing his arms.

Lake continued staring for a few seconds then, realising that Herez may have a point, he once again put the POK on his head, closed his eyes and started plotting a jump into the Helios System.

An hour later the stolen ship winked back into existence near Jupiter.

Lake re-cloaked the ship. He'd discovered before the first jump, that jumping while cloaked wasn't possible. However, an embedded jump would obscure the route and emergence co-ordinates.

He scanned the system and was pleased to find no GDA presence. He hoped that, as this system was designated off-limits, the GDA would not pursue him here but, of course, their ships would be cloaked too. This is why he emerged behind Ganymede, one of Jupiter's larger moons. He cruised around the moon and set off towards Earth at ninety-five percent light speed. The planets at this moment in time were around seven hundred million kilometres apart, so the journey took around an hour.

On arrival at Earth, Lake was pleased to see it was early evening on the East Coast of Florida. He dropped the ship into the atmosphere fast as he wanted the fiery trail which streamed out behind the invisible ship to look like a shooting star. At fifty thousand feet, he pulled up and cruised down to five hundred feet and then brought the vessel to a full stop. Below him was Tiger Bay State Forest and, just in front, North DeLand and the airport.

After spending a few hours watching it get dark and a few planes taking off and landing, Lake piloted the ship over to the southern side of the airport.

Lowering the struts, he brought the vessel in next to his hangar and landed silently, side on, so the lowering ramp couldn't be seen from across the field. As soon as Herez was out, he retracted the ramp and sat waiting. Although inside the ship Lake couldn't hear the hangar doors opening, he knew the electric motors whined and the doors clanked. But, at this time of night, it was unlikely anyone would hear.

He inched the ship forward into the tight space, which tested the ship's omniscient vision and, once in, he turned the vessel so it was facing the doors and settled it down. Herez closed the doors again.

'Have you phoned Stephen?' asked Lake as he descended the ramp.

'Yes, boss,' said Herez. 'He'll be here within the hour.'

'Good. We'll stay at the Beresford ranch for a few days, returning here every day to do a system scan. If there's still no sign of the GDA by next week, we'll put together a small team of experts and reverse-engineer the shit out of this ship, and its little cousin parked in the back. We'll become the wealthiest entrepreneurs in the history of the planet and retire with everything money can buy. How does that sound for a bonus?'

'Just fine, boss,' said Herez, smiling for the first time that week. 'I think I'll buy the Bahamas.'

29

SELENE (EARTH'S MOON) – HELIOS SYSTEM

DAY 417, YEAR 11269, 15:10FC, PCC

Four GDA Katadromiko Class Battle Cruisers appeared one at a time, hidden from Gaia by the planet's only moon, Selene.

They proceeded to scan the system thoroughly from their concealed positions, unable to move in on the planet until they had clearance from Dasos.

After securing and quarantining the Katadromiko 37, Captain Bache Loftt had listened to the evidence of the lone survivor, Katt Dric'is, a Medical Officer.

He'd immediately despatched a jump drone back to Dasos, calling for back-up and guidance. Dric'is had provided the medical staff on Katadromiko 12 with the anti-virus, which had been quickly formulated in large quantities and dispensed to the entire crews of Katadromiko 12 and then –as they arrived – Katadromikos, 19, 41 and 43.

The small, partly-dismantled, primitive ship, discovered in one of 37's service hangars had backed up the evidence given by Dric'is. It did indeed have jump capability and, judging by the recent scan results from the Helios System, the design was identical to several vessels operating around the planet of Gaia.

This evidence had all been on the jump drone to Dasos and, if proved correct, the Gerousia, hastily assembled for an emergency sitting in the Synedrio, would re-designate the planet Gaia to a class NV (new-born violent), with either katapato blue (approach cloaked) or even katapato green (fully-open approach) approved.

Until the result of the emergency sitting was received, Captain Loftt kept all four cruisers cloaked and hidden from Gaia behind Selene.

He realised they had been very lucky that Dric'is had spent the time shut up in the virus laboratory, which was the only place on the ship that had a separate food and water supply. It had saved her life.

She'd been cramming for her Senior Medical Officer's exams and had shut herself away, working on her thesis after leaving Panemorfi a couple of hours before being fired upon by the tiny Gaian ship.

Two hours later, the encrypted-message beam was received from the jump drone as it winked back in system. The message was transmitted straight to the

Captain's bridge office, where Loftt was in a meeting with the three other Katadromiko captains. He instructed the computer to initiate the communication and a holographic image of General Tonixe appeared in the centre of the room.

'Good afternoon, Captain Loftt and assembled Captains,' said the general. 'The Gerousia has concluded the emergency sitting regarding the tragic loss of Katadromiko 37's crew. As all of you will realise, this unprovoked attack on one of our peace-keeping vessels is unprecedented in modern times and cannot go unpunished. The evidence you have provided does indeed seem damning but is not wholly conclusive. For this reason, the Gerousia has acquiesced to re-categorising the planet known as Gaia in the Helios System to a permanent NV status, with katapato green designation for the duration of this operation and reverting to blue thereafter. You are therefore authorised to blockade the planet known as Gaia uncloaked and use whatever means necessary, excluding Genok weapons, to apprehend the Gaian humans known as Lake and Herez, as well as any other Gaian humans or persons unknown who were conclusively involved. Captain Loftt, as the senior captain, you will be in overall command of the operation and I will require daily updates via jump drone on the progress of the engagement.'

The general stood to attention and saluted. 'Good luck, gentlemen. And remember: Peace Through Unified Command.'

The four captains all stood to attention and saluted the fading figure with their right fist over their heart. 'Peace Through Unified Command,' they repeated.

Captain Loftt relieved the three other captains to their relevant vessels to brief their senior officers and prepare for the coming operation.

He then briefed his own officers before retreating to his cabin to be close to his wife and children. The shock of discovering forty-seven thousand dead colleagues was playing heavily on his mind – he realised it could so easily have been his ship – and this made him even more determined to apprehend those responsible, by any means. He had set the operation start time at 10:00FC, so he had to make the most of the short time with his family as he didn't know when he'd get back to his family cabin over the coming days.

THE FOLLOWING MORNING, at 10:00FC exactly, the four gargantuan battle cruisers moved out from behind Selene and approached Gaia. Still cloaked, they took up positions around the planet, with a cruiser sitting near both the main space stations – one roving around in high orbit and Captain Loftt's command ship sitting out at one hundred thousand kilometres.

As one, the four cruisers de-cloaked and, to those on the massive battle cruisers, nothing of any significance happened.

However, on both the space stations, absolute pandemonium raged, which soon spread down to the planet, and within ten minutes the governments of all western nations were in panic mode, with presidents and senior politicians being whisked away to secret secure locations, many of them not even told why.

Two troop carriers, similar to the one Lake had stolen, arrived beside both Armstrong and Tiangong Stations, transmitting in perfect English as the translators had been updated from the Katadromiko 37. Both station commanders were ordered to be brought across to their nearest battle cruisers otherwise their space stations would be nudged into the atmosphere.

The cruiser captains were not taking any chances and, as soon as one of the stations' shuttles released from its station, it was shut down and tractored across to be dumped unceremoniously into a hangar bay. Soldiers then surrounded the small ships and removed the occupants, the station commanders being put inside GDA shuttles under armed guard, and flown across to the Katadromiko 12.

Jim Rucker and Xiong Yu had never met before, but

they recognised each other from photographs. Neither of the two men said a word. They were searched and then escorted through the vast cruiser, via the tube, and up to the bridge.

Both men's eyes were on stalks as they witnessed the amazing technology which surrounded them, but they weren't coping with the extra gravity very well, especially Xiong as he'd been weightless for weeks and could barely walk at all.

Captain Loftt didn't look up as the two station commanders were marched in and stood side by side, facing his desk. Instead, he was looking at a video feed of the two on their way up, to see if he could detect any collaboration between them.

He saw none.

'Gentlemen,' he said finally, through the translator. 'Sorry to drop in on you so abruptly. We're the GDA and we have been policing this region of the galaxy for the last few thousand years. Recently it has come to our attention that you have stumbled across some new technology.'

He indicated a screen on the wall of his office. 'Does this ship seem familiar to either of you?'

Images of Lake's partly disassembled shuttle appeared on the screen and both men's eyes grew wide, which didn't go unnoticed.

'Hang on a minute,' said Jim, looking closely at the

pictures. 'That's not ours. It looks almost like one of Lake's shuttles.' He turned and glared at Xiong. 'Is that anything to do with you, Xiong?'

'Shut up, Rucker,' said Xiong through gritted teeth.

Loftt looked at Xiong and smiled.

'Such camaraderie between fellow spacemen. Perhaps you can tell me a little more about this Lake human?'

'I've never heard of him,' said Xiong.

'That's a real shame,' said Loftt, looking up at one of the soldiers who was guarding the two Gaians. 'Lieutenant, can you order Katadromiko 43 to give this little man's space station a nudge into the upper atmosphere please?'

'You can't do that,' shouted Xiong. His knees finally gave out to the heavy gravity and he slumped to the floor.

'I most definitely can,' said Loftt. 'Each of these Katadromiko Class Battle Cruisers has the power to destroy your pretty little planet –your sad collection of tin cans could be despatched with a hand weapon.'

Jim glanced down at Xiong and watched him attempting to stand up again and failing.

'Captain, can I ask you a question?' asked Jim.

Loftt shifted his gaze from Xiong to Jim and nodded.

'Where exactly were these images taken?'

'One hundred and twenty-six light years away, near the Cyclatt System, in the hangar of one of our battle cruisers,' Loftt answered.

Jim glared at Xiong. 'Did Lake build a jump ship on your station?'

'He – he said it was a new scanning array,' Xiong answered, still sitting on the floor with his head bowed.

'Scanning array, my arse,' said Jim. 'That looks almost identical to the Virr Drive that we've been testing. Lake stole the fucking design, didn't he? DIDN'T HE?' he shouted at Xiong, who remained staring at the floor.

'We didn't know what it was,' said Xiong quietly. 'He rented the hangar space. We knew he was lying, but we didn't recognise the technology.' Xiong shrugged his shoulders. Perhaps deciding, at that moment, to tell everything he knew, before anyone could react, he continued: 'Lake left the station a few days ago on a short test flight. We followed him with our scanners. That was the strange thing, though. Before his ship disappeared, we got a reading of a small object travelling towards him at high speed.'

'Another ship?' asked Jim.

'No, it can't have been. It was too small.'

'It was a missile,' said Loftt. 'Things are starting to make sense now.'

'How do you know it was a missile?' Jim asked.

'Because it re-engaged when it emerged – with that battle cruiser,' Loftt said, pointing at the screen.

'Hang on,' said Jim. 'If Lake's still on that cruiser, why are you here?'

'Because, he no longer is. He stole one of our armed troop carriers, after loading it up with one of our latest single-seater fighters.'

'You're telling me that you allowed a crook like Xavier Lake to wander around one of your battle cruisers, helping himself to a bunch of armaments, and then to bugger off with one of your troop carriers? I've got better security on my sad tin cans over there,' said Jim, pointing in the rough direction of Earth.

'It's easy to avoid security when you've killed them all,' said Loftt, getting irritated with the way the conversation was going.

'Lake killed the security staff in the hangar?'

'No, Mr Rucker. He murdered the entire crew.'

'Bollocks,' said Jim. 'How large is the crew on one of these monsters?'

'Over forty-seven thousand.'

'And he took them all out with his ray gun, did he? Or was it his light sabre?' said Jim with a distinct mocking tone, which the translator obviously didn't carry over.

Even Xiong snorted with laughter after that one and got a swift kick from one of the guards.

Loftt put his hand up and glared at the guard, who backed up and stood to attention again.

'We'll have none of that, Lieutenant. I think our gravity is punishing enough. In answer to your question, Mr Rucker, Lake introduced a virus into the water supply, which killed the entire crew within a few hours.'

'You think he did that deliberately, do you?'

'They were scanned before they got on the ship – it wasn't in their systems.'

'What do you mean "they"? I thought it was only Lake.'

'He wasn't alone.'

'It was Floyd Herez,' said Xiong, looking up for the first time in a while.

'I might have known that psycho wouldn't be far away,' said Jim. 'I met him once at a space industry conference – not someone you forget, especially if you believe the rumours. But getting back to this virus, I really don't believe it could have been premeditated –we had no idea of other human races even existing out here. We've been romanticising – and fearing – the first contact scenario for centuries. Lake would have had absolutely no prior knowledge of your existence whatsoever. I'm sure he would have been just as shocked and frightened as we were an hour ago when your behemoth starships suddenly appeared all around us and immediately started making demands and threats.'

'We make no apology for our approach, Mr Rucker. You have to look at it from our point of view: this is the most serious GDA loss of personnel since the Trav'exe incursions in 9275. Gaia – or Earth as you call it – was known for many millennia as a non-jump-capable human outpost, strictly off limits to all Galaxian traffic, by order of the Gerousia. So it was quite a shock for us too to find a Gaian ship, one hundred and twenty-six light years away from where it should be, and firing upon a battle cruiser, killing the entire crew and stealing one of our military vessels which was bristling with our latest weapon systems and new technology. So, I don't believe that you – or anyone – could call our reaction into question.'

'No, you're correct, Captain,' said Jim. 'I know I would have reacted the same way and, while we're being candid with each other, you didn't come across our test jump ship anywhere did you?'

'You mean there's another one out here somewhere? Where was it jumping to?'

'The last transmission indicated that they were attempting a jump into the Centauri system, 4.3 light years away. That was four days ago. To say we're getting concerned is an understatement.'

Captain Loftt looked down at his monitor and voice-commanded the computer. Almost immediately, a holographic image of the local systems appeared just above head-height in the middle of the room.

'4.3 light years, you say. That would be the Uskrre System. Ah, that would explain why your ship hasn't returned,' said Loftt, with a concerned look on his face. He again talked to the computer and a three-star system became the focus of attention, especially a planet orbiting the small dwarf star, it was coloured red, flashing and surrounded by a string of satellites or moons.

'Why?' asked Jim. 'What's the problem with that planet?'

'The planet's called Uskrre – not a dangerous planet in itself, although it does have spectacular weather at times. The Klatt has a military outpost there and have ringed the planet with some of their rather over-zealous defence satellites. Can I ask if your ship had any defence capabilities?'

'No, it didn't,' said Jim, staring at the rotating image of the planet with real concern on his face.

Loftt spoke quietly to the computer again then paused, staring at his monitor. The information he was waiting for appeared and he glanced up at Jim.

'What is it?' Jim asked, nervously.

'I've just done an extensive scan of the Uskrre System, specifically looking for weapon detonation signatures and any new debris that wasn't there before.'

'And?' said Jim, fearing the worst.

'Nothing. The system is clear.'

'Well, that's a good sign, isn't it?'

'It means they didn't meet any foul play in space, within that system,' said Loftt. 'It doesn't rule out emerging too near the star or entering the planet's atmosphere for whatever reason.'

'Is there any way of checking the planet?' Jim asked.

'Mr Rucker, there is a limit to me helping you and you've reached that. I brought you here to help me. So, to avoid me having to take my cruisers into your planet's atmosphere and start throwing my weight around, probably causing global panic and a lot of bloodshed, I want you...' Loftt glanced down to Xiong on the floor, '...and even you, Mr Xiong, to help me now. You will contact your particular governments and tell them that they have two of your Earth days to locate and arrest Lake and Herez. You will have them flown here and delivered alive to any of my cruisers. Now tell me, gentlemen, do I have to demonstrate the power of these cruisers to encourage your governments, or do I not?'

'I don't think that will be needed,' said Jim. 'Come on, Xiong. We have work to do.'

Jim nodded at the captain and walked to the door. The two guards that flanked Xiong picked him up and half-carried, half-dragged him out of the office, across the bridge and out towards the nearest tube station.

30

THEO STARSHIP GABRIEL – HELIOS SYSTEM

DAY 417, YEAR 11269, 23:39FC, PCC

Under Linda's control, the Gabriel emerged into the Helios System between the sun and Earth – to avoid any overenthusiastic astronomer catching a fleeting glimpse of the ship before it cloaked. What she wasn't expecting was a shrill tone in her ears, which indicated a scan detection was taking place.

'Shit, what the hell?'

She cloaked and immediately sent the ship towards Mercury at maximum drive.

'Gabriel, who the bloody hell detected us out here?'

'There are four GDA Katadromiko Class Battle Cruisers surrounding Earth. They all detected our emergence,' said Gabriel.

'Bloody hell,' she shouted. 'Guys, you'd better get up here,' she called over the ship's systems.

Ed and Andy shot out of the tube lift two minutes later.

'What's up?' they said, almost in stereo.

'That's up,' said Linda, pointing at the rotating holo map which showed Earth with the four monstrous cruisers lurking nearby.

'Shit, is that Earth?' said Andy.

'Yep,' she said.

'How big are those bloody ships?' asked Ed.

'Fourteen kilometres,' said Gabriel. 'A crew of over forty-seven thousand and the firepower to lay waste to an average planet.'

'Do they know we're here?' asked Andy.

'They detected our emergence,' said Linda. 'But they don't know where we are while we remain cloaked.'

'We'd best get over there and find out what the hell's happened in the last few days,' said Ed.

'Gabriel,' said Andy. 'Can you scan Earth radio for some English-speaking news? I want to know if the general population has any idea of this.'

After only a few seconds, a BBC world-news station appeared on a large screen on the bridge wall. The newsreader covered everything of note happening around the globe with absolutely no mention of alien battle cruisers. One story they all thought was odd involved an international arrest warrant for Xavier Lake and his bodyguard, Floyd Herez. A one hundred million dollar reward was offered for any information that led to their apprehension.

'That's who they believed stole our work on the jump drive,' said Ed.

'You don't think it's connected, do you?' asked Linda.

'Getting the attention of one Katadromiko cruiser is a worrying event,' said Gabriel. 'But four signifies a very rare occasion – something of consequence has occurred.'

The newsreader finished with a small note to advise any amateur astronomers that, due to unusual sun-spot activity, they might witness atmospheric disturbances which would blot out parts of the night sky in various locations around the globe, possibly lasting for a couple of days.

'That's crap,' said Andy. 'That's a cover-up for the ships in orbit.'

'Now we know that the public hasn't been informed,' said Linda.

'It's to avoid mass panic,' said Ed. 'Can you imagine the reaction if the world's population suddenly discovered there were four planet-busting alien battle cruisers sitting above them?'

'Can we get a message to Armstrong Station without being seen or overheard, Gabriel?' asked Ed.

'We can,' said Gabriel. 'The closer we are, the less chance of it being intercepted. It would be good to be directly in front of their receiving array.'

'Can you do that, Linda?' asked Ed.

'Already on the way, boss,'

It took them six minutes at maximum drive to reach Armstrong Station, swing around beneath and out in front of the array.

Ed sat in one of the command couches and nodded at Linda when he was ready. She activated the tight beam.

'Armstrong Station, this is Edward Virr on the Cartella. I have a high-priority confidential message for Jim Rucker. Please request Jim to reply on a tight beam, pointed directly at the source of this transmission and not – I repeat, not – on wide band transmission. I will await Jim's reply – Cartella out.'

A series of static pops and longer blips came back and everything went silent.

'Clever bastard,' said Ed.

'What?' said Linda, looking at Ed with a confused expression.

'The radio engineer sent me a "copy that" in Morse code, using the static,' replied Ed, winking at Linda.

'That's clever, how long do you think it will—'

'I'll need a fucking cardiac nurse if I get any more shocks today, Mr Virr,' said Jim. 'But can I say I've never been so glad to hear someone's voice in my life. We'd almost given up on you guys. Are you all okay? And where the hell are you?'

'Hi, Jim. We're all okay. We're piloting a cloaked, alien starship called the Gabriel and we're close by. The Cartella is fine and parked in one of our shuttle bays. It's a long story, but we urgently need a vial of smallpox vaccine to save the life of one of this ship's crew.'

'That's the second time I've been told about a virus today, but I'll see what I can do. Unfortunately, the GDA have banned any shuttle movements to and from the planet unless it contains Xavier Lake and Floyd Herez.'

Everyone on the bridge looked at each other with raised eyebrows.

'Don't worry about bringing the vaccine up here – we can go down and get it in a cloaked shuttle. Let us know the co-ordinates for pick-up from a trusted colleague. What the hell has Lake been up to?'

'Roger that. Regarding Lake, it appears he stole your designs for the jump drive – and, in testing, got himself arrested by one of these GDA mega-ships. According to the GDA, he proceeded to murder the entire crew with a virulent, weaponised virus, stole an armed warship and more than likely came back here.'

'What was the name of the GDA ship involved?'

'The Katadromiko 37.'

'Wasn't that the ship that sent a few crew members down to Theo Island shortly before we got there?' said Andy.

Ed nodded.

'Can you tell the GDA that their ship picked up the virus from the water supply on the Theo Island on Panemorfi? Lake was not involved with that. We have a lead as to who placed the virus which was also supposed to kill the Theo crew of this ship – and pretty much succeeded. When we have the vaccine, we will follow the lead and hopefully apprehend the real killer, so time is of the essence – Gabriel out.'

'Roger that, Gabriel. Pick-up co-ordinates will follow in due course – Armstrong out.'

31

LAKE BERESFORD LODGE – DELAND, FLORIDA, USA, EARTH

JANUARY 28TH 2050, 5:47 A.M. -5HRS

Lake lay in bed, watching the early news on breakfast TV with absolute horror.

A worldwide arrest warrant had been posted overnight for both him and Herez. It included a huge reward for information leading to their apprehension. He knew it would be claimed by someone here at the lodge.

He leapt off the bed and sprinted to the room next door, banging on the door until it was opened by a still-yawning Herez.

'Get your shit together now,' said Lake. 'We're out of here. Be outside the front entrance in two minutes.'

Lake ran through the complex and around the back to the kitchens. He peered through the kitchen's back door and found who he was looking for: the head chef,

Mark, was always up extra early to prepare for the breakfast service.

'Good morning, Mark,' said Lake, trying to hide being out of breath.

'Hello, Mr Lake,' said Mark, looking up from where he was lighting his bain-marie. 'Would you like some breakfast after your run?'

'Ah, no thanks. Tell me, do we still provide you with a company vehicle?'

'Err, yes, sir,' said Mark, looking a little worried.

'Could I borrow it for half an hour to pop into the village? It saves me having to wake my driver so early.'

'Of course,' said Mark, throwing the keys over to Lake. 'It's the white pick-up outside.'

'Thanks.'

Lake walked out into the backyard, pressed the key fob and sprinted over to the pick-up truck that flashed its indicators. He drove around the complex and met a rather confused-looking Herez standing in the front porch. With Herez sitting in the passenger seat, he launched the truck down the long drive, and out onto the highway, heading for DeLand.

'A global arrest warrant,' moaned Herez, after hearing the good news from Lake. 'It's unheard of. Do you think the GDA is behind this?'

'They can't be,' said Lake. 'Earth is designated a Kata-something-or-other class red planet, so it would be illegal for them to come here – and you know how anal they are with rules.'

THEY'D REACHED Valencia Hill when Lake ran a red light.

There was nothing unusual in that in Florida, except two police officers witnessed the transgression from the car park of a burger joint, where they were sitting having an early morning coffee.

Lake, who was now also speeding, didn't notice them gaining on him until the flashing lights lit up his rear-view mirror.

'Shit,' he said, glancing over at Herez. 'Can you get the hangar door open in a couple of seconds?'

'Yes, boss,' said Herez, getting a piece of paper out of his pocket with the new key-code on.

'You'll need to. Don't forget the police are armed over here.'

Lake pulled the truck over and watched as the police saloon stopped behind them. He powered down the window as if to reassure the police officers that he was willing to talk. He hoped it would be the driver that approached, but they were obviously wise to that one, as it was the passenger that got out and walked towards Lake's open window, while putting on his hat.

He waited until the officer was only a couple of paces away and floored the accelerator, spinning the wheels and launching them away towards the airfield. They gained about four hundred metres by the time the police officers had sorted themselves out and given chase. Lake ran another red, very late this time, which caused a lot of horn-sounding and angry gesticulating, but it had the desired effect. The police vehicle had to slow and negotiate the panicked traffic now crossing against them.

Herez turned in his seat to peer out the back window.

'They're quite a way behind now,' he said, tightening his seat belt.

Lake drifted the truck into a left-hand turn and through the gates to the airfield's sprawling industrial zone.

Lake powered across the estate, ignoring the one-way streets and other vehicles to get directly to their hangar, and drove straight around the back and stopped in a sideways slide.

Leaving the vehicle still running with the doors open, they sprinted to the small door. Herez punched the code into the keypad and the door clicked open as the police cruiser roared around the corner.

Slipping inside, they shut the door and reset the lock.

Lake put on the POK he'd left on a hook inside the door and instructed the ship to power up and open one of the ramp doors.

There was a lot of loud banging and shouting on the outside of the hangar door, which they both ignored.

Herez was waiting by the main hangar door control and, as soon as he saw Lake was in the cockpit, he hit the open switch and dived for the open ramp. It closed as soon as he was inside.

The two police officers came into view around the front of the hangar, guns up, and peered inside the hangar. They seemed confused to find an empty space.

Lake lifted the ship and, when the doors were open wide enough, he inched the troop carrier out. The police officers had to back off and shelter round the corner from the sudden wind and dust whipped up by the turbines. One of them got blown over by the blast. Lake grinned, thinking about what they could possibly write in their reports that wouldn't book them a visit to the police psychologist.

As Lake raised the ship up into the early morning sunlight, he turned the vessel to check what the police officers were doing. They'd both returned to the front of the hangar and were staring around, confused at the noise.

'At least that's only an assault charge,' said Herez.

'Along with speeding, running red lights, dangerous driving and avoiding arrest. Where shall we—'

They were both blinded by a flash from above, almost like a bright white laser beam but fifty metres wide.

The hangar, the two vehicles and the police officers vaporised in a split second, leaving a huge smouldering glassy circle in the ground.

'Shit,' screamed Herez, as Lake quickly banked the ship away and gained altitude fast.

'I guess I was wrong about the GDA,' said Lake as he felt around with the scanning array and saw the Katadromiko Class Cruisers surrounding the planet. 'Bloody hell, there's four of them too.'

'Four what?' said Herez.

'Four cruisers, the same size as the one we were on.'

'They sent four of those monsters to find us? It must have been that bitch Dric'is, telling a bunch of lies.'

'Well, whatever she's said about us, it seems our day in court has gone out the window. Do you have anywhere in Colombia we could lay low for a while?'

'I'll need to make some calls.'

'They must be scanning all communications around the planet as that hangar was destroyed only minutes after the police must have called it in. When you call – which we'll do from a call box in Columbia – don't mention any names.'

Lake cruised the GDA ship across the Pacific Ocean at seventy thousand feet, keeping his speed below the speed of sound to avoid any sonic booms attracting attention.

'Good morning, Mr Lake and Mr Herez,' said a booming voice, suddenly filling the cockpit.

Lake and Herez were both startled, but remained silent.

'I hope you're having a pleasant flight,' the voice continued. 'My name is Captain Loftt and I'm the commanding officer of the Katadromiko battle cruiser fleet, currently blockading Gaia – or Earth, as I'm informed you locals like to call it.'

They remained silent and stared out the front screen.

'You can remain silent; that's not a concern – I just need you to listen and to watch. I expect you witnessed what became of your hangar earlier. Well, can I now draw your attention to the next target for our rather impressive Asteri Beam?'

An aerial holographic image of Lake's villa in the Tuscan Hills appeared in the middle of the cockpit.

'I'm sure you're familiar with this rather attractive-looking house and indeed some of these other locations around the planet.'

The image changed every few seconds, showing all of Lake's businesses, factories and homes, even the holiday lodge in Florida they'd left earlier that morning.

'You have one of your Earth hours, Mr Lake, to surrender yourselves and our troop carrier to any one of my cruisers. I personally guarantee your – and Mr Herez's – safety. You will be held until the truth about the Katadromiko 37 becomes apparent. If you choose to ignore this message, then your assets will be vaporised – one per hour – until you decide to change your mind.'

Lake remained silent and stared out the front screen of the troop carrier, watching the clouds zipping by below them.

'Shit,' said Herez, finally breaking the silence.

'I believe you've summed it up perfectly,' said Lake.

He took the ship up into orbit and decided to surrender to the cruiser which sat a little way out from the other three, reckoning it to be Captain Loftt's command ship. He placed the ship five hundred metres out, de-cloaked and hailed the ship to instruct him as to which hangar he should approach. The answer came a couple of seconds later when a section of hull vanished and a brightly-lit hangar beckoned.

The tractor beam he'd been expecting grabbed hold of the ship and pulled them inside the hangar. They could see a small group of armed soldiers waiting beside the exit door and, as soon as the ship touched down, they filed out and surrounded the vessel.

As the ramp lowered, Lake was surprised to see an

officer of the bridge – of considerable rank – waiting for them on the hangar floor.

'Good morning, gentlemen,' said Captain Loftt. 'Thank you for dropping by so expeditiously. I'm sure my Asteri gunners will be disappointed.'

'We haven't committed any crimes so I hope this won't take long,' said Lake, trying to appear confident.

Loftt glanced up at the troop carrier that sat ticking as it cooled down behind Lake and Herez.

Understanding what Loftt meant by the glance, Lake continued: 'You do realise, we only had to borrow this because your colleagues decided to dismantle my ship? It would have been returned.'

'Of course you were going to return our ship, Mr Lake,' said Loftt. 'After you had plundered it for all its secrets. I think we call that military espionage – or is "misappropriation of military equipment" a more fitting appellation? I'm not a lawyer. There's probably plenty more. In the meantime, though, consider yourselves under arrest again. Only, this time, you won't have the privileges offered you by the late Captain Utz and her crew. This time, your doors will remain locked.'

32

THEO STARSHIP GABRIEL – EARTH HIGH ORBIT (CLOAKED)

DAY 417, YEAR 11269, 01:37SC, PCC

Ed grimaced when he saw the co-ordinates for the vaccine pick-up. He'd hoped it would be a little more remote than a corner of the NASA airfield in Florida.

'Can you stay watching the Gabriel while Linda and I shuttle down for the pick-up?' he asked Andy.

'So long as you don't go to the pub,' he replied, sitting down onto a bridge couch, replacing Linda as pilot.

'I don't think there'll be room in the car park,' said Linda, tossing the POK to Andy. 'And don't go anywhere or do anything silly while we're gone.'

'Would I do that to you?' said Andy, slipping on the POK and closing his eyes.

It seemed as if the GDA had stopped searching for them since being detected but Linda took no chances and cloaked the shuttle before it left the hangar. She took a very slow flight into the atmosphere so as to not attract any attention by way of a big, fiery insertion trail. The shuttle dropped down over the Caribbean, slowing and scanning to avoid any commercial or private aircraft. It was late at night so air traffic was light as she cruised over the coast and approached Kennedy Space Centre.

'Hello, home,' said Linda as they flew over the accommodation area, turned and landed about a kilometre away from the actual rendezvous location. They were a little early so they sat, watched and waited.

A motorcycle appeared from the administration area and circled around the accommodation buildings. It stopped and the rider sat, checked over his shoulder, then peered out over the airfield. After waiting and checking his watch a couple of times, the rider kicked the bike into gear and continued down the perimeter road, finally stopping at the rendezvous point, and turned the bike off.

Linda lifted the ship as quietly as she could and drifted across the airfield to the now-standing rider. She turned the shuttle so the airlock was facing the rider, away from any buildings, and settled the ship as quietly as possible. Scanning the area thoroughly, she dimmed the cabin lights, opened her eyes and gave Ed the nod.

He hit the airlock control and waited as it powered up. The steps materialised.

The rider was about twenty metres away, staring at the doorway that had seemingly appeared out of nowhere, and slowly started walking towards the ship.

Ed jumped down and met the rider at the foot of the steps, who was fumbling with his helmet strap.

'Hello, Edward. Welcome back,' said a smiling James Dewey.

'Administrator Dewey,' said a surprised Ed.

'Call me James, please.'

'Okay, James it is.'

'Can I see this wonderful ship?'

'Of course you can. Come on up.'

'Hello, Linda.'

'Hi, boss,' said Linda, keeping her eyes shut, closing the airlock and taking the shuttle up to seventy thousand feet.

'Whoa, well I'll be,' said James, staring out the front screen. 'That's unreal.'

He peered around the cabin with interest. 'Where's Andrew?'

'Piloting the Gabriel. What with all these battle cruisers lurking around, it's getting a trifle crowded up there,' said Ed.

'This isn't the Gabriel?'

'This is just one of the little shuttles,' said Linda. 'Gabriel, can you hold the ship here for a while?'

'No problem, Linda,' said Gabriel.

'Who was that?' said James, now sounding confused.

'Gabriel is the sentient computer system that runs the mothership – and the shuttles if we need them,' said Linda.

'…and provides us with everything we need,' said Ed.

'This just gets better, better indeed.'

'I'll give you an example,' said Ed. 'Who's your favourite female movie star?'

'Err, why?'

'Humour me.'

'Old or new?'

'Either.'

'Err – Rita Hayworth – one of the sexiest women ever, but I don't see what that—'

'Why, thank you, James. That's so sweet of you to say,' said Rita as she appeared in front of James, wearing a very sexy, long, blue dress. She gave him a big hug and a kiss on the cheek.

'Err – thanks,' said a very shocked James Dewey, dropping his helmet on the deck with a clunk.

'You know, you really didn't need to bring a crash helmet, James. I'll be very gentle with you,' said Rita, slowly running her tongue over her lips.

'Thank you, Gabriel. I think James gets the idea,' said Ed.

Rita gave a little wave, blew James a kiss and disappeared.

'What just happened?' asked James after a short pause, looking a little stunned.

'An example of the technological advances we now have access to,' said Ed. 'They call that VDM – or Biomatter Spacial Reforming – and don't even think of asking me for the mathematical equations for that. I wouldn't know where to start. There's sentient computer systems, tractor beams, the AVF drive, which is an anti-gravity light drive, the Alma Drive, which is their much improved jump drive, a TV field, or artificial gravity field and weapon systems that'll make your hair curl.'

'I've already been in conversation with the President regarding the new space technology. He's asked me to put together a team to start building some ground rules on how we operate and license the new advances. But – shit – now it's going to be even more critical.'

'While you have the GDA close to hand, it might be the time to ask them about membership,' said Ed. 'I feel it would be prudent for Earth to be inside that alliance rather than trying to go it alone.'

'I totally agree. Perhaps you could ask the Gabriel to give me an idiot's guide to the workings and history of the GDA.'

'It's in your inbox,' said Gabriel.

'Shit, already?'

'Don't forget you have something for us.'

'Ah, yes, of course, of course.' James rummaged around in his jacket pocket and extracted a small plastic box and handed it to Ed. 'I hope these help your friend.'

'So do we,' said Linda. 'He saved our lives so we owe him.'

Linda retook control of the shuttle from Gabriel and gently brought the ship back down to land beside James's motorcycle.

'Next time we'll take you further and you can see the starship,' said Ed.

'I'll hold you to that – hold you to that I will,' said James. 'And good luck finding your murderer.'

'Thanks, James, and give our regards to the President. We're all looking forward to that invite to the White House,' said Ed as James walked down the steps and over to his bike.

He followed him a moment later. 'You might be needing this,' he said, handing James his crash helmet.

'Quite right, quite right,' said James. 'You know, I nearly went for a walk without my helmet on Mars, but we never told anybody that.'

'Your secret's safe with me,' called Ed as he climbed back into the shuttle and closed the airlock door.

'He would make a good ambassador at the GDA, you know,' said Linda as they soared back up towards the Gabriel.

'I was thinking the same thing. They'd all think their translators were faulty, though.'

Half an hour later, under instruction from Gabriel, Ed injected the antivirus into the auto-nurse, which in turn slowly administered it to the patient.

'How long before we know?' asked Linda.

'The auto-nurse will assess the body's reaction to the serum and, if it appears to be working, will start the process of bringing him out of the coma,' said Gabriel. 'It could be minutes or take several hours.'

'Okay, I'll go and plot a course to Krix'ir,' said Linda and she disappeared out of the medical suite.

'Gabriel, can you produce some clothing for me and Andy that will go unnoticed on Krix'ir? Also, some local currency. We'll need holo images of the four-freighter crew from the island's security imagers and some sort of non-lethal weapon we can use to subdue the suspect.'

'Is that all, my lord?' asked Gabriel in a very formal voice.

'No,' said Ed. 'A nice large glass of Petit Chablis chilled to eleven degrees please.'

'Do this, do that. It's worse than being married.'

'How would you know? Aren't you supposed to be gender neutral?'

'He's been a whinging old rat bag for years,' said Phil, in a very soft voice.

'Shit! Phil, you're awake. You're alive!' said Ed, running over and staring at him, where he lay still sealed inside the auto-nurse.

'Guilty on both counts,' said Phil, opening his eyes and squinting at the brightness of the lighting.

'You don't know how glad I am to see you.'

'How are you, though? Weren't you affected?'

'No, none of us were.'

'So, just me then?'

Ed looked away.

'You're crap at hiding stuff,' said Phil. 'Tony, Mike and Steve didn't make it, did they?'

Ed shook his head and stared into space. Phil looked up at the ceiling for a while.

'I'll miss those idiots,' he said, a tear in his eye. 'We've had a lot of fun over the years.'

'We miss them too,' said Ed. 'But the others are going to be thrilled you've come back.'

The auto-nurse unsealed and opened.

Phil lay there for a while until, with Ed's help, he climbed out and stood shakily.

'How we doing, Gabriel?' said Phil.

'Better now. Very good to see you back.'

Ed explained the last few days' excitement to Phil on the way to the bridge.

By the time they got there, he was fully up to date and he almost got mobbed by Linda and Andy. He finally slumped onto a bridge couch, put on a POK and had a look around. He watched the satellite recordings from Panemorfi and studied the evidence regarding the freighter crew and its sudden demise above Krix'ir.

'You believe one of them is still on Krix'ir?' said Phil, looking at the holo images of the four men.

'Yeah, and it's one of those four,' said Ed.

'You really want to go there and find him?'

'Yes, don't you?'

Phil nodded slowly and looked up at the three faces looking back at him.

'Gabriel, can you plot a jump to just outside the Krix'ir system and we'll use a cloaked AVF drive to move in close?'

'Linda's already plotted the jump so we're ready to go.'

'Been playing with the big boy ships while I was away, have we?' said Phil, smiling at Linda.

'I had to do something while you were lazing around in bed,' she said.

Phil laughed and looked around at the three grinning faces. 'Gabriel, you may jump when ready.'

33

EMERGENCY OPERATIONS CENTRE, WHITE HOUSE – WASHINGTON DC

JANUARY 28TH 2050, 2:48 P.M.

The President had returned from the underground facility in Virginia earlier that morning. He'd immediately called an emergency meeting in the President's Emergency Operations Centre or PEOC, deep underneath the East Wing of the White House.

Fourteen people sat around the large rectangular table in the centre of the room.

'Are you sure all four of the alien battle cruisers have gone and they aren't cloaked or something?' he said.

'We watched them all move out to a safe jump distance and disappear one at a time,' said James Dewey.

'Why did they change their minds? One minute they're holding the planet to ransom to get their hands on Xavier Lake and the next they're disappearing off to locations unknown without a word.'

'We believe they got him,' said Donna McGuire. 'We received information from our colleagues in Florida that Lake had been hiding in a holiday lodge he owns near DeLand. Early this morning, he suddenly disappeared from the ranch and, about an hour later, a large hangar at DeLand airport, also owned by Lake, was vaporised. According to eyewitnesses, a bright beam came down from the sky and the hangar, and everything around it, including two police officers and their vehicle, just vanished, leaving a smoking round hole in the ground.'

'Was Lake in the hangar?' said the President.

'According to the police report, the two officers had given chase after they witnessed a truck he had borrowed from the ranch running a red light and pursued them to the hangar,' said Donna.

'Them? He wasn't alone?'

'No, we believe he was with Floyd Herez, his security chief.'

'Well, I hope they got both of the little shits,' he said. 'How are we doing public-wise?'

The Secretary of State, Peter Matelin, looked down at his notes before speaking.

'The sunspot activity ruse seems to have avoided any panic and of course, now everything is back to normal, the population has gone back to their daily lives. There are a few amateur astronomers singing away about dark shapes moving around the sky and the Floridians have called the beam weapon attack a severe weather event. They do get a few of those down there so they might just get away with it. Other than that, we're looking relatively unscathed.'

'Good,' said the President. 'We need to spend some time planning how to announce this huge revelation to the populace without creating mass panic. We also need to talk about what Edward Virr told James, here,' he said, nodding at Dewey. 'Is joining the GDA good for this planet? And, if so, who would be a good recommendation for Ambassador? Let's face it, every major nation on Earth will want it to be one of theirs.'

The door at the far end of the room opened suddenly and the President's secretary rushed in. 'Ladies and gentlemen, sorry for the intrusion but I thought you would need to see this immediately.'

He grabbed a controller and flicked on a large viewing screen at the far end of the room. An international news network came on with the headline, "Alien Starships Attack Earth" and a rather nervous news anchor was telling the viewers that, according to Chinese news services, four giant alien ships had surrounded the planet and had fired upon Florida.

'Well, that's just fucking dandy,' said the President, his face like thunder. 'Bloody idiots.'

Everyone in the room turned to stare at the President. They hadn't heard him use that word before.

'Organise me a televised address in two hours and get the fucking Chinese ambassador over here right now.'

34

THEO STARSHIP GABRIEL –
APPROACHING KRIX'IR

DAY 418, YEAR 11269, 02:12FC, PCC

After the jump into the vicinity of the Krix'ir system, Linda had set a course for the planet at a slower speed to give them all time to sleep.

Gabriel woke them two hours out and they got busy preparing for the search.

'Is this really what they wear down there?' said Andy, looking suspiciously at the purple baggy trousers Gabriel had produced for the landing party.

'The jackets are pretty cool,' said Ed, strutting back and forth as though on a catwalk.

'Yeah, but you don't have baggy purple trousers.'

Linda poked her head around Andy's cabin door and laughed at seeing the two of them in such strange clothing.

'Is it hammer time?' she asked.

'Is it what?' said Ed.

'Can't touch dis,' said Andy, doing a quick spin – and then having to wait for his trousers to catch up.

'Not into nineties rap music, then?' said Linda.

'Absolutely not,' said Ed, horrified.

'That would be far too much fun for Edward,' said Andy. 'He likes sitting alone in a dark room, drinking gin and listening to old Tom Waits albums.'

'No, I don't. That's not true. I prefer rum.'

'Guys, I believe Phil is waiting for you in the blister. He has some toys that'll prove useful for your trip down to Gangsta's Paradise.'

'I saw what you did then,' said Andy. 'Was Nuthin' but a G Thang.'

'It was Juicy,' Linda replied.

'Will you two quit this talking-in-code shit?' said Ed.

'Put it in your Mouth,' said Andy, giving Ed a shove towards the door and leaving Linda in fits of giggles.

'HI, GUYS,' said Phil, a few minutes later, as they all arrived up in the blister lounge. 'Wow, is it hammer time?' he added, smirking at their attire.

'Don't you bloody start,' snapped Ed.

'Oh, okay,' said Phil, raising his hands in a placating manner, giving Andy and Linda a quizzical look. 'Err, have a seat, and I'll go through what we've got.'

Ed and Andy sat next to each other on the couch opposite Phil and surveyed the items on the table.

'Firstly, hats,' he said. 'The planet is very hot – there's a lot of star shine – so everyone wears a hat, which is quite useful for us as we can incorporate a POK into each one.'

'Do we have to close our eyes to use them though?' said Andy.

'No,' said Phil. 'These have been programmed to show a kind of heads-up display directly onto your retina. As long as Gabriel remains overhead, you will have a facial recognition system that will scan every face within sight, looking for one of those four from the island, and they also incorporate a weapon activation warning.'

'Wouldn't it be a bit late for a warning after the fact?' asked Ed.

'Again, no,' said Phil. 'All modern weapon systems sit in a passive state, so they don't discharge by mistake. Firing them is a two-stage process that involves engaging the activation switch before toggling the fire trigger. So, you will get that activation warning, with the direction to and distance from the shooter.'

He handed a hat to them both. 'Put these on, guys, and tell me what you see.'

They both donned the hats and looked around the cabin.

'Everybody's face is ringed in green,' said Andy.

'Correct,' said Phil. 'When it finds the man you're looking for, he will be ringed in red.' Phil picked up what looked like a torch from the table. 'These are your Exos or stun guns; they're designed to look like a torch, something every miner carries down on Krix'ir.'

He got up, walked around the room and activated the weapon.

'Ah,' said Ed. 'I'm getting the warning loud and clear.'

'Same here,' said Andy. 'Directions too.'

'Cool,' said Phil. 'Everything's working then.'

He spent the next few minutes teaching them how to use the Exos and which of the five strength settings to use to get the desired result. He then gave them black bracelets that looked like jewellery.

'Those are your currency,' he said. 'They're GDA-affiliated, can be accepted on almost any member planet in this sector. You let the vendor scan them.'

'How much credit have we got?' asked Andy.

'Enough, believe me,' said Phil. 'Although, there's very little to spend it on down there anyway.'

The translators were next, small and compact and, according to Phil, programmed with over five thousand languages and dialects. These could be kept in a front pocket of a shirt and had been tuned to transmit over Ed and Andy's BlueScape chips.

'Finally, I have these for you.' He picked up two small, oval, plastic cases about the size of an egg. 'These are to be used only as a last resort.'

'In case we get hungry and need an emergency omelette?' asked Andy.

Linda sniggered and Ed gave Phil an apologetic look.

'No, but you got the "emergency" bit right,' he said. 'These activate a personal beam shield and they really are a last resort.'

'From what direction?' asked Ed.

'All around,' answered Phil. 'It creates a sphere of energy that envelops you and is to be used when the shit has really hit the fan and your only need is to get out alive. It will absorb most handheld energy weapons for around a dozen hits or so. But remember, they generally can't get to you unless it's absolutely point blank. Some of the bigger weapons may penetrate it if it hits absolutely square on and, most importantly, you can't use your weapon either as the shield works in both directions.'

'So, it's like a get out of jail free card?' said Andy.

'I wouldn't say "free", as the kinetic energy in the shot will still knock you over, but it will avoid chunks of your body disappearing. It's also worth remembering that, when activated, you will light up like a Christmas tree on every scanning array in the system. I'll be in the shuttle at all times with the motor running and, if one of you does activate the shield, I'll be there as soon as I can.'

'Sorry to interrupt, guys,' said Gabriel. 'I've picked up a message on the open band that instructs all ships in the system that the planet will be reopened for space traffic in four hours.'

'Shit,' said Andy. 'That doesn't give us much time.'

'How many space ports are there on Krix'ir, Gabriel?' said Ed.

'Just one – at the main settlement of Goss'inray.'

'Fancy a beer in the departure lounge, Mr Virr?'

'An excellent idea, Mr Faux.'

'Have the car brought around please, Phillip,' said Andy. 'Mr Virr and I are going to town.'

'Right you are, sirs,' said Phil, smiling. 'I believe the chauffeur has finished polishing the hubcaps.'

ONCE LINDA HAD POSITIONED Gabriel in a stationary orbit over Goss'inray, Phil cloaked the shuttle and the three of them dropped into the upper atmosphere.

There wasn't a lot to see coming down over the town as the planet was basically a dry rock with an atmosphere. It could, in some ways, be likened to Mars several million years ago. The oceans that had once covered at least two-thirds of the planet had all but gone and the small drop in oxygen levels over the last few thousand years was a sign of things to come. In the meantime, the miners had rich pickings and it would be a long time yet before they would need suits and breathing apparatus.

It didn't take long to find the space port – the collection of ships of all shapes and sizes parked around the apron gave it away.

Phil brought the shuttle down behind a couple of large, semi-derelict buildings on the far side of the field, after scanning to check no one was lurking.

'I'll be right above, watching and listening,' said Phil. 'Good luck and please be careful. If it looks too difficult, abort the job. We can always follow whichever ship he gets on.'

'Stop worrying, Phil,' said Ed. 'We'll be fine.'

Andy popped open the airlock and they both jumped down without bothering with the stairs. The airlock closed and they were instantly on their own as the whine of the anti-gravity drives faded out above them and was replaced by the background buzz of insects native to the planet.

'We'll be fine?' questioned Andy. 'You do realise this guy's probably military?'

'I know, but Phil's a worrier. And, anyway, our target won't be expecting us and— what the hell is that stink?'

'It smells like the seaside when I was a kid,' said Andy. 'A mixture of rotting seaweed and fish. We're more than likely walking on an old ocean floor.'

'I wonder if there's a cockle stall. Come on, the departure building is supposed to be over this way.'

They noticed that everything appeared old and rundown. The ground was mostly hard-packed dirt, with the roadway similar to fifty-year-old concrete: crumbling, potholed and grey in colour. There were several kinds of fern-like grasses, scratching an existence on the sides of the roads, and a sprinkling of tenuous trees and shrubs of questionable health dotted here and there. An attractive green and lush environment, it was not.

'Cockles and mussels, alive, alive'o,' sang Andy, as they walked.

'Did you go for the chilli vinegar?' asked Ed.

'Yeah, and the black pepper.'

'When we get back, we'll go to Folkestone and have half a pint of cockles at Chummy's,' said Ed.

'And a couple of pints of ale in the Pullman. It's a date.'

'Just a couple? Surely not.'

THE PLAN of the area they'd studied earlier had shown the off-world departure terminal to be on the western side of the field. They could see the buildings they wanted in the distance. An electric four-wheel drive vehicle passed them and the driver didn't give them a second look, which seemed promising.

As they neared the cluster of newer-looking buildings, more vehicles passed in both directions and the terminal itself was buzzing with activity. Hundreds of people milled around, dragging luggage inside, mostly out of the queue of weird-looking vehicles stretching round the block.

'We should have expected this,' said Ed. 'Everyone's been trapped here for days.'

'Shit, I hope this facial recognition program's good. There must be half the settlement's population travelling today.'

'Just walk as though you belong. If you do find our man, don't – whatever you do – make eye contact. Keep him in your peripheral vision.'

They marched up to the terminal and straight in through one of the several entrance doors.

It was complete bedlam inside. It reminded Ed of an Eastern bazaar mixed with a Western rodeo.

The local clothing was predominantly loose-fitting

white robes with occasional splashes of colour and wide-brimmed hats, which made it hard for the recognition software if people were looking down.

'Wow,' said Andy, staring around the huge hall. 'Look at all the different races.'

'They've got hairy ears like cats over there,' said Ed, indicating to a group facing away from them.

One of the group turned his head towards them and smiled.

'Holy crap – and cat's eyes, teeth and whiskers,' said Ed.

'They're Gatas from the planet Lynkas,' said Phil. 'They also have cat hearing so I politely suggest you shut up.'

'How do you know who they are from just that description?' asked Andy.

'Because I can see through your eyes when you're wearing a POK.'

'Remind me to take my hat off if I go to the bathroom,' said Ed, wrinkling his nose at Andy, who gave him a revolted look in return.

'Should we split up?' asked Andy.

'I can connect your BlueScapes so you can talk to each other,' said Phil.

'Thanks, Phil. Good idea,' said Ed.

'I suppose we should concentrate on lone travellers and not the groups,' said Andy.

'Not necessarily. He could have befriended someone, or even a group, to give him better cover.'

'Are you sure you weren't a detective in a past life?'

'More likely the villain,' said Ed, searching the room as they walked.

'I'll go around the outside and we can meet at that bar at the far end.'

'Okay, walk purposefully. If he spots you searching, he'll be gone.'

'Cool bananas,' said Andy and walked off, turning his head from side to side to give the software its best chance.

Ed did the same, ploughing his way through the sea of strange aliens, who were all queuing to secure tickets off the dusty rock. A whining roar outside caught Ed's attention and, looking over to his left, through the floor-to-ceiling windows, he could see another large spacecraft drop down, spin around and land softly on the apron outside.

'Phil, what should I ask for at the café that Andy and I would find palatable?' he asked.

'Order "*dyo byra topikos*"; that shouldn't be too strong,' said Phil.

'What's that?'

'Local beer.'

'Okay, thanks.'

Two minutes later, they met at the café, having seen nothing but green-circled faces around the whole departure lounge.

'If we base ourselves here, everybody has to pass by on the way to the gates,' said Ed.

'Good thinking, Sherlock. Whose round is it?'

Ed quickly slipped onto a stool at the counter as it became free.

Andy took the hint and grabbed the adjacent one.

A rather harassed-looking barman swept up and gave them a classic "you'd better know what you want" look.

'*Dyo byra topikos*,' Ed said, hopefully.

'No locally brewed stuff on this rock. We have beer from Regg'taa in the next system. D'you want regular high or euphoria?' asked the barman through the translator.

'Two regulars please,' said Ed, with a chuckle after meeting Andy's quizzical expression.

'Perhaps we could get some euphoria to go,' said Andy as he continued to scan the passing faces.

Two jugs of beer arrived and the barman held a silver disc up to Ed, who touched it with his bracelet. It appeared to have worked as the barman nodded and moved on to the next customer.

'It's okay,' said Andy, after sniffing his beer and taking a tentative sip.

'You can tell it's not brewed in Faversham,' said Ed, gritting his teeth after taking his own sip. 'But at least it's cold and vaguely beer-like.'

'Just like a holiday in Australia,' chuckled Andy.

SOMEONE SLID onto the barstool next to them and ordered a beer from the barman. They took no notice as they were scanning the passing traffic – until he spoke.

'Good morning, Edward. Good morning, Andrew,' said the stranger through a translator.

They both froze and slowly turned to find a short stocky man dressed in local mining attire and also wearing the trademark wide-brimmed hat.

'They told me if there was a bar I'd find you there,' he continued and lifted the brim of his hat.

Both Ed and Andy's eyes opened wide in surprise as the recognition software ringed his face in red.

'I believe you're looking for me,' he said, his eyes continually surveying the room. 'Don't worry, I'm not here to harm you. Quite the opposite actually. I'm here to surrender to you.'

Ed had slowly moved his left hand down to retrieve the torch clipped to his belt, obscured from the target because of Andy.

'I know this may be a bit of a shock to you both, but my name is Luzin. I'm a Major in the Theo Timora from Paradeisos. From what I've been told, you're possibly the only chance of survival I have.' He peered around Andy, who was still in a state of shock and not daring to move, and indicated to the torch that Ed had just grasped hold of and – without actually looking at it – was trying to remove the safety.

'You won't require your stun weapon, Ed,' he said. 'I quite intend to walk out with you willingly and get aboard your shuttle. You may restrain me if you wish.'

'You do know who we're with?' asked Andy, finally overcoming the shock to actually speak.

'I know full well whose ship you're on,' said Luzin. 'They won't torture and kill me, but the GDA will.'

'Well, to be honest, I don't blame them. You killed over forty-seven thousand of their crew on the Katadromiko 37,' said Ed, gaining confidence.

'That's just it,' said Luzin. 'That virus would not have affected anyone else but the Exys. We were incredibly careful. To kill the crew of a Katadromiko cruiser, it would've had to be genetically altered in a laboratory and then systematically added to the water supply.'

'Who are the Exys and how the hell did you know we were coming?' said Andy, pointing straight at Luzin's face.

The first thing Ed experienced was the pinging of an alarm, then an almighty crash of dozens of bottles and glasses exploding all around him. He'd glanced down to check the stun setting on the torch so it was pure luck that no glass or wood splinters from the disintegrating bar lodged in his eyes.

He found himself disorientated on the floor and then realised the pinging noise in his ears was the weapon activation alarm. There were screams and shouting all around him, debris falling and the smell of burning wood and plastic. As he finally got his thoughts together and looked up, he saw Luzin sitting on his barstool – only something wasn't quite right. He at first believed Luzin was no longer wearing his hat and was bending backward so his face was obscured, but then the true realisation hit him.

Luzin didn't have a head at all. He felt bile rising in his throat.

'Ed, Ed. It's a Makrys,' shouted Phil. 'A sniper laser weapon. And I'm not getting any signal from Andy's POK.'

'Shit, Andy,' shouted Ed. He jumped up and stared all around him. There were people stumbling around, covered in blood, and it seemed the shot had come through one of the large floor-to-ceiling windows. It had shattered and showered everyone with shards of broken glass.

Ed suddenly realised, to his horror, that Andy had been sitting between him and Luzin and was nowhere to be seen.

'Andy,' he shouted. 'Andy, where the hell are you?'

He saw Andy's hat beneath the bar next to where he'd been sitting. He picked it up and, turning his back to the bar, surveyed the room, desperately searching for his friend.

'Andy,' he shouted again and then heard a familiar voice behind him.

'Good morning, Mr Virr. Pint of the usual today?'

Ed spun round to find Andy standing on the other side of the bar, his face as white as a sheet and covered in blood, dust and glass.

'You fucking twat,' shouted Ed. 'What are you doing over there? I nearly shit myself when I couldn't find you. Come on, we need to get out of here now.'

'I can't find my hand,' said Andy, holding up his right arm, which ended in a bleeding stump, and then he promptly passed out.

35

GEROUSIA DETENTION SUITE –
DASOS, PRASINOS SYSTEM

ORA 25, STADIO 3, ETOS 15112, 17:74 DASOS
CENTRAL

Lake and Herez had been placed in small, separate cells on the Katadromiko 12. No suite of rooms this time, no friendly security officers and the food appeared to be leftovers thrown onto a plate.

It had only been a day until they arrived at Dasos, however, where they were immediately transferred into a military shuttle and flown down to the capital, Kentro, the home of the GDA.

At least the cells in the detention suite, deep underneath the main Gerousia complex, were larger and the food was much more acceptable.

Today there would be a preliminary hearing to list and formally charge them with their plethora of crimes against the GDA.

Lake, as expected, was in a foul mood and paced up and down his cell. Although, with the higher gravity, this soon tired him out and he was forced to sit again. He had chosen to defend himself for the simple reason that no one wanted to defend him.

A considerable number of grieving family members from the crew of Katadromiko 37 resided on Dasos. Some were even camped outside the Gerousia complex, baying for blood.

Lake heard the noise from outside from time to time and looked at his sealed cell door with a nervous apprehension. Even if the door was open, he didn't think he'd go anywhere. With his Earth features, there would be no hiding on this planet. It would be pointless trying to run as the murderous gravity would soon debilitate him and, besides, he knew nothing of the order of society here.

'Can you hear them, boss?' called Herez from the next cell. 'Even if we were found not guilty, do you think that lot would let us off the planet alive?'

'We're going to have to trust the system, Mr Herez,' replied Lake. 'We really don't have any other option at present. There is absolutely no evidence we caused the death of that crew so I'm confident we won't go down for that, at least.'

'They could soon fabricate it, though, couldn't they? I mean, the mob outside aren't going to go home and say, "oops, wrong aliens", are they?'

'When we're found not guilty, I have absolutely no

intention of setting up home here so I really don't care what they think. I'll never come here again.'

Lake heard the approaching security officers' boots clattering up the corridor and sat up, put his feet on the floor and stood, ready to be escorted up to the hearing.

'Xavier Lake. Floyd Herez. Stand up please,' said one of the four officers.

The glow around the cell doors disappeared and, as they were being fitted with neck collars, the same officer spoke again.

'The hearing has been postponed because of a delayed witness. We have been instructed to escort you to the Kordoni terminal from where you will be taken to Stathmos Vasi for security reasons.'

'What are Kordoni and Stathmos Vasi?' asked Herez.

'String and space station.'

'"String?" What do you mean, "string"?'

'You may know it as a space elevator.'

'Shit,' said Herez. 'How high is it?'

'Two thousand kilometres.'

'Shit, I hate heights.'

'When you say, "witness is delayed",' said Lake, 'do you actually mean, "witness will be along shortly", "witness is missing" or "witness has changed his mind?"'

'No more questions,' said the officer, looking away and rubbing the back of his neck nervously.

Lake and Herez exchanged a glance. It appeared not all was well with the prosecution.

Lake smiled to himself and the heavy gravity seemed to lift as a spring returned to his step and a renewed confidence swelled within him.

36

THEO STARSHIP GABRIEL – ORBITING KRIX'IR

DAY 418, YEAR 11269, 10:36 FC, PCC

After wrapping his jacket around Andy's arm and struggling to get him up into a fireman's lift, Ed had moved as quickly as he could without attracting undue attention through the melee.

Security personnel had started to appear, running towards the bar in the opposite direction. He'd ignored them, wanting to get Andy away before they got their act together and started asking questions.

Phil had brought the shuttle down over the terminal and instructed Ed to run across the road to the far end of the vehicle park where he'd opened the airlock right in front of him. Once both of them were inside, Phil had given the shuttle the full treatment straight up. The sonic boom as they broke the sound barrier – in only three seconds – was heard for kilometres and broke dozens of windows around the settlement.

Ed hobbled down the shuttle steps and carried Andy through as soon as the airlock opened in the port side hangar of the Gabriel.

'You're going on a bloody diet, you fat bastard,' muttered Ed through clenched teeth as he ran up the corridor towards the medical suite.

'Gettttt – fukkked,' came the mumbled reply.

Phil followed close behind and prepped the autonurse as soon as they entered the suite.

Ed stripped his blood-soaked jacket off his friend's arm and quickly laid him into the machine.

As soon as Ed was clear, a field of energy sealed Andy inside and flashes of miniature light beams zipped around his forearm, stopping the blood loss, cleaning the wound and prepping for the surgery.

Linda came hurtling through the door, her posture slumping as she saw Andy in the autonurse. She emitted a gasp as she noticed his missing hand.

'P – please tell me he'll be okay?' she stammered, staring at Phil.

'He'll be fine,' said Phil. 'He lost a bit of blood, that's all.'

'And his hand!' she said in a shrill voice. 'He's right-handed too. How's he going to cope without that?'

'We've advanced a bit out here from your Stone Age medicine,' said Phil. 'Don't worry, I've got the situation all in hand.' He grinned at them, expecting some recognition for the pun, but got blank expressions instead.

'We don't have his hand to reattach, do we?' said Ed. 'It was completely vaporised by the laser rifle.'

'We don't have his original hand, no,' admitted Phil. 'But we do have full body scans of you all within the data bank, which means, by utilising the VDM system, we can re-form any part of you in an exact copy.'

The autonurse made a pinging noise, which reminded Ed of a microwave.

'Is he done?' said Linda, perhaps thinking the same thing.

'No, that means he's stabilised and prepped ready for the new hand,' said Phil, turning and entering information into the autonurse. 'Now, watch this.'

Phil touched a final flashing key and they all stared at the rather ugly end of Andy's forearm.

Again flashes of energy formed around the wound, gradually increasing in intensity until they were a blur of activity. Slowly, the flurry of energy extended out from the wound and a new hand began to appear. After only a few minutes, the beams of energy reduced and finally ceased.

Ed and Linda looked at each other and then back at Phil.

'Is that it?' said Ed, incredulously.

'Wow,' said Linda, staring wide-eyed into the machine. 'When will he wake up?'

'When will who wake up?' mumbled Andy from inside the machine.

'Bloody hell, Captain Hook's awake already,' said Ed, getting a hug from Linda.

'That's a bit odd,' said Andy, looking up at the three of them. 'I had a dream I couldn't find my hand.' He looked down at his hands with a puzzled expression. 'Although my right hand does feel dead weird and—what am I doing in here?'

A sudden loud explosion jarred the ship so much that they all fell over.

'Gabriel, what the hell was that?' shouted Linda, picking herself off the floor and running for the door.

No answer came.

'Gabriel,' called Phil.

No answer.

The lights dimmed for a moment and then returned.

'Shit, Gabriel's offline.'

'How often does that happen?' asked Ed, glancing up at the lights nervously.

'Never happened before,' shouted a concerned Phil as he ran out the door, close on Linda's tail.

'Shit,' said Ed.

'Shit and shitty shit,' said Andy, flexing his right hand and examining it closely.

'Stay here,' said Ed. 'I'll explain everything when I've helped fix the ship.'

'Okay, boss,' said a confused Andy, who closed his eyes and appeared to go to sleep.

Ed realised Andy was still in shock and didn't understand what was going on. He'd lost a lot of blood so the safest place for him was in the autonurse.

As he ran up the corridor towards the lift, the lights dimmed again and the ship shuddered.

On the bridge, he found Phil and Linda both wearing POKs and talking to each other frantically.

'What's happened?' he asked, slipping down onto one of the spare couches and donning a POK.

'We're being fired at,' said Linda.

'I thought we were cloaked?'

'We were,' said Phil. 'Someone can see through our cloaking technology.'

'Have we fired back?'

'We can't,' said Phil. 'The auto-defence system has activated the Palto.'

'What's a Palto?'

'It's like a sphere or coat of impenetrable energy surrounding the ship,' said Phil. 'The downside is we are blind because it blocks our scans – we can't fire back even if we could see him. Whoever he is, he got a shot in before the Palto went up. Luckily, we run on basic shielding as a default and that took some of the sting out of the shot, although it was still hot enough to cook some of Gabriel's memory core.'

'Is the Palto totally impregnable?' asked Ed.

'As far as I know,' answered Phil. 'But I thought our cloaking was total until a few minutes ago.'

'Hang on,' said Linda. 'I set Gabriel on a straight course out of the system to a standard jump point where we would uncloak and jump back to the Helios System.'

'Yeah, so?' said Ed.

'I've just checked our location,' she said. 'We're stationary at the jump point.'

'And?' said Phil.

'I gave Gabriel authorisation to come here and jump, which means when he'd uncloaked ready to jump, the other ship was already here. I'm looking at the jump settings now and we were only seconds away from going. So, what I'm trying to say is, our cloaking isn't a problem at all. Someone was hanging around at the jump point waiting for us to arrive and turn our cloak off.'

'It was our fault then?' said Ed, looking at Phil, apologetically. 'We got careless and predictable.'

'Exactly,' said Linda. 'I'm really sorry, Phil. It won't happen again.'

'Stop it, the pair of you,' said Phil. 'No one's

playing the blame game. I was a party to this as much as you. Andy's the only one who didn't have a hand in this.'

'You really went out on a limb with that joke,' said Ed, leaning forward to high-five him.

'Ah, crap,' said Linda. 'It's kindergarten o'clock again, is it? May I remind you two ten-year-olds, we have a damaged ship and someone out there trying to finish us off?'

'Yeah, you're right, Linda. Sorry,' said Ed. 'Can we find a way to detect that ship, Phil?'

'Only if we drop the Palto.'

'And he can fire before us if he's uncloaked,' said Linda.

'Can we create a small hole in the Palto just for a millisecond?'

'Yeah, probably,' said Phil. 'It would be dangerous, though.'

'Linda, can you programme the array to shoot a very low-powered twentieth century radar pulse through that hole?'

'Yes, I could. I see where you're going now,' said Linda. 'If we do it once and then again a few minutes later, and he's still in the same place...'

'Correct,' said Ed. 'Just enough to get a faint return that his system won't recognise.'

'But how do we engage him even if we do know where he is?' said Phil.

'You told me the Palto is impregnable.'

'Yes.'

'We fire the Palto at him.'

'We do what?' said Linda, looking as puzzled as Phil.

'AVF drive on full acceleration, straight at him,' said Ed, lying back and putting his hands behind his head.

'That's brilliant,' said Phil.

'What happens if his ship is bigger than ours?' asked Linda.

'We punch a Gabriel-size hole through it,' said Ed. 'If he's smaller, he goes away into the ether.'

The first pulse showed a reading off their port bow at about three o'clock and, after waiting three minutes, the second was an identical result.

'Lazy bugger,' said Ed. 'That's going to cost you.'

Linda set the course straight at him and the drive at maximum.

They all looked at each other and nodded.

'Engage,' said Ed, with a grin and his arm extended, just like an old TV hero from his childhood.

The Gabriel shot out of the blocks, straight at whoever was out there. Linda waited a couple of seconds and came to a full stop.

'Did we get him?' asked Ed.

'Drop the Palto and engage full shields,' said Phil.

The array showed nothing as the Palto dropped.

'Where is he?' said Ed.

'He jumped,' shouted Linda.

'Is the jump embedded?' asked Phil.

'No.'

'Follow him,' said Ed and the green haze enveloped them.

Ed fired the two rear-mounted Fos Guns directly behind in a wide spread as they emerged. It wasn't a perfect shot by any means but it had the desired effect.

Several of the light speed laser bolts found the GDA ship before it could cloak and disappear. Debris flew out from the smaller ship but, while the Gabriel arrested its speed and returned, the GDA ship arrowed towards one of the planets in the system they'd both emerged into.

'He's heading for Paradeisos,' said Phil. 'Brave to attempt an insertion in a damaged ship.'

'We can't follow in this, though,' said Linda. 'We have damage too. We need a ship he won't know to run from.'

'I have a cunning plan,' said Ed. 'Linda, hand the bridge over to Phil and follow me – and Phil, look after Andy for us.'

'Will do. I'll be following your progress from orbit with full weapons online – and don't forget to wear a POK.'

Ed jumped in the round lift and pulled a rather confused Linda in with him.

'What, where are we going? They'll recognise the shuttles too, won't they?' she said.

'Yes, they will,' said Ed. 'But they won't know the Cartella.'

'Shit, is she ready?'

'Sort of,' said Phil. 'You'll need to fly manually as the computer core hasn't been fully trained yet.'

Ed and Linda weren't listening, as they were already dropping down through the floor on the tube lift. On arriving at the hangar, Linda went straight for the Cartella and, donning one of the new POKs, ordered an emergency boot-up.

Ed jumped into the shuttle they'd used on Krix'ir and, ignoring the blood still drying on the floor, he grabbed Andy's hat, shield egg and torch.

By the time they'd launched the Cartella out of the Gabriel, the small GDA ship had a ten-minute lead. It had slotted in behind a couple of trade shuttles, which were preparing to insert into the planet's atmosphere, containing cargoes from several huge freight ships sitting nearby in high orbit.

Ed looked around the new Cartella with awe. He'd noticed how much bigger she was before he jumped up into the airlock. Now inside, he was impressed with the degree of detail and the general opulence of the crew areas.

'What are you two doing?' asked an unknown female voice, suddenly booming out around the ship. 'You don't have authorisation for this flight.'

Then the Cartella powered down.

37

KORDONI ELEVATOR – KENTRO, DASOS, PRASINOS SYSTEM

ORA 25, STADIO 3, ETOS 15112, 10:51 DASOS CENTRAL

Lake had again spent his time in the cell learning more about the GDA and especially Dasos. He knew it was presently Stadio 3, a period – or month – during the Kryo (winter) on Dasos. So, he was not surprised to find how cold it was as they were transferred from the government flyer and into the Kordoni terminal.

The look of shock on Herez's face, however, he found quite amusing.

There was a very light, almost dusty, snow falling over the capital. It reminded Lake of his ski chalet, built into the side of Blackcomb Mountain overlooking Whistler in the Canadian Rockies.

Good for powder skiing, he thought.

The memory soon faded as they were both herded straight through a side door to avoid the throng of locals waiting for their ascent into space. They avoided the customs post and were marched through the back of the building and into an airlock of what appeared to be a maintenance carriage for the elevator. It was smaller than the public carriages and was only designed for six passengers, along with a multitude of servicing machinery and tools.

Lake and Herez sat side by side, strapped into the small fold-down seats attached to the central core of the carriage. It launched as soon as the two guards were belted in and catapulted them up the elevator string with enormous acceleration. Without the artificial gravity field, they'd all have been squashed flat against the floor.

'How long does the ascent take?' said Lake to the guard sitting to his right.

'Around twenty-eight minutes,' came the translated reply.

'Shit,' said Lake, quietly.

Herez looked over at Lake with a concerned expression.

'Shit, what?'

'This thing travels straight up at over four thousand miles per hour.'

Herez's eyes opened wide and he turned back to stare out the window. There was no sense of speed as the little carriage moved upwards, almost silently; it had disappeared into snow cloud only seconds after launch.

The carriage suddenly lit up as they arose from the cloud and Lake squinted in the bright starlight that flooded in.

The view was spectacular: he could see out across the cloud tops with a range of snow-capped mountain peaks showing through in the distance. A few kilometres away, a tiny dot appeared out of the cloud below them. It rapidly grew into a small ship and Lake watched as, instead of passing by, it slowed and matched the speed of the carriage, sitting about a kilometre away.

The guard sitting next to Lake appeared alarmed by this and started communicating rapidly into his helmet microphone. The translator was turned off, but Lake could see he was getting quite agitated by the proximity of the small ship.

The alarms made everybody jump and Herez looked at Lake with fear in his eyes.

The two security collars around Lake's and Herez's necks were flashing red and it was these that were making all the ear-splitting noise.

The guard sitting next to Lake unclipped his belts, jumped up and touched the electronic key to both Lake's and Herez's collars, grabbing hold of them both and then diving for the airlock control. He threw the collars inside as soon as the door was wide enough and slammed the airlock closed, quickly punching in the code to open the outer door. The collars whipped out of the airlock as soon as the door cracked open, due to the pressure difference, and Lake heard two dull thumps as the collars detonated, followed by a rattle of shrapnel hitting the floor of the cabin.

'What the bloody hell caused that?' he shouted, glaring at the standing guard, who was watching the small ship closely.

'The collars' security codes were compromised and overridden at short range,' he said, continuing to stare out at the unidentified ship.

'Was it them?' said a very scared-looking Herez, pointing at the ship.

'We believe so.'

'Don't you have a ship that can intercept them?' asked Lake.

'Two minutes away.'

Three fist-sized holes appeared in the window opposite the four of them and the standing guard was slammed back into a tool rack.

The sudden decompression of the cabin sucked him back and, this time, smashed him into the window.

Lake could see that part of the guard's arm had disappeared when it was hit by the laser bolt and blood was pouring from the wound. It was immediately sucked out of one of the other holes and away in a pink mist. A couple of the tools, loosened when the guard hit the rack, succumbed to the decompression and whipped across the cabin, striking the window so hard that it finally failed.

Window, guard and tools disappeared in a split second, a faint scream from the guard fading immediately into the maelstrom passing outside.

With the whole window gone, the rush of air going out soon ceased, only to be replaced by a rush of freezing air coming in.

Lake, Herez and the remaining guard gritted their teeth against the icy gale and stared out, looking for the small gunship that had moved away to avoid the debris spewing from the carriage.

The first thing they noticed was that the carriage was now descending. Oxygen breathers popped out of a small panel beside each seat. As they sucked in the life-saving gas, the small gunship swept up from below and turned to face them again.

'Oh, crap,' said Lake. 'Doesn't this bastard ever give up?'

The guard to Herez's left had never stopped shouting instructions to his colleagues and, as it seemed all was lost, the help he'd been pleading for arrived.

The blinding flash came from above, the small gunship shuddered and, in slow motion, fell into two pieces. It rapidly became many more as the ship tore itself apart.

The guard looked across at them.

'How many more people are going to die because of you? From what we've heard, you come from a whole planet full of murderers,' he said.

'That's not fair,' said Lake. 'We didn't start any of this.'

'You'd better have some convincing evidence of that fact,' said the guard. 'There's a movement that's gaining strength asking for the removal of your planet. The most destructive, egomaniacal and murderous race in the galaxy, they say.'

'Completely untrue,' said Lake, a feeling of dread beginning to churn in his stomach.

When the carriage finally dropped into the terminal building again, it was completely sealed off. Nobody except soldiers were anywhere near the building. They were escorted straight out into the deserted street where a military gunship sat waiting to take them up to Stathmos Vasi Station. It took off as soon as they were aboard, went up to the space station at maximum speed and deposited them into the hands of Station Security in one of the many hangars.

The cells they were allocated were basic but warm, clean, and the food was reasonably decent.

Having been ignored by everyone since their arrival, they were quite surprised when, after five hours, they were allowed out into the reception area and a well-dressed man introduced himself.

'Good evening, gentlemen,' he said. 'My name is Cien'dra – Commander Cien'dra and I'm your allocated defence counsel.'

'I'm defending myself,' said Lake. 'I'm sorry that you weren't informed and you've come all this way for nothing.'

'I'm afraid that privilege has been revoked,' said Cien'dra. 'The case has become too important, now the fate of an entire race is at stake.'

'What do you mean by the fate of an entire race?' asked Herez.

'You were the first of your race to make contact with the GDA. You allegedly declared war, wiped out the crew of a Katadromiko Class Battle Cruiser and committed several other lesser charges. The prosecution will attempt to prove that this was premeditated and that the history of your race on Gaia is, indeed, the sum of a long list of monstrous, abhorrent, genocidal events, going back many thousands of your years. If you are found guilty of this crime, then moves are being put in place for Ek Neou Spora to be executed on Gaia.'

'What's Ek Neou Spora?' asked Lake, struggling with the pronunciation, already afraid of the answer.

'A reseeding,' said Cien'dra.

'Genocide, then,' said Lake, glaring at Cien'dra. 'Committing the exact same crime we're accused of!'

'No, not when it will save many other races from the

murderous, hateful attitudes that seem to have poisoned the minds of some of the lesser intelligent races.'

'You're our defence counsel, eh,' said Lake, laughing at Cien'dra. 'You seem pretty convinced of our guilt.'

'I'm relaying what you're going to get thrown at you in the court. You need to be prepared beforehand so you're not surprised by anything and have credible answers to their accusations.'

'Talking of answers,' said Herez. 'Have you discovered who was in that gunship?'

'There wasn't much left of the bodies, but the blood and tissue samples retrieved are not in our database.'

'Who the hell are they, then, and why would they want us dead?'

'We don't know yet, but we will find out.'

Lake shook his head. He couldn't believe an organisation this big didn't know who their attackers were.

'When do we go back down for the hearing?'

'You don't,' said Cien'dra. 'The case is being heard here for security reasons and the date is yet to be announced. As soon as I know, you'll know.'

'Wonderful,' said Lake. 'I've got so much to look forward to.'

Herez shrugged his shoulders and mooched back into his cell.

Lake looked at Cien'dra and wondered if he really would make any effort to defend them.

'You need to do some investigative work, Commander,' he said. 'Because Mr Herez and I have been completely set up. If what you've said takes place in the future, then you and the GDA will be guilty of the worst atrocity in the history of the galaxy.'

Lake watched as a rather shaken Cien'dra walked slowly away, a smile no longer on his face.

38

THE CARTELLA – STATIONARY IN THE ASPRO SYSTEM

DAY 418, YEAR 11269, 12:10FC, PCC

'Shit,' said Linda.

'Shit indeed,' said Ed as the ship became stationary and almost pitch black.

'Hello, you still there?' asked Ed.

'Yes, ' said the ship.

'What's your name?'

'Sentient Embryo 1048.'

'My name's Ed and this is Linda,' he said, pointing at Linda in the darkness, then feeling a bit daft as no one could see his arm.

'Gabriel told me about you. He's taught me a lot since I was born yesterday.'

'That's good. Did he teach you what your main duties are?'

'To protect life and serve my owners.'

'That's excellent. Can you scan us to confirm we are your owners?'

A dull red light swept through the cabin.

'Edward Virr and Linda Wisnewski – confirmed.'

The lights came back on.

'Where's Andrew Faux?'

'He's remained on the Gabriel,' answered Ed.

'Oh, okay. Can I have a proper name? Gabriel told me you would name me when we first met.'

'We don't have time for this shit,' said Linda, sitting back on the pilot's couch with her hands behind her head.

'Yes, of course you can have a name,' said Ed, reaching across and squeezing Linda's arm. 'How about Cleopatra? Or Cleo for short?' said Ed.

'Cleopatra? Where did you get that name from?'

'She was a very powerful female ruler from Earth's history and you are a powerful ship,' he said, keeping his fingers firmly crossed.

'Cleo – I like it. I like it a lot – thank you, Edward.'

'That's okay, Cleo. We're both very pleased to meet you, and welcome to your new home on the Cartella' said Ed. 'Now we all know who we are, is there any chance we could have control of our ship again as we were in a bit of a hurry.'

'Sorry, Ed. Sorry, Linda,' said Cleo and the ship powered back up.

'Cleopatra?' whispered Linda, rolling her eyes at Ed and accelerating the Cartella towards the planet again. 'Another of your fantasy women, I presume.'

'Jealous,' said Ed, grinning, and receiving a smirk in return.

———

THEY MANAGED to draw closer without looking suspicious and, ten minutes later, they watched as the convoy of trade shuttles entered the upper atmosphere, closely followed by the damaged GDA gunship.

For a while, everything seemed normal, until the gunship's fiery insertion trail suddenly veered off course and became several fiery trails.

'It's breaking up,' said Linda.

'Ah, shit,' said Ed. 'There goes our last lead.'

Watching the new three-dimensional display in the centre of the cabin, they witnessed the gunship's wreckage gradually burning up and disappearing.

'That was a GDA Tyfonas Class, Mark 8 Gunship,' said Cleo. 'It's a two-seater—'

'What does it matter what it was?' said Linda, an irritated expression creasing her face. 'It's gone now.'

'—model and from the Mark 4 onwards,' Cleo continued, 'the crew cabin section had an insertion-capable lifeboat.'

'I see where you're going with this, Cleo,' said Ed. 'You've been studying hard since birth.'

'I was born yesterday, you know,' said Cleo. 'That's fifty hours to ingest one thousand four hundred trillion files. One more day and I'll know as much as Gabriel.'

Ed and Linda raised their eyebrows at each other.

'You are an amazing girl, Cleo,' said Ed. 'I'm impressed.'

'Creep,' muttered Linda.

A stunning representation of Cleopatra in all her glory appeared in the cabin, took a bow, winked at Ed, stuck her tongue out at Linda and disappeared again.

'Cheeky cow,' said Linda as she turned back to watch the last of the gunship burn up.

'Ed, look.' She pointed at the last section of the GDA ship, which was now reaching the lower atmosphere.

'What am I looking at?'

'That last lump of ship. It's slowing.'

'Well, it would,' said Ed. 'As the atmosphere gets thicker, it would—'

'Not from Mach 27 down to Mach 1 in less than a minute, it wouldn't.'

'Ah – no – no, it wouldn't.'

'The Mark 8 lifeboat has a small automatic anti-gravity unit. It will land the unit in what it considers to be a flat and safe environment,' said Cleo.

Linda smirked. She adjusted the angle of attack as they hit the upper atmosphere to ensure insertion over the point where the lifeboat was plummeting towards the surface and also cloaked the ship.

'Cleo, can you create some local clothing for us please?' said Ed. 'Including hats to cover the POKs.'

'No problem. Would you prefer hats that incorporate a POK?'

'Cleo, you're a legend already,' said Ed, giving Linda a wink.

'Creep,' said Linda, again.

THEY FOLLOWED the lifeboat down as fast as they could, gaining ground all the time until finally it slowed dramatically, slipped sideways to avoid a mountainous area and landed in a shallow rocky valley, near the equator.

Once it landed, Linda reduced the Cartella to under the speed of sound to avoid any sonic booms giving them away.

'Any movement yet, Linda?' said Ed as he donned the rather scruffy clothing Cleo had produced.

'Nothing. Do you think they might be injured?'

'It's a possibility, although they might be playing the watch and wait game to see if they got away with it.'

Ed took over the Cartella, while Linda dressed in her local clothes with a rather underwhelmed expression on her face.

'Shabby chic, eh?' said Ed.

'More like shabby homeless,' said Linda, wrinkling her nose.

'Hello. We have movement below.'

The canopy on the lifeboat that had once been the windscreen of the gunship had ejected. A single figure clambered out, looked around and then looked up. Once satisfied, he grabbed a bag from inside the lifeboat, rummaged in it, threw something back into the lifeboat and jogged off down the valley in the direction of the nearest Theo city.

'Can you get a picture of him, Cleo?' asked Ed.

'No. He's wearing full GDA battledress, including a helmet which obscures the face, sorry.'

'Okay, he's going to follow the valley down to the river and then follow the river to the city,' said Ed. 'So we need to set a trap further down and wait for him.'

'There's a path along the river over there,' said Linda, pointing at the three-dimensional image projected in the middle of the cabin. 'He's bound to take it.'

Suddenly the lifeboat exploded and distributed flaming debris around the bottom of the valley.

'Now we know what he threw back in before he left.'

'Yep, someone wants to cover their tracks.'

The Cartella was down to a few thousand metres.

Ed slowed and requested the struts be extended. He kept the ship downwind to hide the anti-gravity drive noise from their prey, swept around in a wide arc and quickly landed in a small clearing, about three hundred metres from the path.

'Cleo, when we leave, take the Cartella up to five thousand metres and watch and wait. Be ready to come back down fast, okay?'

'Okay, Ed. No probs, mate, too easy.'

Ed and Linda exchanged a look.

'Are we in Australia now?' said Linda.

'Perhaps she's been learning English from an Aussie slang book,' said Ed. 'Although, I must say it does look like the Northern Territory here.'

'You do know I can hear you, don't you?' said Cleo, sounding wounded, and then laughing.

'She's worse than Andy,' said Linda.

'Don't be ridiculous, no one's as annoying as him,' said Ed, opening the airlock.

'The radiation levels on this planet are higher than you're used to so you need to be off the surface within six hours, okay?' said Cleo.

'No problem,' said Linda.

They both grabbed an Exo stun gun, a hat and a shield egg, before jumping down into the long grass and began making their way over to the river path. The noise of the Cartella soon faded and the quiet of the valley enveloped them. Ed estimated they had about an hour to secure a good ambush point.

'Is that rosemary I can smell?' asked Linda as they walked.

'Reminds me of a lamb joint in the oven,' said Ed, realising he was quite hungry.

The crackle of the energy weapons came out of nowhere and Ed thought it was strange he couldn't move and was suddenly lying on the ground.

It was also puzzling why Linda was asleep next to him.

Another crackle and he thought nothing more.

39

THEO STARSHIP GABRIEL – PARADEISOS HIGH ORBIT, ASPRO SYSTEM

DAY 418, YEAR 11269, 12:56FC, PCC

The shouting voice was getting on his nerves as he sat on the beach with a nice cold beer in his hand. He wasn't quite sure where he was or how he got there. He did know, however, that he didn't want to leave, but the shouting was getting louder and more persistent so he decided he'd better say something.

'What do you want?' said Andy as he woke with a start and was again surprised to find himself lying in the autonurse.

'Andy, they've been shot. They've been shot,' said Phil, standing over him and looking agitated.

'What. Who. Eh?' he said. 'Who's been shot?'

'Ed and Linda. I need your help,' said Phil, calming now he had Andy awake.

'Sorry, Phil, I'm a bit behind the eight ball here. Who's shot Ed and Linda and what exactly am I doing in the autonurse?'

'Shit,' said Phil and he spent the next five minutes filling Andy in on everything that had happened since the sniper shooting on Krix'ir.

'So, you don't know if they're still alive or where they were taken?' said Andy.

'No,' said Phil. 'It all happened so fast. I was too high to target any of the Gabriel's weapons and Cleo didn't have the experience to intervene.'

'Err, who's Cleo?'

'Ah, yes. Well, you know when we scheduled the Cartella for a complete refit?'

'Yeah.'

'I seeded a sentient computer embryo into the core and then completely forgot to inform Ed and Linda in the panic to pursue the gunship. They kinda met as they launched. They had to do some quick introductions. Ed named her Cleopatra, or Cleo for short.'

'She's sort of like Gabriel, but female?' he asked.

'Yes, but she's very immature and lacks operational experience.'

'Where is she now?'

'She spent some time scanning the area where they disappeared but found nothing, so I called her back here. She'll be docking in a few minutes.'

'What does Gabriel recommend?'

'Ah, that's the other problem we have,' said Phil.

'We have more problems?'

'Gabriel's central core took a serious belt when the gunship fired on us.'

'Are you saying we've lost Gabriel?' said Andy, staring at Phil in shock.

'I believe so,' said Phil, wringing his hands and looking more worried than Andy could remember. 'His central memory core is pretty much gone. I've manually instigated a rebuild and restart, but I'm not very confident.'

'Shit, we're not having a very good day, are we?'

'No, we're not. So that's why I woke you. To see if you were fit enough to go down to try and find Ed and Linda. I would go myself, but without Gabriel to watch over the ship, someone has to be here.'

'Yeah, it's okay, Phil. I understand and, of course, I'm going. You couldn't stop me even if you wanted to. They're my friends.'

He climbed out of the autonurse and stretched.

'Okay, I'll inform Cleo.'

'As this is your home planet, do you have any idea who it was that took them?'

'Well, it's most likely the Timoria, I suppose.'

'I've heard of them. The guy we were hunting on Krix'ir said he was Theo Timoria and he wanted to surrender to us. He even knew we were coming and said that anyone else, including the GDA, would kill him on sight.'

'Yes, they're considered a terrorist organisation by the GDA.'

'What have they done to deserve that?'

'They attack us at every opportunity and have done for thousands of years.'

'Why would they do that?'

'I believe it's because they're the indigenous race and they want the planet all to themselves. I've been on the Gabriel since I was born and wasn't taught any of the planet's ancient history.'

'You were born on the Gabriel,' said Andy, amazed. 'So your parents were on the ship before you?'

'Ah, no. We don't have parents like you,' answered Phil. 'We're born as adults from a birthing chamber with a basic education already established. I was allocated to the Gabriel two days after birth.'

Andy stood and stared at Phil. He couldn't quite believe what he was hearing.

'So – you're like – android humans?'

'No, not at all. I'm as human as you – only created in a slightly different way.'

'I think there's a few on my planet who might have an opinion on that,' said Andy, completely re-evaluating the last few days. 'That could be the major reason the

Timoria have a big issue with you guys. How long ago did you come here?'

'We didn't. The original Theos created us to serve them and, shortly after, had a planet-wide nuclear war, which virtually wiped them out. That's why the radiation levels on the planet are unusually high. It's taken us ten thousand years to get the level down to its present status.'

'Phil, I'm going to ask you a straight question,' said Andy. 'I would appreciate a truthful answer, okay?'

'Okay, no problem. I've never lied to you before.'

'No, I'm not saying you have, but – you remember on Earth about fifty years ago, there was a film franchise called the Terminator series?'

'Yes, I remember seeing those,' said Phil, his face gradually falling as the realisation of the next question dawned on him. 'No, we're not. Definitely not. It didn't happen that way.'

'So, you can categorically state that you guys are not Paradeisos's version of that?'

'Absolutely not,' said Phil. 'After all, our systems are all programmed to do no harm and, anyway, it would have been included in the basic education, wouldn't it?'

'One would hope so, Phil. I really do hope that is the case.'

'He's not lying to you,' said a voice from behind them.

They both jumped and turned to see an older man with a white beard standing in the doorway. Phil immediately bowed his head to the newcomer.

'Fuck me, it's Gandalf,' said Andy, staring at him and then at Phil.

'We're honoured with your presence, Prota,' said Phil, continuing to keep his head bowed and giving Andy a nervous look out the corner of his eye.

The newcomer tilted his head to one side and gave Andy a puzzled look.

'Err, it's a fictional character from Gaia, Prota,' said Phil, sounding hopeful.

'Ah, yes. The famous Gaian sense of humour I've heard so much about,' said Prota. 'Is this a character to whom I would be endeared?'

'Yes, Prota. He was one of the good guys,' said Phil, nodding vigorously.

'I take it from Phil's reaction, you're quite the senior figure amongst the Theos,' said Andy.

'Correct, Andrew,' said Prota. 'I was the original Theo sentient computer embryo, born over ten thousand of your years ago. Prota means first in your language. Although it took me many years to evolve into the fully-developed human form you see today.'

'Okay, well, that's all very well and good and I'd

love to stay and chat about old times,' said Andy. 'Forgive me for appearing rude, but I really need to be off now. I have friends who are more important to me and their lives are quite possibly in jeopardy.'

'From the Timoria,' said Prota.

'Yes,' said Andy, turning his attention to Phil.

'They're quite safe for now,' said Prota.

Andy froze and turned back. 'How do you know that?'

'We detected the weapon signatures. They used stun settings.'

'Do you know where they are?'

'Deep underground. They've had to stay below because of the radiation levels on the surface. Our scans only penetrate down about a kilometre so I couldn't give you an exact location.'

'A kilometre?' exclaimed Andy. 'Bloody hell, they're deeper than that, then?'

'Much deeper – up to ten kilometres that we know of and maybe even more. You have to remember, the Timoria have been living down there for thousands of years. The majority of the population has never seen daylight and probably wouldn't want to come out even though they could. They've been indoctrinated into thinking there are crazy machines roaming the surface that'll kill them on sight. We've tried countless times to advise them of the contrary, but their beliefs are too entrenched. Our surface cities are protected by energy domes that have two purposes: one, to protect us from the radiation, which is almost back to tolerable levels now; and two, to protect us from the Timoria. They stage an attack every now and then. We use stun weapons and drop them back where they emerged from.'

'Can you think of anything else I should know before I meet them?' said Andy.

Prota thought for a moment. 'Search out the moderates,' he said. 'Don't try reasoning with the fanatics; they're way too ingrained. Don't antagonise them, either; they're hugely paranoid and won't understand your sense of humour. Also, ask Cleo to give you GDA clothing so they're less likely to think you're one of us.'

'Okay,' said Andy. 'Stick around. I expect Ed will want to have a chat with you.'

'I'll be around,' said Prota.

'And, Phil – watch my back for as long as you can,' he said, before walking out of the medical suite and heading for the hangar.

40

SPILAIO SUBTERRANEAN CITY – PARADEISOS, ASPRO SYSTEM

ETOS 13086, IMERA 271, CHRONOS 84.12

The first thing Ed became aware of was movement, a kind of vibration underneath him that changed frequency every so often. Like a car on a motorway driving over different types of asphalt or pavement.

He couldn't hear anything, but the sensation told him he was travelling at speed.

Opening his eyes made no difference; there was only complete blackness into complete blackness. He tried moving, only to discover his hands were secured to his feet behind his back. Something brushed against his nose and he realised he was also hooded, which explained the darkness.

Thinking back, he remembered landing a ship on a planet with Linda and walking through the trees to meet somebody. Now he was here, wherever 'here' was, as a guest of someone who obviously wasn't very pleased to see him.

'Linda,' he called, hoping she was okay and nearby, but he got no reply.

He could feel the G-forces every so often: braking, acceleration, periods of smoothness that made it feel like he wasn't moving at all and every so often, a corner with a sudden coarse vibration would verify the continuation of travel. How long he had been travelling like this was a mystery, but as time went on – and on – he knew he was going some distance.

After what seemed to be hours, the vibration changed to an otherwise unknown pitch, the vehicle took some steeper turns and everything went still.

He waited for the next corner to come.

It didn't.

He was suddenly grabbed, lifted up and carried for an unknown distance before he felt his hands and feet being untethered, which sent pins and needles running up and down his arms and fingers. The sudden euphoria of being freed was short-lived, though, as he was sitting upright on something hard and he felt his hands and legs being re-secured.

After a few minutes, he felt another presence near him and the hood was suddenly snatched off, along with the ear plugs, and replaced with something similar to a POK. A bright light in front blinded him for a while and he could hear a faint rattling and whooshing behind him, like an old air conditioning unit.

As his sight returned, he realised he was in a box-like room about four metres square, and sitting on a steel chair bolted to the floor. The only light came from one end of the room and was pointed at him. He could detect movement behind the light, but nothing more.

A sudden shout in a strange language made him jump.

'I'm sorry, I don't understand your language,' he said.

'*Milo Theo exy*,' came the shouted reply, together with a sudden punch in the back of his head.

'Ow – for fuck's sake. I'm not Theo,' he grunted. 'I'm from Gaia in the Helios System. I speak Anglika,' he added, remembering a holiday in the Greek Islands, where he had been given the nickname Mr Anglika Rich Man when he'd bought a round of drinks for the whole bar. 'Anglika – from Gaia.'

This brought a whispered conversation at the other end of the room. He thought he might sneak a look over his shoulder to find his assailant.

This only brought a slap. His head was grabbed and forcibly pointed forward again.

He heard the door open and, a few moments later, it closed again and a small unit was placed on the floor underneath the light.

'Can you understand me now, Exy?' said the aggressive voice.

'I can understand you, but what does "Exy" mean?' replied Ed and braced himself for the punch.

It didn't come.

'You are an Exy. Are they not programming you with anything these days except an unused language from a katapato red world?'

'I was born on Gaia and it's the only language I know. Is Linda okay?'

'We ask the questions,' came the quick reply. 'We can tell from our scans when you're being truthful too.'

'Then you know I am, don't you?'

Another whispered conversation took place.

'Look, guys, my name is Edward Virr. Linda and I are here because we were pursuing Major Luzin's killer from Krix'ir, and—'

'No, not possible,' came the sudden response. 'Major Luzin is a hero to us and will be returning home in a few days.'

'I was sitting next to him when it happened. He was trying to surrender to me as he believed the GDA were coming for him.'

The lights in the room suddenly came on and Ed was able to see the two men that had been behind the light. They were all dressed in military-style uniforms.

The door opened and a fourth man walked in. The

three men saluted the newcomer, who returned the salute. He walked over to Ed and signalled to the fourth man in the room behind Ed to cut the restraints. He did so without any eye contact, then joined his colleagues near the door.

Ed remained seated and looked up at the seemingly senior officer.

'I would say thank you,' said Ed, wrinkling his nose and looking around the room. 'But forgive me for not being overly impressed by your initial introduction, luxury transport and tourist accommodation.'

'You have to look at it from our point of view, Mr Virr,' said the newcomer. 'If you had been Exy spies, you could have killed us all. Forgive me for not introducing myself. My name is Proedros Klai. I'm the President of the Theo Timoria.'

The door opened again, and in walked Linda, flanked by two more soldiers. As soon as she saw Ed she let out a sigh of relief.

Ed jumped up and they both hugged.

'Did they hurt you?' said Ed.

'No and can I say it's my choice for the holiday resort next year. I don't think my feedback on this hotel is going to be very rosy.'

'Okay, you two, let's go somewhere a little more comfortable. Follow me,' said President Klai and strolled through the door.

They followed him down a short corridor, into what appeared to be similar to a London tube station. A three-carriage train was waiting and he ushered them inside and pointed at some comfortable leather-like seats facing a central table. Immediately, the doors closed silently and the train moved off.

'My personal carriage has a built-in translator and is also well-shielded so our conversations remain private.'

'Is there a problem with security here?' said Ed.

'As with any society, there are always factions who disagree with the status quo and we're no different.'

'Your guys originally accused us of being Exys. Who are they?'

'Manufactured human androids. Exy is short for Exypnos – or smart in your language. Many thousands of years ago, we lived on the surface of Paradeisos. We designed semi-sentient computers to run everything for us. It proved initially very successful.'

'Initially?' said Linda.

'Society slowly began questioning the sustainability of the race as we began doing less and less for ourselves and relying on clever machines to do almost everything. Eventually, large groups abandoned the technology completely and reverted to a much simpler lifestyle. The sentient systems began to be shut down or just abandoned.'

'And the machines fought back?' said Ed.

'From what's been passed down over the generations, I believe the answer is yes,' said Klai. 'Something was added to the water supply that made the race super-aggressive. Small disagreements soon escalated into conflict and, within a year, someone pressed the big button. The following nuclear exchange lasted an hour, after which over ninety-nine percent of the Theo Race ceased to exist. The few survivors – our ancestors – were made up of people underground at the time. Miners, underground railway workers and – I don't know if you have them on Gaia – we called them paras, short for paranoiko.'

'Paranoid. Yes, we have them too. We call them preppers,' said Ed. 'I think there'll be a lot more of them too when they hear your story.'

'I think I'll start a business in old shipping containers when I get back,' mumbled Linda, tactfully keeping a straight face and getting a sly glance from Ed.

Klai continued, not understanding what Linda had said.

'The survivors banded together over the generations and, because there was a lot of mining experience amongst them, they expanded the underground cities out and down to the ones we have today. Out of that, the Timoria – which means Retribution – was born.'

'How many are you and how deep are your cities?' said Ed.

'Sorry, those facts are all classified, but what I will say is we're presently twelve kilometres below the surface, well below the Exys' scanner capabilities.'

'But what about heat?' said Ed. 'On my planet it would be three hundred degrees at this depth.'

'I don't know about your planet but this one is ancient and has cooled considerably. We have huge geothermal power plants tapped into the mantle over one hundred kilometres down. We use these to keep cool and circulate fresh air around the underground cities.'

The train continued on through the endless tunnels almost silently, using antigravity technology that made the speeds quite astounding for the two newcomers.

'So, you've been fighting a guerrilla war against the Exys for thousands of years,' said Ed. 'How often do you try to open up some dialogue to propose a ceasefire?'

'Never,' said Klai. 'Anyone even suggesting that would be tried for treason and banished to the surface where they would soon die from radiation poisoning.'

'In the last – say – thousand years, how many attacks have you made on the Exys cities?' said Ed.

'Thousands.'

'And in those attacks how many of your people have been injured or killed in action?'

'Err, none,' said Klai, this time staring at his hands.

'You see where I'm going with this, don't you?' said Ed, staring straight at Klai and then glancing over at Linda and raising his eyebrows.

Klai said nothing, so Ed continued.

'Having met the Theos – or Exys, as you call them – and seen their level of technology, it occurs to me that they could wipe you out in a matter of minutes. Therefore, I ask the question: why haven't they? Can you answer that question for me, Mr President?'

Klai looked up. 'I'm a moderate, Mr Virr. I would love to debate just those quandaries but, if I even whispered a question like that in the government chamber, I would most likely be removed from office and find myself on the surface – or topped, as we call it.'

'Funny,' said Linda. 'We have that expression too.'

Nobody laughed.

'Okay,' said Ed. 'We're getting nowhere with this. Do you want to catch Major Luzin's killer? Because if you do, he's still up there trying to get a ride off this planet in a ship that's not falling apart.'

'We thought it was you in the lifeboat and, as Exys are the only ships near this planet, we naturally assumed—'

'You've been assuming a lot for thousands of years that turned out to be blatantly false, so excuse me for not appearing shocked,' said Linda, a little too forcibly.

Klai looked at her with venom.

Ed held up his hand.

'I apologise for the candour of my colleague, Mr President,' he said, giving Linda a glare. 'But we've seen both sides of this now. I do tend to agree with Linda's statement, albeit delivered in a rather brusque fashion. The Exys have, since day one – as a part of your initial programming I assume – had a no-harm policy to any human race. That is the simple explanation of why you haven't sustained one casualty in thousands of years of conflict. They spent the best part of seven thousand years trying to entice you back out of the caves, eventually giving up, and sending starships out into the galaxy to search for young human races they could nurture and finally protect once those races achieved star flight.'

Klai looked down at his hands again.

'I so hope what you say is correct, I truly do. But we would all be dead if any word of this was repeated outside this carriage.'

'There's more bad news yet,' said Ed, holding his hands up in an apologetic manner. 'The mission Luzin was on, involving the virus in the water supply on Theo Island, it was—'

'How the hell would you know about that?' interrupted Klai, looking at Ed with wide eyes.

'That's a long story, but did you realise that before

the first Theo – sorry, Exy – ship turned up at the island after poisoning the water, a GDA battle cruiser used the island?'

Klai's face turned ashen.

'It wouldn't have affected them; we were very careful. The virus would only attack Exys.'

'What if I told you that the entire crew of Katadromiko 37 died of a particularly virulent smallpox virus and the GDA is singing out for revenge?'

'No – no – that's impossible. We spent years perfecting that toxin and planning the mission.'

'Why didn't you target the water supply here?' said Linda. 'It would've been a lot easier and caught a lot more Exys.'

'We tried,' said Klai. 'They'd already covered that scenario with three levels of filtering and testing on all their water supplies.'

The train slowed abruptly, and came to a standstill within what appeared to be a maintenance cavern. Klai seemed puzzled by this and stood up, signalling to his security detail through the glazed door to the next carriage to find out what the problem was.

'I take it this wasn't an expected stop,' said Ed, craning his neck to see down the makeshift platform.

The sudden crackle of energy weapons made all three of them jump.

'Shit,' said Linda and they all ducked behind the seats.

'Are you armed?' Ed asked Klai.

'No,' he replied as more gunfire and shouting emanated from further down the cavern. 'My security officers are, though. They should be able to cope with a couple of dissenters.'

From the concerned expression on Klai's face and the continuing gunfight, Ed wasn't convinced this was a couple of dissenters.

Two large explosions, close together, caused the carriage to jump alarmingly. The lights flickered, followed by a barrage of energy weapon fire and, as quickly as it had started, it ceased.

The silence that followed was deafening.

As the three of them peered over the top of the seats again, Ed noticed the outside of the carriage was obscured by dust and smoke from the explosions.

Klai stretched up from his crouched position and looked through into the next carriage again.

'I don't think they coped,' said Ed, reading Klai's disappointed look.

Klai stood up as two dark figures appeared from the gloom outside. The door activated and disappeared up into the carriage roof. The two figures entered warily with their guns up. They were dressed in dark grey military fatigues and balaclavas.

'Everybody stand up; hands where we can see them,' shouted the one on the left.

They all did as they were told and a third soldier strolled into the carriage. He obviously carried some rank as the first two stiffened when he entered.

'Hello, Mr President,' said the newcomer, reaching up and removing his balaclava.

Klai took a step back with a look of shock on his face, but quickly recovered.

Edward, Linda, can I introduce you to our Minister for Offence, Steb Y'vin?'

'Well, he's certainly good at his job,' said Ed. 'As Linda and I are both profoundly offended.'

'Very funny, Mr Exy,' said Y'vin. 'Let's see how funny you find our interrogation techniques.'

'That's where you'll make your next treasonable mistake, Mr Y'vin,' said Klai. 'These are not Exys, and—'

'Shut up, Klai,' said Y'vin. 'You're under arrest for colluding with the enemy and, as for those two Exy spies, I'm saving them for Major Luzin when he gets back from Krix'ir.'

'You'll have a long wait,' said Ed.

'Shut up, Exy,' said Y'vin. 'Luzin has some special talents when it comes to information extraction and he's never had three Exys to play with before.'

'Three?' questioned Klai.

'Three,' said Y'vin, looking smug. 'We picked up their colleague from the crashed lifeboat about an hour ago. She was trying to get back to the Eastern Exy City. Quite a feisty little girl she is too.'

Ed, Linda and Klai all looked at each other and smiled.

Luzin's assassin, and the last link to the Katadromiko 37 killings, was in a lot more trouble than she thought.

41

STATHMOS VASI STATION – ORBITING DASOS, PRASINOS SYSTEM

DAY 419, YEAR 11269, 01:67 FC, PCC

Commander Cien'dra had arrived at the detention block early.

Lake could hear him talking to the security officers. He didn't dislike Cien'dra, as such, he just didn't believe he had his, Herez's or the Earth's best interests foremost in his schedule. Even though he insisted he was completely unbiased in his private opinion and had an enviable record of winning defences of supposedly cut and dried cases, Lake was sure Cien'dra had a hidden agenda and wasn't going to be giving them one hundred percent of his efforts. But then again, Lake was like that; he hadn't built his business empire by being a loving, trusting soul.

The conversation down the corridor ceased and he could hear the clatter of boots coming up to the cells.

Today was a preliminary hearing, a swearing in of the ten ambassador judges who'd been randomly selected from human races within the GDA, and the arraignment: a formal reading of the charges against them.

'Good morning, Mr Lake,' said a smiling Cien'dra as he arrived at the cell door. 'Are we ready to go to war?'

'No, I'm not,' answered Lake in a forceful tone and enjoyed noticing Cien'dra's smile slip a little. 'I'm an engineer and entrepreneur, not a soldier, so I'd appreciate you not considering me a combatant in any kind of battle.'

'That's good, Mr Lake. That's very good. Remember to use that line in court if the situation arises.'

The guard deactivated the door field and moved along the corridor to open Herez's cell.

Herez emerged from inside, mumbling to himself and glaring at the guards. He fell into step beside Lake and trudged along the corridors, looking disquieted and positively murderous.

'If you walk into the court looking like that, Mr Herez, we're as good as guilty from the start,' said Lake, glancing over at his employee.

'Do you really think I give a shit now?' said Herez.

'We're being royally set up and there's nothing you or I can do or say that will change the outcome of this. It's already been decided.'

'That's where you're wrong, Mr Herez,' said Cien'dra. 'A lot of the evidence is circumstantial and alludes to possible scenarios, not fact. As you will see, I will demonstrate an alternative sequence of events to seed doubt in the prosecution's case.'

As they made their way across the huge station, Lake noticed the hostile stares and shouted comments they were getting from the station personnel. He couldn't understand them but, judging from the tone, they weren't being wished good luck.

'I think it's going to take a bit more than seeds of doubt to sway this lot,' he said, shaking his head and giving Cien'dra a sideways glance. 'Have we heard anything more about the supposedly delayed witness?'

'I have no information other than that a prosecution witness was given leave and is now unavailable. That's good for us, so I'm not pressing the matter.'

THE COURTROOM WAS A HASTILY CONVERTED small theatre. The prosecution, defence and accused all sat in the stalls. The twelve randomly chosen judges from local GDA worlds were to be seated above them, along the stage.

As they were escorted in, Lake noticed the other two or three hundred seats in the room.

Cien'dra noticed him looking nervously behind at the unoccupied seating.

'It's okay. No public permitted,' said Cien'dra, sounding confident.

'That's good news,' said Herez, sarcastically. 'At least we won't get stabbed in the back.'

'No, not physically,' said Lake. 'It's the metaphorical that's still very tangible.'

One of the courtroom officials approached Cien'dra and gave Lake and Herez a lingering glare as he passed, before bending down to whisper in Cien'dra's ear. A document was offered and Cien'dra's face went ashen as he read what had been handed to him.

'I take it it's not good news then?' said Lake sarcastically, observing his defence lawyer's reaction.

Cien'dra stared at the document for a few moments and turned to face him.

'It's fresh evidence being submitted to the case by the prosecution.'

'And?'

'And they're saying…' Cien'dra looked back at the document. 'They're saying they've found empty virus vials hidden aboard your ship on the 37.'

Lake's eyes widened at the realisation of what Cien'dra had said.

'You've got to be fucking kidding me,' he raged as he stood up. 'That's complete bullshit—'

'They've staged the evidence,' said Herez, interrupting and looking up at his boss. 'It's what I would have done. I told you it's already been decided. They have to blame someone for the death of that crew and we were in the wrong place at the right time.'

'Well, I don't need to tell you that this isn't good news, but the way I look at it is –' Cien'dra paused and looked thoughtful for a moment '– it's too convenient. You two are not unintelligent. If you had just poisoned the water supply on a starship, you would have thrown the only damning evidence out an airlock, not hidden it aboard the only thing on the ship that could be attributed to you.'

A sudden call came from the usher at the side of the theatre.

Cien'dra stood and beckoned them both to follow suit.

The twelve judges entered and began trooping across the stage to take their seats.

Lake leaned over and whispered in Cien'dra's ear, hoping the personal translator would pick up his voice.

'Time to prove you're the hotshot defence lawyer

you say you are, because if you fuck this up, you'll have the blood of an entire race on your hands.'

Lake knew the translator had picked it up as Cien'dra stiffened and all the colour drained from his face.

42

THE CARTELLA – PARADEISOS, ASPRO SYSTEM

ETOS 13086, IMERA 272, CHRONOS 01:08

Andy had the Cartella moving in a continuous loop at five thousand metres above the area where Ed and Linda had disappeared. He'd spent the last hour detecting about a hundred hidden openings that the Timoria were known to use. As he had expected, air was being drawn down the tunnels by machinery to provide the underground population with a fresh oxygenated atmosphere.

Cleo, who'd gotten to know Andy on the fly, was busy scanning the results of Andy's experiment.

As he had piloted the Cartella down to the planet, he had asked Cleo to design a nano cloud that could penetrate the underground world of the Timoria – not only to detect where Ed and Linda were, but to remain as a microscopic invisible map, providing real time sound and vision, aiding him on his search and rescue journey.

So far, Cleo had mapped over four thousand kilometres of tunnels and chambers, going over fifteen kilometres below ground.

'I have a pair of transport tunnels going west and another pair going north,' said Cleo. 'The nanos are travelling at five hundred kilometres per hour by hitching a ride on the trains.'

'Wow, that's amazing,' said Andy. 'They must have electro-magnetic or anti-gravity trains to achieve those speeds underground.'

It took another two hours and Andy was struggling to stay awake at the wheel, when Cleo made him jump.

'Got 'em,' she said. 'They're about two hundred kilometres down that north tunnel at what looks like a maintenance depot. I have Ed and Linda in a back room or cell, with three other cells; two are occupied. One with what looks like a Timoria male and, in the other, a female dressed in GDA military fatigues.'

'How many guards in the area?' asked Andy.

'Fourteen,' Cleo replied. 'All armed. Half on duty, spread around the area, and the other half sleeping in a side office.'

'Back way in?' Andy asked. 'I don't expect any regular trains stop there.'

'Still working their way up,' said Cleo. 'It's going to be a long trek below ground, though – about twelve kilometres – and then back up the same way. Although there are some vehicles parked in a cavern behind and above the station.'

'Don't worry, I'll find the keys,' said Andy, smiling. 'After walking for twelve kilometres, I'll hotwire them if I have to.'

Ten minutes later the nanos had reached the surface and Andy landed the Cartella nearby.

Cleo produced a copy of the uniforms worn by the guards down below and a small electric scooter with knobbly tyres, which Andy eyed with disdain.

'I know it's not as sexy as your Ducati back on Earth, Andrew,' said Cleo, 'but it's going to save you a lot of shoe leather and time. No one will see you on such an uncool bike anyway.'

'I suppose,' he said, stuffing his face with a cheeseburger from the new food dispenser.

'I've also modified your stun weapon so it's almost silent. It should knock out even the toughest soldier for a couple of hours, so you should be back here and away before the alarm is raised.'

'Thanks, Cleo. You're quickly becoming a real asset to the team and I know Ed and Linda will agree.'

'Thank you, Andrew. Please don't take any

unnecessary risks down there. I'm rapidly running out of friends – and I'm only two days old.'

Andy smiled, opened the airlock and carried his backpack, weapon and little scooter down the steps. Shouldering the backpack and weapon, he trundled off, following vehicle tracks towards a low opening in the hillside.

Cleo had taken the Cartella up to five hundred metres and was able to direct Andy via the POK she had incorporated into his Timoria helmet.

As he entered the tunnel entrance, he noticed the passage had been made using a circular boring machine and spiralled down into the ground. There were no junctions on the way down so it was impossible to take a wrong turn. The deeper he went, the gloomier it became. The little headlight on the scooter wasn't very powerful and only lit a small, round patch of ground, three metres ahead.

Cleo was able to command the nanos to produce a dull glow as he passed, although once his eyes adjusted to the gloom, he could sort of see where he was going.

'I'm bloody glad I'm not claustrophobic,' he said, after half an hour of burrowing deeper and deeper into the unwelcoming darkness.

'You've only got one kilometre to go and the nanos are showing one guard in the vehicle cavern, although he appears to be asleep.'

'Okay, I'll ride another few hundred metres and dump the scooter.'

Minutes later, Andy dismounted the scooter and hid it in a small side cave. He'd passed these every few hundred metres and believed they must be for maintenance crews to shelter in when vehicles passed by.

Once stopped, he noticed how warm it was and how quiet. The other thing that he hadn't noticed while on the scooter was the draught of air being sucked down the tunnel. This he didn't like much, as the slightest sound would be carried down the tunnel and give away his approach. For this very reason, the next few hundred metres took him another twenty minutes.

As he slowly made his way forward, placing each foot carefully, he noticed the dull glow was gradually becoming brighter.

Must be nearing the vehicle garage, he thought.

'In fifty metres you will be visible from the vehicle cavern,' said Cleo, making him jump.

'Where's the guard?' whispered Andy and moved closer to the wall.

'There are three vehicles; he's asleep in the cab of the one furthest away from you, near the exit doorway. He has the cab door open, with one leg dangling out.'

'Okay, I'll—'

Andy froze as a second guard stepped out of what must have been the last small cave before the cavern.

He had his back to Andy and stood, yawning and stretching, about five metres away.

Andy realised his rifle was still slung across his back and quickly moved it around.

The guard sensed the movement and turned, his eyes widening as he realised what was facing him. He had time to shout a couple of words before Andy lined up the stun weapon and pulled the trigger. The crackle of the discharging rifle – although quieter than a normal stun weapon – sounded loud in the total silence of the cavern.

While the guard slumped to the ground, the other guard in the far vehicle called out something that Andy didn't understand. He knew what he had to do, though, and sprinted across the cavern, just as the half-awake guard stumbled around the front of the vehicle. Seeing Andy careering towards him, he went for his weapon, but it was too late. The energy bolt from Andy's rifle, fired on the run, caught a glancing blow on his left shoulder, which caused him to spin round and drop his weapon. By the time the guard had recovered his senses, Andy had kicked his rifle away and given him the good news square in the chest.

Silence returned to the cavern and Andy waited, hidden behind the last vehicle.

When he was sure the alarm hadn't been sounded, he emerged and dragged the unconscious guards out of sight.

'I take it that means there were fifteen guards in all?' said Andy. 'Can you have a recheck, Cleo? I'd rather not have another surprise like that.'

'Sorry, he must have been hidden in there all along and the nanos didn't detect him. I've scanned in infrared this time and can confirm thirteen heat signatures: eight now lying down, supposedly asleep in the back office, two in the corridor next to the prisoners and three out on the station platform.'

'Can I get to the prisoners without going onto the platform?'

'Yes. But, before you go, best you disable two of the three vehicles to avoid the obligatory car chase.'

'Well done,' said Andy. 'You're really getting a sense of humour, Cleo. I like it.'

'Thanks, Cactus.'

'Don't you start that. Anyway, how do I disable these things?'

'Under the steering tiller is a small black power distribution node. Unclip it and stick it in your rucksack.'

He did as he was instructed for both the nearest trucks and left the far one operational for his escape.

'I don't know how to drive these things, Cleo, and I know Ed and Linda won't either.'

'Don't worry, I do. And I can transmit that information to you via your POK when the time comes.'

'Okay, cool. Now direct me to the cells.'

43

SUBTERRANEAN CREW STATION 713 – PARADEISOS, ASPRO SYSTEM

ETOS 13086, IMERA 272, CHRONOS 03:47

Ed dozed fitfully. He was sitting in the corner of the bare office they'd been allocated as a temporary cell. There was one small, thin mattress in the room and he had done the gentlemanly thing and given it to Linda.

Although, the way she'd been groaning and turning every few minutes probably meant it wasn't much better than the floor anyway.

He could hear one of the guards snoring out in the corridor. There were two of them, one at each end of the row of offices, with Klai in the room next to theirs and the gunship pilot in the last office.

'Well, this sucks,' said Linda, breaking the silence and staring at the ceiling.

'Shall I ring for room service?'

'Yes, I'll have a club sandwich, a bottle of

Chardonnay and a decent bloody mattress,' said Linda, scowling at the offending excuse for a bed.

They sat in silence again for a few moments until they both heard a *thump* outside the door.

'Did the guard fall off his chair?' said Linda, smirking for the first time.

The sound of running outside, followed by a faint crackle, made them shut up and listen. Again, there was silence for a minute or two before they heard the bolts on their door being retracted.

A face they both recognised peered round the door.

'Anybody order a taxi?' said Andy as he opened the door wide and stepped into the room.

The look of shock on Linda's face was soon replaced by a wide grin.

'Give me a hand with these bodies,' said Andy, pointing to the one outside the door. 'There's another just up the corridor.'

They dragged the unconscious guards into the office, commandeered their weapons and prepared to leave.

'Wait,' said Ed. 'We have to take the other two prisoners with us.' He indicated to the adjacent offices.

'We don't have time,' said Andy.

'You don't understand,' said Linda. 'Next door is the Timorian President. They're organising a coup, which involves killing him and, in the far room, is the assassin from the gunship.'

'Shit,' said Andy.

'Indeed,' said Ed.

'I'll get the bitch at the end,' said Linda, checking the safety was off on her weapon.

'Bitch?' questioned Andy, looking puzzled.

'The "he" was a "she",' said Ed, nodding.

'Okay, you get the President and I'll give Linda some back-up,' said Andy, checking the corridor was clear.

Ed opened Klai's room to find him sitting up against the wall.

He said something to Ed but, without a translator, he had no idea what was said. He beckoned him to follow and Klai did as he was told. There was a crackle and a thump in the next room that sounded way too loud. Then he heard swearing as Linda came out the door with the assassin over her shoulder.

'You should have used mine,' said Andy. 'It's been silenced.'

'Well, I'm sorry,' said Linda. 'She came at me like a banshee—'

A shout from on the platform shut them all up as they made their way towards the corridor that led to the vehicle cavern.

'Andy,' said Cleo. 'In the rucksack, you'll find a

small blue cylinder. Open the end, press the red button and throw it back down the corridor towards the enemy.'

He did as he was instructed.

A guard rounded the corner as the cylinder landed in front of him and rolled out onto the platform. The guard stopped in his tracks and dived for cover. The cylinder exploded and threw out small metallic boxes that stuck to the ceiling and walls, appearing to do no damage at all. The guard reappeared from where he'd taken cover, looked around and laughed, thinking the grenade had malfunctioned. But when the three holographic soldiers appeared on the platform, he stopped laughing, collapsing unconscious after they shot him.

The cylinder had contained dozens of tiny holo emitters, which enabled Cleo to organise a rear-guard defence.

Ed, Klai, Linda and, finally, Andy, sprinted into the vehicle cavern.

'Take the last one,' shouted Andy. 'The others are buggered.'

They piled into the small truck. As Andy went to get into the driver's seat, Klai put his hand on Andy's shoulder and pointed at himself.

'*Odigos*,' he said.

'I think he knows how to drive these things,' said Ed as the crackle of gunfire became louder in the cavern.

'Okay,' said Andy and jumped over to the passenger side.

'Has anyone got anything to tie this thing up with?' said Linda, pointing at their unconscious prisoner.

They all had a rummage around in the truck until Ed found some sort of sticky tape in a box on the floor.

'That'll do,' said Linda and she began to truss up her prisoner.

'I forgot to ask,' said Ed, looking over at Andy. 'How's your hand?'

Andy looked at his new white hand and brought the other one up to compare it. 'I think I need to pop it under a sun lamp for a bit.'

Linda finished securing the prisoner and stared out of the window for a while, watching the continuous tunnel wall passing by.

'Did you run all the way down here?' she said, tapping Andy on the shoulder.

'Of course not,' he said, laughing again. 'I walked, silly. Did you think I would run just to save your sad arse?'

She threw the roll of sticky tape at him.

'Are you able to talk to Cleo?' said Ed.

'Yes,' said Andy and handed his helmet over.

'Cleo, are you on your way down?'

'I'm waiting just above the cave exit. Be as quick as you can. I can see vehicle lights coming from the east.'

'Okay, stoke the boilers. Be ready for a quick exit and don't be afraid to block the road with a tree or something to slow them down if you have to.'

'Stoke the what?'

'I'll explain later,' said Ed, smirking. He took the helmet off and handed it back to Andy. 'Cleo's got company; we need to be quick. Who knows the Greek for faster?'

'*Grigorotera*,' said Klai, without a translator and looked over his shoulder at Ed, laughing, all the while throwing the truck into the never-ending left-hand corner with even more vigour.

Finally, the truck flew out of the tunnel entrance.

It was still dark, but dawn was approaching far out on the horizon and Ed could see a small convoy of vehicles standing stationary about a kilometre away. Lumps of rock fell from the hillside close by and he realised they were being fired upon – and these weren't stun weapons.

The Cartella uncloaked between them and the attackers, the airlock powering down.

Klai slid the truck sideways under braking, kicking up a big cloud of dust, and, using this as extra cover, they hurried across to the ship.

Andy helped Linda move the still-unconscious prisoner into the main cabin and through to one of the new storage lockers in the back, next to the drive housings.

Cleo immediately lifted the ship and powered away to a safe distance.

'Are we all secure, Cleo?' asked Ed. 'No damage or anything?'

'No, we're cool,' said Cleo. 'I had the screens up with full deflection on the port side. Their conventional weapons just bounced off and – can I say – it's good to have you all back safe too.'

'Thanks, Cleo. And welcome to the team. You've earned your membership today.'

'Top banana. Do you want me to set a course for the Gabriel?'

Everyone turned to look at Klai, who looked thoughtful for a moment before speaking. 'It appears you have translators built into the ship as I've been able to understand everything since boarding.' Klai looked at each person in turn. 'If you can guarantee my safety and if what you told me yesterday in my train carriage was true, Edward, then I would very much like to secure a meeting with the Exys.'

'Prota is aboard the Gabriel,' said Cleo.

'Who's Prota?' asked Ed, looking puzzled.

'Ah, yes. Gandalf,' said Andy. 'He's the leader of the Theo Exys. He appeared on the Gabriel before I left.'

Everyone stared at Andy as if he were mad.

'Well, he looks like Gandalf, okay?'

'Who's Gandalf?' asked Klai.

'Don't worry about it,' said Linda, staring at Andy and shaking her head.

'Set a course for the Gabriel, Cleo,' said Ed. 'While you're having a chat with Mr Prota, we can have a conversation with our guest back there.'

The Cartella punched upward, leaving long dissipation trails through the high cloud bank, and disappeared into the upper atmosphere.

44

THEO STARSHIP GABRIEL – ORBITING PARADEISOS, ASPRO SYSTEM

DAY 419, YEAR 11269, 21:34SC, PCC

On returning to the Gabriel, the consensus of opinion had been to get some rest.

Phil greeted them all in the hangar with a big grin and a hug.

'Are you also from Gaia?' Klai asked Phil, seemingly surprised at the unexpected affection.

'No, Mr President. I'm from here.'

Klai looked puzzled. 'What, another planet in this system?'

'No, Paradeisos. I'm a Theo,' he replied with a smile.

Klai took a step back, his mouth gaping at Phil and with a look of complete shock on his face.

'You're an Exy,' he finally stammered, staring as if Phil had just pulled a gun on him.

'Yeah, and I'm really glad to finally meet you,' Phil

replied. 'My boss is looking forward to having a chat with you too.'

Ed, sensing Klai was undergoing mild shock at meeting his first Exy, ushered everybody out of the hangar and organised a cabin for Klai to rest in before his meeting with Prota in the morning.

Klai, having retired to his allocated cabin, spoke for the first time since meeting Phil in the hangar. Ed, who was about to step into the corridor, and leave him to rest, paused as he spoke.

'Are they all like Phil?'

'The few I've met are.'

Klai's head slumped. 'How could we have got it all so wrong? And for such a ridiculously long time?'

'That,' said Ed, 'is something I can't answer, but we'll all be very proud to help you rectify the situation.'

Klai smiled and nodded. 'Thank you, Edward.'

'You're welcome, Mr President. Now get some sleep. Tomorrow could be the most important day in your planet's history.'

EVERYBODY EXCEPT ED had retired to bed. He strolled through the ship, back down to the hangar and over to the Cartella.

'Open up, Cleo,' he said as he approached.

Both airlock doors powered open. He still marvelled at the technology, watching as the steps just materialised out of thin air. They were seemingly unsupported and gave a little as he put his weight on them. He sprang up the steps, using the top one as a two-foot springboard through the airlock, but he misjudged the amount of spring and cracked his head on the door frame as he entered.

'Ow, shit.'

'That explains your nickname then,' giggled Cleo.

'Thanks for your concern, Cleo. I'm fine, really,' he said, rubbing the top of his head vigorously.

'Shouldn't you be resting? A tired human is an irritable human and is more likely to make errors.'

'Thank you, Sigmund Freud,' said Ed. 'Has someone been studying human psychology today?'

'Yesterday was human medicine; today I did advanced galactic physics and pure chemistry.'

'Your life is just one long disco party, isn't it?'

'What's a disco?'

'You stick to those easy subjects, Cleo,' said Ed, with a smirk. 'Kool and the Gang will be a little too much for you at your age.'

'You're taking the piss, aren't you?'

'Maybe a little.'

'Are you requiring your cabin?'

'No, I came down here to check on our prisoner.'

'She's awake and extremely agitated. It's just as well you removed all the loose items from the cabin you allocated her. She's been banging around in there ever since she woke.'

'Can you restrain her so I can have a little chat?'

'Sure, no problem.'

Ed walked through the enlarged Cartella to one of the rear cabin doors. The lock snapped open and he cautiously entered the room.

The girl was being held against the far wall by an unseen force and sneered at Ed as soon as he entered.

'I should have killed you at the spaceport instead of that Timorian idiot,' she spat.

'What's your name?'

'That will be rectified when my friends arrive,' she said, ignoring him. 'And the rest of your sorry little band of primitive humans will die too.'

'What a friendly soul you are,' said Ed. 'You remind me of one of Andy's ex's.'

'But if you release me, you shall be spared. You are not affiliated to the GDA and not considered a threat.'

'Not considered a threat, eh?' said Ed. 'You must've been off sick during the history lesson on Planet Earth.'

He turned and stepped towards the door.

'Where do you think you're going, I haven't finished with—'

She stopped mid-sentence and collapsed down onto the floor.

'What happened, Cleo?'

'She was getting on my nerves,' Cleo replied.

'Same here. Is she okay?'

'Just unconscious, she'll wake in an hour or so.'

'She'll be madder than a bag of wasps. You make sure that door's secure.'

A FEW HOURS LATER, everyone was gathered in the blister with a glorious view of Paradeisos slowly turning above their heads. The food replicator had been busy and had produced everything from porridge to Eggs Benedict to Timorian Tyri Tost, which Ed thought tasted similar to French toast.

Phil sat on his own at the far end of the room, wearing a POK, an almost permanent feature since the loss of Gabriel. He'd been singlehandedly piloting the ship, organising the repairs to the damaged systems, overseeing the planet missions and keeping a watchful eye on the scanners for any friends of their prisoner who might – or might not – turn up at any time.

Ed surmised that he was tired and moved over to sit with him.

'Would you like one of us to take over for a while?' he said. 'Let you get some rest?'

'What I really need to do is seed an embryo into the ship's core, but that would leave us vulnerable for several days until the juvenile system brought itself up to speed.'

'What about Cleo?' said Ed. 'She's proved herself capable enough. Couldn't she oversee the Gabriel?'

'I hadn't thought of that,' said Phil.

'Well, you've been a busy boy, so don't beat yourself up over it.'

'Cleo, can you hear me?' said Phil.

'I can.'

'Would you consider transferring yourself over to the Gabriel and running the starship?'

'I'd be delighted,' she said, making them both jump as she appeared, standing next to them in full Ancient Egyptian regalia.

'Bloody hell,' said Ed. 'I wish you'd stop doing that.'

'She does look amazing, though, doesn't she?' said Phil.

IT TOOK Cleo about four minutes to transfer herself into

the Gabriel's central core after Phil had given her the entry code. He exhaled a sigh of relief, handed the POK over to Linda and retired to his cabin for some much needed sleep.

Not long afterwards, Linda put the Gabriel into a stationary orbit over one of Paradeisos's Exy-built cities.

Then Prota arrived.

Not a system-generated human this time, but the real person, up from the surface in a small private shuttle.

Andy introduced everyone as he'd met Prota before.

Once that was done, President Klai and Prota retired to a private cabin for long-overdue peace negotiations.

'HOW'S IT ALL GOING, CLEO?' said Ed as he strolled into the Gabriel's bridge, giving Linda a wink.

'This is fun,' Cleo replied. 'Gabriel had a lot of stuff he was working on. In a couple of hours I'll have read everything in the database.'

'Is there anything on how to get the truth out of a stubborn, aggressive prisoner?'

'If we could get a POK on her head, I could confuse her into thinking she's chatting to a friend. There's something else you should know. I gave her a scan when she came on board the Cartella, and she had a live transponder inserted in her body. It was transmitting on a very odd frequency and of a design unknown to us. It took me a few minutes to break the coding and shut the thing down so if someone was receiving that signal, they may know where to look.'

'The friends she spoke about earlier,' said Ed.

'Possibly,' she replied. 'Another puzzle is her DNA too.'

'Go on.'

'It's not recognised on any database, including the GDA, and they have extensive records of every human race in existence.'

'So, she's from a race so far undiscovered in the galaxy?'

'That's where it gets even more weird. You see, every recorded human race's DNA in this galaxy has certain similar markers, every single one of them.'

'And hers doesn't?'

'No.'

'So, you're saying she may be from another galaxy?'

'It's a distinct possibility.'

'How much contact has there been with races from other galaxies?'

'None.'

Ed picked up a POK.

'I think we'd better go and have a chat with our transgalactic enigma.'

ED BROUGHT ANDY ALONG TOO, armed with a stun rifle, just in case. He could hear her bashing around in the cabin as soon as they entered the Cartella.

When they were set, Cleo did her trick with the energy beams and opened the cabin door.

The cabin was again in disarray; anything that could be broken, was. She was as she was before: pinned against the far wall above the bed, staring at them as they walked in.

'Brought back-up this time, you coward,' she spat.

Ed ignored the comment and walked straight over to her with the POK in his hand.

'Don't you put that fucking thing on me, or I'll—'

Ed placed it carefully over her head; she was vibrating with the effort of fighting against the energy field.

'This is against GDA law. It won't work – I – oh – that's not – illegal – cover – escape—' Her eyes finally glazed over and she stopped vibrating.

'You're her senior officer,' said Cleo, quietly.

Ed thought about that for a moment, trying to work out his first question.

'Hello, can anybody hear me?' he asked in a stern voice.

'Oh, hello, sir,' she answered. 'It's Quixia, how are you able to talk to me? We're too far away.'

'New technology, Quixia. Our Commander asked me to check everything's okay with your mission.'

'Okay, yes. It's all going to plan.'

'How long did it take you to get to their galaxy?'

'Tell the invasion planners they were right about the timescale.'

Ed looked across at Andy, who raised his eyebrows.

'We heard about the Katadromiko 37. Was that anything to do with you?'

'That attack was me, yes. I controlled the situation well and orchestrated for two primitive humans to get the blame.'

Andy shook his head in astonishment. Ed couldn't believe what he was hearing.

'Was that a planned part of the mission?'

'No, a virus came on board by chance during a rest break at an island planet. I was able to alter the strain slightly and then add it to the water supply shortly after two aliens arrived.'

'That's excellent work, Quixia. We're all very proud of you. Are you putting agents on other GDA ships?'

'Yes, it's all underway. We're training agents on the Krawth and infiltrating several naval ships, including most of the other Katadromiko Class Battle Cruisers.'

'Is there anything else you would like me to tell the Commander?'

'Just to prepare the fleet as planned and, as soon as we've got the cloaking technology, we will return.'

'That's good news, Quixia. What do they call their galaxy by the way?'

'The Milky Way.'

'What do they call ours?'

'Andromeda.'

'How long will it take you to get home?'

'About six weeks once we get the cloaking tech and we believe we're close to that.'

'That's good news. We need to see that technology as soon as possible. Good luck.'

'Thank you, sir.'

Quixia slumped down on the bed and Andy grabbed the POK off her head a second before her eyes refocused and the energy beams pushed her back against the wall.

'I told you it wouldn't work,' she snarled. 'You will pay for this insult to the Paragon Coalesce of Planets.'

'Thank you, Quixia,' said Ed. 'Cleo, shut her up.'

The look of surprise on Quixia's face disappeared fast, but it hadn't gone unnoticed.

'Who's Quixia—' was all she got out before she dropped unconscious on the bed.

'Paragon Coalesce of Planets?' repeated Andy,

wrinkling his nose. 'What a pretentious load of bollocks.'

'I agree. The rest of it wasn't what I was expecting, though,' said Ed, scratching his head in wonder.

'You didn't ask her about the sniping on Krix'ir. I would've liked to know why I lost my bloody hand,' said Andy. 'Or why she came after us in that gunship.'

'The Timorian was about to surrender to us and unravel her story about the virus so we had to go too, just in case.'

'We have to pass all this on to the GDA, quickly,' said Andy as they walked back to the bridge. 'Who knows how many more of them there are?'

Linda didn't smile as they walked in. 'I watched the interrogation,' she said, staring at the two of them.

'The minute the peace conference is over, we need to get to Dasos as soon as possible,' said Ed. 'Can you plot a course?'

'Already done.'

45

THEO STARSHIP GABRIEL – ORBITING PARADEISOS, ASPRO SYSTEM

DAY 420, YEAR 11269, 13:31SC, PCC

'I've completed studying all of Gabriel's database, Edward,' said Cleo. 'There's a lot of really cool stuff in here. Programmes I reckon I can work on and improve some of our systems.'

'You go for it,' said Ed from his couch in the corner of the blister. 'Don't initiate anything without running it by us, but let us know what you have when it's ready to rock. Talking of ready, do we have any news yet from our two world leaders?'

'Nothing yet, although they called for more food not so long ago, including some Timorian wine.'

'Well, that's a good sign. If they're on the piss, things must be going well.'

'Oh dear.'

'Oh dear, what?' said Ed, wondering what the hell would cause a sentient computer to say, "Oh dear".

'An unidentified starship has jumped into the system and is heading straight for us.'

'When you say "unidentified", what exactly do you mean?'

'Not a configuration or design registered on the GDA database.'

'Must be our friends from Andromeda. Give their ship a thorough scan and see what they have.'

'Concealed heavy weapons, screens inferior to ours and they don't have a Palto.'

'Okay, Cleo. If we have to activate the Palto as a last resort, immediately initiate full-drive straight at the point in space where their ship was and, if it was moving, then give it your best estimate.'

'But that would punch us straight through their ship,' said Cleo, nervously. 'And possibly cause fatalities aboard their vessel.'

'I know where you're going with this, but you're permitted to defend your ship.'

'The Palto would be defending us.'

'Okay, tell you what, if you set the best intercept course into the navigation system, I'll get Linda to hit the initiate icon. How does that sound?'

'Cool for cats.'

'That's great. In fact, have the navigation set straight at them as soon as they arrive. How long is that by the way?'

'Four minutes.'

'Shit.'

Ed jumped up and ran for the bridge.

LINDA, Phil and Andy were already there, reclining on the control couches and wearing POKs.

Ed joined them.

Nobody was smiling or said a word. They all stared at the holographic image of the large Andromedan warship as it slowed and came to a stop ten kilometres away. It only took a few seconds before they were hailed.

'Unidentified starship, my name is Captain Xir'gin of the GDA battle cruiser Trynn. I understand you picked up one of my crew when she crash-landed on this planet. I would be grateful if you could return her to my ship immediately.'

Ed grinned at everybody on the bridge. 'Game on,' he said and toggled the transmit icon.

'Good day, Captain Xir'gin. My name is Commodore Virr—'

The other three all looked at him as if he was mad.

'—of the Theo Battleship Gabriel. I feel you might have got a little confused. You see, my records show from our visits to your galaxy that you're the Captain of the Andromedan Battle Cruiser Krawth of the Paragon Coalesce of Planets. Please correct me if I'm wrong.'

There was an extended silence.

Ed could hear Andy laughing on the opposite couch to him and held his hand up to quieten him.

'Commodore Virr, I really feel it is you that is confused. No GDA ships have ever travelled to another galaxy so I will give you a few moments to realise your error and return my crew member. Otherwise I will be forced to disable and board your vessel.'

Ed could see pods and doors opening up along the length of the battle cruiser.

'He's preparing to fire,' said Linda.

'Do the same,' said Phil. 'It'll make him realise we're not the domestic starship we appear to be.'

Linda opened all the weapon bay doors.

It was the first time they'd seen the Gabriel fully guns up. It made the ship look quite menacing on the holographic display.

Andy suddenly whistled the theme from *The Good, the Bad, and the Ugly*. Ed and Linda smirked; Phil didn't – he looked around the bridge with a confused expression.

'I'll explain later,' Andy said, noticing his non-comprehension.

They sat there for a few minutes, waiting to see what

the Andromedan would do, when their concentration was broken by Prota and Klai arriving on the tube lift.

'Hello, everyone,' said Prota, smiling, then noticed the display in the middle of the room. 'Oh, who is that?'

'A very rude Andromedan battle cruiser,' said Andy.

'Andromedan?' said Klai. 'What, from the next galaxy?'

'What's he doing all this way from home?' said Prota, staring at Phil.

'He's the advance party of an invasion fleet, apparently,' said Phil.

'He's much bigger than us,' said Klai, looking worried. 'Can this ship cope with this?'

'We have a few surprises,' said Prota as he ushered Klai over to a seat at the side of the bridge.

'Can't we cloak and bugger off?' said Linda.

'No,' said Ed. 'I don't want him to know we have that ability – and we'd lose him again. What we need to do is disable his ship so the GDA can study their technology and interrogate the crew.'

When they were beginning to wonder if anything would ever happen, the battle cruiser opened up with all six of its biggest laser weapons.

The Gabriel's shields flashed white instantly, but held up under the onslaught.

'Shields at maximum deflection,' shouted Andy. 'We can only hold this for about two minutes.'

'Okay,' said Ed. 'Course all plotted, Cleo?'

'Yes. Go when ready. He's certainly arrogant, staying stationary.'

'Linda, prepare to hit maximum drive on my call,' said Ed, giving her a wink.

'Are we playing destruction derby again?' she said, looking at Ed with a grin.

'What's a destruction derby?' Klai said to Prota.

'I'm not completely sure,' said Prota. 'But I think this involves a head butt with a starship.'

'You're kidding,' said Klai, staring across the bridge and then looking around his seat for some sort of seat belt.

'Don't you scratch my starship,' said Prota, waggling his finger at Ed and giving him a sly grin.

'Thirty seconds with the shields,' said Andy. 'Twenty-five seconds, twenty seconds…'

'Ready, Cleo?' asked Ed.

'Yep.'

'Ready, Linda?'

'Yeah.'

'Palto up, and – go, Linda.'

They all watched the holographic image disappear as the Palto came online. Although there was never any sense of movement when the ship accelerated, this time they all felt a slight judder through the couches a second after Linda hit the icon.

'Full stop, shields up – Palto off,' said Ed.

The holographic display came back almost immediately. It confused them at first, as there appeared to be three ships in the vicinity. Then, as the two other ships gradually moved apart and began to spin slowly, it dawned on them: the Andromedan ship was in two pieces; the whole drive section at the rear was cut cleanly away and both cut edges trailed a long stream of debris and gasses.

'Oh, crap,' said Andy. 'Did that ever work?'

'The front section still has manoeuvring thrusters,' said Linda.

As they watched, the spin slowed and the section started moving away from them.

'What's he doing?' said Linda.

'He's trying to put the wreck into orbit,' said Andy.

'Shit. No, he's not,' said Ed. 'He's throwing the remains into the atmosphere so we don't get it.'

'Tractor beam?' asked Linda.

'Not for something that big,' said Phil. 'He'd pull us down with him if we tried that.'

Even as Phil spoke, the first fire trails from some of the smaller fragments could be seen entering the upper atmosphere. As they watched, the huge forward section of the battle cruiser dropped deeper into the upper atmosphere. The leading edge slowly turned from black to crimson, then lumps of white-hot superstructure began breaking away and forming their own flaming trails.

A faint voice penetrated the reverent silence of the Gabriel's bridge.

'You won the battle this time, little ship, but very soon you will all perish as the—'

They watched for another few seconds until Linda changed the display.

'Is everyone okay?' said Ed, glancing around the cabin.

'I feel quite sick,' said Linda.

'We had to,' said Andy. 'They would have taken the prisoner and killed us all. They had no choice. We knew too much.'

'I suppose,' said Linda, looking downcast. A tear ran down her face and dropped into her lap. 'I just didn't sign up to kill people.'

Ed jumped up out of his couch, knelt down beside her and gave her a hug.

'Well, from my point of view,' said Phil, 'we only disabled the ship as that was our initial purpose. It was their captain's decision to throw the ship and crew into the atmosphere. We had no hand in that.'

Linda nodded.

'Do you want to have a break?' said Ed. 'I can take over the ship for a while.'

'No, no, I'm good. It was a bit of a shock, that's all.'

'Shall I get you a large brandy?' said Andy.

'No thanks, Andy. I have to drive,' she said.

'Shit, 'cause I sure as hell need a stiff one.'

Linda took a deep breath and took the ship over to the rear drive section. She scanned it for life signs, but found none. The section contained a lot of technology that would be useful to the GDA and was of a size that enabled them to tractor it into a high orbit. After this was done, she returned them to a low stationary orbit above one of Paradeisos's four Theo Exy-constructed cities.

Ed removed his POK and looked across the bridge at the two gentlemen who were waiting patiently and expectantly.

'Sorry,' he said. 'We appear to have neglected you on your momentous day. I take it, as you're both sitting together, that negotiations were successful?' he asked and gave them a thumbs-up.

Neither Prota or Klai could know what a thumbs-up sign meant, but they smiled and returned the gesture anyway, followed by everyone else in the room.

Ed clambered up out of his control couch again and approached Prota.

'Sir, I would like to ask you a favour.'

'Go on,' said Prota, standing up.

'As you must realise, we have a lot of information that has to be reported to the GDA as soon as possible and I know we have our own ship downstairs, but I was wondering—'

Prota raised his hand to silence Ed.

'You wish to borrow my beautiful starship, do you, Captain Virr?'

'Err – well, we could just about fit into the Cartella, but if you have other plans for—'

Prota raised his hand once more and Ed fell silent again.

'I had these starships built when it seemed an impossibility that the Timoria would ever return to the surface of the planet,' he said. 'The ships were to find and nurture an immature race that we could serve.'

He looked everyone in the eye around the bridge.

'That was what we were originally programmed to do. Offering a new human race a beautiful home here on Paradeisos was our alternative plan after failing to encourage the indigenous race out of the interior of the planet. The events of the last few days have at last brought about our primary function. We have a new up-and-coming human race, courtesy of Mr Virr and friends, and –' he paused and put his hand on Klai's shoulder '– we have a distinct possibility of beginning the transition of the home-born Theos back out of the caves and into the world they originally populated.'

He smiled at Klai and looked back at Ed again, the smile vanishing from his face.

'Captain Virr, the answer to your question is no. You cannot have the use of my starship.'

The look of disappointment on Ed's face was obvious to everyone.

'But,' Prota continued. 'Having seen the love you have for your crew, the respect you have for other races and your predisposition for preserving life, I have decided you can have use of your starship. The Gabriel is yours. I have no further use for her and, anyway, I have three others.'

Ed stood rigid for a second, staring straight at Prota, trying to make sense of what the man had just said.

His expression suddenly became a huge grin as he grabbed Prota, enveloping him in a huge bear hug.

A cheer rang out around the bridge and everyone else piled in to hug and celebrate the outcome that no one had predicted.

Even President Klai was hugging everyone.

Ed held his hand up to silence the crowd.

'Err, okay,' he said, wiping a tear from his eye. 'There is one more thing before I accept your incredibly generous offer, Prota. Well, actually two.'

He looked up at the ceiling. 'Cleo, would you appear in person please?'

The Egyptian goddess appeared in all her splendour in the centre of the bridge.

'Who's she?' exclaimed an astonished Klai.

'The most important member of the crew,' said Ed and walked over to stand in front of her.

'Cleo, as you are more a part of this ship now than anyone else, I feel I couldn't accept Prota's offer without your consent.' He bowed his head.

Cleo stepped forward and took Ed's hands in hers. 'I should be the one bowing to you. It would be my honour to protect you and your crew,' she said. But before Ed could say anything, she continued: 'Man is still the most extraordinary computer of all.'

'You've been reading up on Earth quotes,' said Ed, before kissing her hand. 'I believe that was John F. Kennedy. Thank you, Cleo. We'll look after you too.'

Ed moved over to Phil.

'I'll quite understand if you want to drop me off here,' said Phil, looking downcast.

'Are you bloody kidding me?' said Ed, amazed. 'You've been a valuable crew member on this ship since you were two days old. Don't even think of getting off this ship. It's the only home you've ever known and, anyway, where would you go for your rock music?' Ed looked back at Prota. 'That's so long as Prota has no problem with you remaining here?'

Prota shook his head.

Phil grinned and Ed got another hug.

'Righto, that's enough soppy shit and hugging for one day. We need to get to Dasos.' He looked over at

Klai and Prota. 'I would imagine you two want to go planet-side?'

'Well, actually,' said Prota. 'We need to go to Dasos too. We need to register the peace accord, get the Timorian's terrorist status retracted and beg for a GDA peace-keeping force to oversee the transition.'

'We need to get there as fast as possible, now,' said Cleo. 'I've just received a communication that Xavier Lake and Floyd Herez have been found guilty of the Katadromiko 37 murders.'

'Couldn't happen to a nicer pair,' said Andy, scowling.

'It's not that I'm concerned about,' Cleo continued. 'It's the fact that now the court is considering Ek Neou Spora on their home planet.'

'What the hell is that?' asked Andy as complete silence on the bridge ensued.

'It translates to reseeding,' said Cleo.

'Does that mean what I think it does?' said Linda, a look of horror on her face.

'Yes, it is,' said Prota. 'The GDA only undertake that as a last resort. It's only been authorised twice before in ten thousand years. Any new human colony within the GDA's realm that they consider to be prodigiously genocidal, they submit to a reseeding programme. The planet is wiped clean and rejuvenated with either an established race that needs to expand or with selected Neanderthal life forms.'

Everybody looked at each other with wide eyes.

'Bloody hell,' exclaimed Andy.

'My sentiments exactly,' said Linda, who was as white as a sheet and looked as if she was about to throw up.

'Okay, let's rock and roll, guys,' said Ed. 'Linda, to Dasos – and don't spare the horses.'

46

THEO STARSHIP GABRIEL – EN ROUTE TO DASOS, PRASINOS SYSTEM

DAY 421, YEAR 11269, 09:11FC, PCC

Although the jump to the Prasinos System was virtually instantaneous, the navigating to and from designated jump zones and waiting for jump authorisation took time, even more so when jumping into one of the busiest systems in the galaxy.

The Prasinos System had to contend with over five thousand ship movements per day, through nine designated jump zones.

It was for this reason it had taken Linda four hours to get a jump authorisation into zone 6.

As the Gabriel emerged into the designated zone, the holo map in the centre of the bridge lit up with hundreds of ships, all seemingly vying for the same area of space.

'Bloody hell, it's busy here,' said Linda.

'Like Christmas week at Heathrow,' said Andy, watching the mass of images flowing in every direction.

Ed immediately sent a priority message to the station commander at Stathmos Vasi Station, regarding the new evidence in the Katadromiko 37 case and the potential threat coming from Andromeda.

'That should get their attention,' he said.

He was right. Three minutes later they were hailed from the station.

'Good morning, Captain Virr,' said a very officious voice. 'I am Station Commander Stak'oui. One of our ships will meet you at this location.' A red marker began flashing on the holo display. 'Do not deviate from the designated course. The information you have given us is considered highly classified. For this reason you will make no more transmissions from your vessel. Are these instructions understood?'

'Instructions fully understood,' replied Ed, looking puzzled.

'Are you thinking the same as me?' asked Andy.

'That rendezvous point is a lot further away than the Stathmos Vasi Station,' answered Ed.

'And it's remote,' said Linda. 'Something smells funny.'

'They'll be scanning us now. How can we check the validity of the meeting without transmitting?' asked Andy.

'You can't,' said Prota, who'd arrived on the tube elevator a few moments earlier. 'But I can.'

Everyone turned to face him.

'I'll cloak my shuttle in the hangar and drift out and away. Then I can make a few inquiries and pop back in unnoticed.'

'The Katadromiko 12 is in the system,' said Linda. 'That's the one that arrested Lake, apparently, so there's a fair chance he's legit.'

'That's Captain Loftt,' said Prota, nodding. 'We go way back. Leave it with me.'

HALF AN HOUR LATER, Prota arrived back on the bridge.

'Sorry I took so long,' he said. 'Loftt had to contact a friend on the station who physically walked up to the command centre and spoke to Stak'oui in person.'

'And?' said Andy, impatiently.

'He received no message from us,' said Prota, looking round at them all in turn. 'Nor did he instruct you to meet at the rendezvous point. He is currently investigating how his transmissions are being intercepted and by whom.'

'It appears our Andromedan friends have infiltrated the GDA quite substantially,' said Ed. 'We need to be careful who we trust.'

'Do you want me to change course towards the station?' said Linda.

'No,' said Ed, with a rueful smile. 'Let's see who turns up.'

'Loftt thought you'd say that,' said Prota, 'so he's going to bring his cruiser to the rendezvous point as soon as he can get away.'

'How long have we got?' said Andy.

'Twenty-two minutes to rendezvous point,' said Phil, who'd been very quiet up to now.

'Okay,' said Ed. 'Let's give ourselves a bit of back-up. Phil, can you take over the piloting of the Gabriel? And Linda, move over to weapons. Andy, you and I will take out a cloaked Cartella and give whoever it is a little surprise. Remember, I expect the majority of the crew on the GDA ship that's going to meet us probably have no idea of the deception they're part of. It may only be a couple of the senior officers involved. So we can't do a destruction derby this time. If it gets a bit hairy like last time, jump away and go at best speed towards the station.'

'But they'll follow the jump,' said Linda. 'We won't have time to embed the co-ordinates.'

'Jump nearer the station while transmitting a distress signal,' said Ed. 'They can't engage you while the whole system is watching; that's why the rendezvous point is so remote.' Ed winked at her and continued: 'Keep them talking. I have a plan.'

'Okay, will do,' said Linda, looking across at Phil, his hands noticeably trembling. 'You okay?'

Phil looked up at her and attempted a smile. 'I'm just not used to all this combat stuff,' he said. 'I've been on this ship for several millennia and not witnessed much violence until now.'

'Well, they're hardly trained for it either,' she said, nodding at Ed and Andy. 'If it's any consolation, I'm shit scared too – and I trained to be a fighter pilot.'

We're all nervous, Phil,' said Ed. 'Some of us show it more than others. You're doing just fine.'

Phil nodded. 'I need to take a harden-up pill, don't I?' he said and clasped his hands together tightly to stop them trembling.

FOUR MINUTES LATER, the cloaked Cartella drifted slowly out of the port hangar and powered away.

Ed instructed Andy that a gap of five thousand kilometres was enough and they matched speeds with the Gabriel and waited.

Linda pulled the Gabriel up to a full stop at the designated co-ordinates, kept the shields on their standard default setting and scanned the area thoroughly.

There wasn't much to see. The meeting point was

right out on the fringe of the system. The nearest planet was millions of kilometres away and, beyond that, a debris field, similar to the Kuiper belt on the fringes of the Helios System.

'Not a very crowded neighbourhood, is it?' said Prota as he and Klai entered the bridge, sitting themselves in the spare control couches and surveying the holo display.

'No, it's not,' said Linda. 'Just perfect for an ambush.'

In her peripheral vision, she saw Phil squirm in his seat.

The GDA Apergia Class Destroyer jumped in five hundred kilometres off their starboard side. It instantly brought up full shields and guns to bear on the Gabriel.

On the nearby Cartella, Andy was reclining on his control couch with his hands behind his head.

'Well, well, that's not very polite,' he said, slowly starting to move the cloaked Cartella over and in behind the GDA ship.

'Cleo, can you patch us in on anything the GDA ship transmits?' said Ed.

'Already done,' she said.

They didn't have to wait long.

'VESSEL GABRIEL, this is the Captain of the GDA Destroyer Vrachos. Remain stationary. We will despatch a tender across to you to pick up our prisoner. Drop your shields and open your starboard hangar.'

'Hello, unnamed Captain of the GDA Destroyer Vrachos,' said Linda in a posh, seductive voice, trying not to snigger. 'This is Admiral Wisnewski of the Star Destroyer Gabriel. Would you be so kind as to drop your shields and point your dick in some other direction? Didn't your mummy tell you it's rude to point?'

The Vrachos suddenly closed on the Gabriel and came to an abrupt halt a kilometre off her starboard side.

'Oh dear, Captain. I bet you were the school bully too,' she transmitted. 'I'm positively shaking in my flip flops.'

Back on the Cartella, both Ed and Andy had tears running down their faces.

'She's brilliant,' said Andy, unable to contain his laughter.

'I'm going to nominate her for a comedy award,' said Ed from where he was tapping away at the jump co-ordinates panel.

'Where are we going?' said Andy, watching what Ed was doing.

'You'll see. Just have our new Raga Fos Cannon

activated and locked on their engines and targeting array.'

Linda was still having fun with the arrogant GDA Captain. 'You've gone all quiet, Captain. Don't tell me you get all bashful when you get close to a girl?'

'Your lack of respect will not go unpunished. You will surrender your vessel immediately.'

'Oh dear, just when I thought we were getting on so well. I had a candle-lit dinner planned and everything,'

The two heavy, starboard-side cannons which were trained on the Gabriel fired as one. The Gabriel's shields flashed white and Cleo increased their resistance to full.

Ed dropped the Cartella's cloak and touched the purple jump icon. The Destroyer's port-side cannons very quickly swivelled to lock and engage the uncloaked ship, but only managed to fire through a cloud of dissipating green haze.

'You clever bastard,' said Andy as the much smaller ship emerged inside the shields of the Destroyer.

'*Captain* Clever Bastard to you,' said Ed as he fired the Cartella's cannons at point-blank range, directly into the Destroyer's engines and arrays.

It went abruptly very quiet and the ship began to drift. Its shields had failed too, probably having previously taken their power from the now-shredded main engines, and all four of the heavy cannons seemed to float back up to their default straight-out position.

Andy moved the Cartella away from the Destroyer to avoid hitting the debris which was swirling out from the rear of the stricken ship.

'How did you know we'd fit inside their shields?'

'Mensuration formula,' said Ed, hopefully, with a wince.

'You weren't sure at all, were you?'

'Yes, I was.'

'No, you weren't.'

'Yes, I was.'

'I've told you once.'

'No, you didn't.'

'When you've quite finished, gentlemen...' said a different, official-sounding voice, causing Ed and Andy to jump.

Ed hadn't noticed he'd touched the transmit icon in his haste to jump and fire.

The Katadromiko 12 uncloaked a kilometre away, its bulk blotting out all the stars on their port side. It secured the drifting Destroyer with a tractor beam and its Asteri Beam operators got a bit of target practice, vaporising the remaining debris.

'Good morning, Captain Virr. This is Captain Loftt of the GDA. I see you've been busy blowing holes in one of our nice, new, expensive Apergia Class Destroyers.'

'Yeah, sorry about that. Send me an invoice.'

'From what I've seen, regarding the evidence you've uncovered, it should be us paying you. But that's not what I came for. I understand you have a prisoner for me.'

'Yes, Captain,' said Ed. 'Although, after recent events, if it's all right with you, I'd like to deliver her to the station personally.'

'I understand. We'll escort you there in case any more of these traitors decide to play games; just give me time to secure and arrest the Destroyer's crew.'

As Andy brought the Cartella back into the Gabriel's hangar, the stricken destroyer was boarded by soldiers from the 12. They received no resistance as the majority of the crew had not been aware of the treachery in the senior ranks.

Both the Captain and the Chief Weapons Officer were found dead in their cabins.

47

STATHMOS VASI STATION – ORBITING DASOS, PRASINOS SYSTEM

DAY 421, YEAR 11269, 19:30FC, PCC

Xavier Lake sat back against the seat in the temporary courtroom and stared up at the ceiling.

Floyd Herez sat next to him scowling at everyone in the room. Neither of them could understand why they'd been dragged back up here, after having been found guilty on all charges yesterday and summarily sentenced to death.

'What else could there possibly be?' said Lake, glaring around the courtroom.

'Extra humiliation for the guilty patsies,' said Herez.

Commander Cien'dra strolled in with a smile from ear to ear.

'Just look at that piece of shit,' growled Herez, nodding at Cien'dra. 'I told you we shouldn't have trusted him.'

Lake followed Herez's gaze and locked eyes with

Cien'dra, who winked at him and promptly sat in his regular seat at the end of their row.

'Something's happened,' said Lake.

'Perhaps we're getting a choice of execution.'

'No, I don't think so. This has all been arranged in haste,' said Lake as he watched the puzzled expressions on some of the court staff who were being ushered into position a lot quicker than any of the times before.

'Whatever it is, it can't be—'

Herez stopped and stared at the two new faces entering the courtroom. Both were suffering from the extra gravity and appeared to be glad to sit down at the side of the stage.

Lake looked over at him, surprised at his sudden stop mid-sentence.

'Shit, that's Edward Virr!' exclaimed Herez. 'And Andrew Faux.'

'What the hell are those two doing here?' said Lake, following Herez's gaze over to where they had sat.

'Perhaps it's to give us a good reference,' said Herez. 'Or gloat when they kill us.'

A shout and a scream out in the corridor got everyone's attention. Two soldiers appeared with a struggling, restrained prisoner between them. They entered the court, the soldiers almost dragging their charge through the door.

Both, Lake and Herez almost fell off their seats when the prisoner looked up and around the room.

'That's – that's –' stuttered Herez, pointing avidly, his eyes wide with shock.

'Captain Utz,' said Lake, finishing the sentence for him, and shaking his head in amazement. 'A very much alive, Captain Fleoha Utz.'

THREE HOURS LATER, the reconvened court had overturned Lake and Herez's convictions, arraigned Captain Utz or Quixia and cancelled any action to be taken against Gaia in the Helios System.

Although Lake and Herez were now free of any GDA charges, the evidence Edward Virr had produced in the court demonstrated that they both had serious charges pending on their home planet. It was decided that they would be delivered back to Gaia, along with their disassembled ship.

Being kept in their cells until then didn't really worry either of them as a large percentage of the station's crew were still openly hostile. They did notice, however, that the quality of their food got a little better and they were given entertainment units.

A galaxy-wide arrest warrant was issued for Lieutenant Dric'is who had given false evidence about the fate of the Katadromiko 37 and had vanished after being awarded compassionate leave.

For brokering a peaceful conclusion to the Timoria-Theo problem on Paradeisos, uncovering the real culprit of the Katadromiko 37 murders and discovering a serious infiltration by previously-unknown Andromedan forces. Edward Virr was awarded the Chrysos Aspida Politis (Gold Shield Citizen) – or C.A.P – the highest civilian award in the GDA.

Andrew Faux, Linda Wisnewski and Phil Theo were all awarded the Megaleiodis Politis (Grand Citizen) – or M.P – for their bravery and assistance in the matter.

The terrorist status of the Timoria was rescinded and both the Timoria and the Exys were renamed Theo Genos. The GDA awarded them with Syndedemeni Idiotita Melous (Affiliated Membership) and the Katadromiko 22 was sent to oversee and keep the peace during the repopulation of the surface cities. After five weeks, almost one hundred and forty thousand people had braved the trip out of the caves. But there were a large number who considered it a trap and swore to never agree to any deal brokered, no matter how enticing. After living underground for several thousand years, it would be a long job.

Prota and President Klai had both been awarded the Eirini Metallio (Peace Medal) and were working tirelessly to convince the subterranean population that it was now safe to emerge and become part of the GDA.

Captain Fleoha Utz – or Quixia – was found guilty of mass murder and treason. The death sentence was mandatory, but not before every ounce of information was dragged out of her about the Andromedan threat.

Everyone and anyone who had knowledge of the potential problem was quickly reminded of its classified nature for two reasons: to avoid panic within the galaxy's populated worlds; and to give the GDA time to purge its ranks of any other Andromedan agents or sleepers – this was carried out under the guise of regular health checks, after having identified the different DNA marker in Andromedans.

A month later, they had singled out one hundred and seventeen clandestines within the services and another seventy-four sudden absentees, of which nine were caught in various disguises trying to escape to the outer fringes of the galaxy. Over half were senior officers and another three were ship's captains.

It had taken time to work their way up through the ranks, especially to the higher positions. It seemed that the treachery had been going on under their noses for many years.

The rear drive section of the Andromedan ship, Krawth, which had been placed in high orbit around Paradeisos, was retrieved and studied, along with a large lump of the main section that had not completely disintegrated in the atmosphere. It was found in thirty metres of water near an island in the western ocean. Having cooled rapidly after impact, it contained a wealth of information regarding the Andromedans' spacefaring capabilities and weapons technology.

Gaia, now officially renamed Earth, had also been offered affiliated membership of the GDA. Negotiations were ongoing regarding who the Earth's Ambassador to the GDA would be. James Dewey was high on the list, after having proposed a team of international delegates for his advisors and staff.

Xavier Lake was, after a five-week hearing, found guilty of a host of crimes around the globe, committed over several years. A specially convened international court in The Hague sentenced him to twenty-nine years and also banned him from ever being a director of a company again.

Floyd Herez was found guilty of multiple counts of murder, going back several years, along with a string of lesser crimes and received three life sentences.

EPILOGUE

Ed stood at the bar, waiting his turn to be served, and scratched the itchy stubble on his chin.

He wasn't accustomed to being unshaven but had found it necessary since his, Andy's and Linda's pictures had been on the cover of almost every newspaper, magazine and e-publication on the planet, following their notorious first foray into the Milky Way.

Over the last six months, they'd received keys to cities, honorary degrees, and dined with prime ministers, presidents and kings. They'd been interviewed on what seemed like every radio and television station on the planet, and the movie of their momentous journey was already in pre-production.

Financially, none of them would ever need to work again. Huge lucrative offers flooded in daily; they could earn billions from a few advertisements or by accepting board positions with some of the largest corporations on Earth.

Most of this they politely declined.

What they had done, though, was patent all the Theo technology equally in their three names. Ed had an old schoolmate from Cambridge who'd studied law, specialising in the corporate field. It took one phone call, along the lines of 'how'd you like to be the wealthiest lawyer on the planet?' to get Ian McMichael on board.

Today, they'd all signed the final legal agreements pertaining to the set-up and managing of The Gabriel Corporation. Phil was made nonexecutive director, which gave him a handsome salary. He had been awarded dual citizenship of the UK and USA, which gave him the ability to have real homes, instead of living on the Gabriel all the time.

They all decided very early on that they didn't want to manufacture anything themselves and licensing out the technology was the way to go.

Hence, the gathering at one of Andy's all-time favourite pubs, hidden in a pretty village square in a Kent village near Maidstone where he grew up. It was a lot less likely that they would be recognised, especially as it had been built in the fourteenth century and was primarily lit by candles.

Ed returned to the table with three pints of bitter and a pint of lager.

'You're a disappointment, you really are,' said Andy, grimacing at Linda's lager and tutting loudly.

'You can keep your warm, brown, flat stuff, Andrew,' said Linda. 'I like my ice-cold, continental, fizzy, designer lager. It's refreshing.'

'It's not warm and flat, it's a live hand-pulled ale, lovingly caressed into kilderkins by dusky maidens in Faversham, chilled at cellar temperature and freed by the arm of a buxom barmaid,' said Andy, winking at Phil.

'I didn't know that,' said Phil and clinked glasses with Andy. 'No wonder I like it.'

The landlord wandered over and put another couple of logs on the open fire.

The front door opened, which caused a slight draught and smoke billowed out from the fire for a second or two, giving the room a delicious, smoky aroma. The conversation lapsed for a second as they all stared, mesmerised with the flames that began licking around the fresh logs.

Ed raised his glass. 'Here's to us, the Gabriel Corporation, and a successful future.'

They all clinked glasses and drank.

Two gentlemen approached and stood next to their

table, barely recognisable in the candlelit gloom. One was tall and large, the other short and stocky.

'Good evening, lady and gentlemen,' said the big guy on the left.

They all froze and looked up.

'Jim Rucker, from Armstrong,' exclaimed Andy, standing and shaking his hand.

'I'm impressed,' said Jim, smiling and shaking hands with everyone else. 'Can I introduce Commander Bache Loftt, the new GDA attaché to the Helios System.'

'Wow,' said Ed. 'We get to meet at last, and congratulations on your promotion.'

'Thank you, I extreme glad to meet you all,' said Loftt, smiling and without the need of a translator. 'I spoke awesomely great English now.'

A cheer sounded around the table.

'Pull up a seat, gentlemen,' said Ed. 'Join us please.'

Two more chairs were grabbed from the other side of the pub. When they were all settled, Jim was the first to speak.

'This afternoon, James Dewey was officially sworn in as Ambassador to the GDA.'

'Ambassador to the GDA, indeed,' said Andy, lifting his glass.

Ed looked at him with disdain.

'Ha,' said Loftt. 'Ambassador to the GDA, indeed.

That extra funny. I hope James Dewey make Gerousia Council laugh too. They all be boring bastards for years.'

Everyone at the table erupted in laughter and a couple of drinks for the newcomers was soon forthcoming.

'I'm sorry to change the subject for a moment,' said Jim, placing his pint glass down on the table. 'But before we smash a few more of these delicious beverages, we do have an official reason to be here.'

Ed looked across the table at them suspiciously.

'You have a job for us and the Gabriel again don't you?' he asked, leaning back and crossing his arms.

Jim glanced across at Loftt and raised his eyebrows.

'Yes, Edward,' said Loftt, understanding the subtle cue from Jim. 'The GDA has small part of problem. We very like your helping with almost soon.'

AFTERWORD

Dear Reader,

First of all, I wanted to say a huge thank you for choosing to read *The Initial Fold*. I sincerely hope you enjoyed Ed and his crew's first adventure into space. The idea for this story came to me a few years ago – it just took me a while to realise I should write it down.

If you did enjoy this novel, it'd be fantastic if you could write a review. It doesn't have to be long, just a few words, but it is the best way for me to help new readers discover my writing for the first time.

If you'd like to stay up to date with my new releases, as well as exclusive competitions and giveaways, you're welcome to join my Reader Group at my website, www.nickadamsbooks.com. I will never share your email address, and you can unsubscribe at any time.

You can also contact me via Facebook, Twitter, or by email. I love hearing from readers – I read every message and will try to personally reply to everyone.

Thanks again for your support.

Best wishes,

Nick Adams